Come with Me to Babylon

Come with Me to Babylon

PAUL M. LEVITT

University of New Mexico Press

Albuquerque

LIBRARY OF CONGRESS CATALOGING-IN-PUBLICATION DATA

Levitt, Paul M.
Come with me to Babylon / Paul M. Levitt.
p. cm.
ISBN 978-0-8263-4178-5 (alk. paper)
1. Jews, Russian—United States—Fiction.
2. Jews—Cultural assimilation—United States—Fiction.
3. Immigrants—United States—Fiction.
4. Jewish fiction.
5. Domestic fiction.
I. Title.
PS3612.E935C66 2008
813'.6—dc22

2007039410

Designed and typeset by Mina Yamashita
Composed in Adobe Garamond Pro, bringing together elements of
Claude Garamond's Garamond and Robert Granjon's Granjon
in a contemporary typeface by Robert Slimbach.
Printed by Thomson-Shore, Inc. on 55# Natures Natural.

To the memory of
my mother and father

Acknowledgments

Over the years my parents' stories became as much a part of me as my own imaginings. To them I owe the greatest debt for having enticed me to find the bygone landscapes of their early lives.

Another story I found haunting came from David Von Drehle's *Triangle: The Fire That Changed America*, which enabled me to understand my country in ways that I had failed to do before.

Without David Milofsky, a man of incorruptible courage, I would never have seen the possibilities in this book. He provided the path with his powerful vision and, along the way, schooled me in writing like no other tutor.

Donald Eron, an immensely talented poet, offered inspired suggestions on how to enrich the story.

Nancy Mann, my editor *par excellence*, read the manuscript several times, keeping me from stylistic misadventures and, with her tuneful ear, transformed the mundane into music.

Anna Frajzyngier, a CU librarian and friend, lent her expertise with the Polish.

Elise McHugh copyedited the manuscript with an unerring eye for factual errors and structural integrity.

At the end of all, I alone am responsible for any failings my readers find in my wanderings through this wide world.

In the days of my father, there was

a wish to be separate, free of the

Delaware nation; and as I was young

and hopeful, happy for the chance

to make a journey into the southern

world, it fell to me to find the way

through the forest. So I ordered my

people to paint their bodies the color

of the sky, in token of our freedom,

and we set out.

Unless memory deceives me, my parents never hugged me; neither did they ever hit me. My father, a private man, and often a silent one, regarded feelings as capricious and ambition as grasping, and clung only to reflection: a recipe, I now know, for despair. My mother, nearly fifty when she bore me, hungered for a better life and had long since grown restive from resentment.

My name, Benjamin, meaning the right hand of God, was my mother's choice. But now that I look back across the years, I ask myself whether I was the Lord's chosen or His fool. The youngest of three children, I was raised by my sister, Fanny. Five years older than I, she taught me to read when I was three and always hid me from the Cossacks. Her only imperfection was her stuttering, worsened by excitement. I can still remember her long flaxen curls, her round cheerful face and perfect teeth, and the scent of soap on her hands. She had cabled a money order to some Parisian perfumery and a month later received three small cakes in a tin box that I treasured because the scent reminded me of her. Years later, when I worked for the Cosin Company, manufacturing powder puffs and mascara, I showed the box to Pierre Gimonet, our French chemist, who had a genius for creating exotic fragrances, but even he could not reproduce its essence.

Ours was a house divided, on one side, Fanny and I, full of hope and laughter; on the other, my parents, ill-matched and disgruntled.

We lived in Bobrovitz, in the state of Chernigov, approximately sixty miles northeast of Kiev. Jewish children were barred from the state schools. Initially, I learned my lessons at the cheder three miles from our village. When it snowed, my brother Jacob and I would sleep on the school floor, next to the stove, to be present at the next day's class. The rabbi was too poor to feed us, so we would doze off in class, from hunger. To wake us, he used a pointed stick. One day, when I was eight, Jacob, six years my senior, stopped the rabbi's arm and said, "Blessed be he of the Lord, who hath not left off his kindness to the living and to the dead." The rabbi slapped my brother's face and told us never to return.

My parents subsequently arranged for me to have a private tutor, a Sephardi, Mr. Peretz. He taught me that in bringing form out of the void, God endowed it with beauty—mountains and lakes and valleys and streams—and that the most enravishing of God's landscapes called itself

Spain, which attracted people of numerous faiths and tongues. Like an exquisite white cloth, damasked with intricate patterns, Spain was a work of art. The different people lived in felicity, sharing their knowledge. But when Ferdinand and Isabella bankrupted the kingdom, dogma overcame decency, leading to the expulsion of the Jews and the Moors and the confiscation of their wealth. It was as if red wine had been spilled on the cloth. Spain ran in blood, staining its former brilliance. Other countries, he said, had suffered similar fates, usually from greed. Even America, the great land of hope, now green and generous, could fall prey to merchants and money. Never underestimate, he cautioned, the lust to own things, not books or art or music, but trifles, baubles, the transient and the meretricious.

Mr. Peretz also introduced me to miniature painting at an exhibit in Kiev of medieval illuminated manuscripts and sixteenth-century miniatures, including one by Hans Holbein. Utterly mesmerized, I begged my parents to buy me paper and brushes and inks and oils, as well as a magnifying glass, enabling me to paint in both watercolor and gouache. Some of my miniatures my father actually sold to a bookseller in Kiev, who said they showed a great deal of promise.

March 1908

Max's letter arrived two months after I turned fifteen—and changed our lives. I divined its importance when my mother removed from the sideboard our silver-plated samovar and took from the cupboard a currant cake. As she read the letter aloud, my father looked as if a contagion had entered the house.

Dear Esther and Meyer,

Today I visited a Jewish settlement in New Jersey. Everyone speaks Yiddish. A few people even know Russian. There is a synagogue, and a hall for concerts. The town is called Carmel. A Jewish philanthropic group, the Baron de Hirsch Fund, will pay your passage if you will live here and be farmers. I know Meyer doesn't like farming, but here it's easier than in Russia.

My father contemptuously waved his hand. "Listen to Mister Expert. Easier! A farmer's a farmer." Lighting a cigarette, he expelled the smoke as if spitting.

"If you were as serious about working as you are about smoking, you'd be a millionaire," said my mother.

"Finish the letter," my father grumbled.

I asked the man if the soil was good. He said it is for some things and not for others. I asked about the water supply, and he said you can put the water in a jug and a year later it will still be the same. The people that have dug deep around here claim that there are streams under this earth that run all the time. Please write and tell me if you will be farmers. I told the man who works for the Baron de Hirsch Fund about you and he wants to help, but he said you must act now, because it could take several years to make all the arrangements. You are all deeply in my heart.

Your cousin,
Max

Slicing a piece of cake and sliding it to my father on one of our few unchipped plates, my mother asked, "So?"

"The golden world!" he scoffed. "The southern land! For Indians maybe, who dye themselves blue, but not for the family Cohen. Better Eretz Israel." My father lit another cigarette. Between puffs and bites of cake, he said, "They speak languages that we speak: Yiddish . . . Russian. There are libraries in Jerusalem. Books. Parks for a man to sit in, and read."

My mother, as always, spoke her mind, driving right to the heart of the matter. "Why would you want to settle in the Holy Land when you despise religious fundamentalism? I'm the believer, you're the secular one. You ridicule observant Jews who wear long sidelocks and beards and beaver hats. The Sabbath? Just another day to you. When I tried to keep kosher after our marriage, you said absolutely not. You wouldn't hear of two sets of dishes and meat without butter." She told him that in Eretz Israel the Jews would spurn him and he'd have to live with the Muslims, "among the Turks and flies and Arabs and heat and sand and religious fanatics as bad as the czar and his laws," and that once they experienced Pop's irreverence, his life would be a misery.

Defensively, he muttered, "The best country is at home. Men in exile feed on dreams."

It had begun to snow. The wind swept some flakes into the chimney, and the flue hissed. My father opened a book, as if the matter were settled. But my redoubtable mother, hands on hips, eyes dark as coal, said, "In America, Meyer, there is no czar. Riches. Opportunities. If we remain here, our landlord will kick us out. The czar wants to resettle all the Jews. Do you understand? He wants to drive us into the eastern lands and steal our properties. Is that what you're waiting for?"

My father slowly turned pages. His silence howled defiance.

"I'm waiting, Meyer."

"'Habit is heaven's own redress; it takes the place of happiness.'"

"Close the book and listen!"

"Things will get better. Wait, you'll see."

"I don't intend to wait."

"Last month in Kiev, in the bookstores and tea houses, the students talked of revolution."

She laughed sarcastically. "Revolution! Who will lead it? You? Meyer, I want to leave dark Russia for a shining land: America."

"The borders of America, Esther, do you know how far the borders of America are? Seven hundred thousand Persian miles away!"

March 1908

Ben, my blessed brother, and I pour over a serialized novel running in the monthly gazette. And try not to listen. Newspapers and books: that's all we have to occupy us. Reading them so often, we can almost recite the stories by heart. Every few minutes Ben glances at me, his gaunt face and high cheekbones exuding his exasperated Lenin-look. We have heard my parents argue—hundreds of times—but only infrequently about emigration.

"Meyer, America is a developing country looking for laborers."

Whenever the subject of work arises, Papa stops listening. And Mama invariably appeals to her children. Throwing up her arms, she turns to us.

"You talk to him. He won't listen to me."

"What's the po-postmark? I'll l-l-look in the At---las."

"Save yourself the trouble," says Papa, reaching for it himself. "I hear that outside of New York City every town's a *grepse*."

He uses Ben's magnifying glass to study the cancelled stamp from Max's undated letter that had been written two months before from Carmel, New Jersey.

"I can't find it, Esther."

"Your eyes are bad."

"Carmel, New Jersey. It's not in the atlas!"

"So? You expect every place in the world is in your atlas?"

"How can I tell where you want to go if I don't know where you want to go is?"

"And if you knew, would it make any difference?"

"Of course it would. Because then I would know if there were any cities nearby."

"You just said America has only one city, New York."

"So maybe I exaggerated a little."

"Meyer, they say in America a person can realize his dreams."

"And the distillery?"

The old argument. Once again. From the maple hutch Mama removes some official-looking paper. A document yellowed by time. "You've wasted your whole life over this!" she says. "The deed to your mother's distillery." She throws the paper on the table in front of him. "The distillery, Meyer, has been confiscated. It-will-never-be-returned! A lifetime wasted. And for what?"

"In this case, who steals my purse does not steal trash."

"Save your poetry for the children. With your education, a teacher you could have been. A bookkeeper. But no, you had to spend your days writing letters to St. Petersburg entreating the czar to return your distillery. And why? So you wouldn't have to work. Ha! Work! What do you know about work? I've run the general store and kept us alive. And you: what've you done? Nothing!"

Papa falls silent, infuriating Mama. Who resorts to self-pity. Shamelessly.

"All I've done," she says hitting her chest, "I've done for you."

Papa replies softly, "Esther, I don't want to die in a strange land among people speaking a language I can't understand."

"It's not fair for Fanny and Ben to have to grow up among illiterate peasants. In America, they can be something. Here, Ben addresses envelopes all week for a few pennies and Fanny slumps over a sewing machine in a dress factory."

Papa sniffs and waves his hand dismissively. "Democracy! The right of every man to be a success."

Mama lowers her voice, a sign that she means what she says. "You are a clever man, Meyer. You will learn the language and the customs." She pauses. No reaction. "We *will* go!"

"And what about Jacob?"

Mama bites her lower lip. Trying, I know, to keep from losing her self-control. "He's adamant."

"Of course. He doesn't want to leave behind his wife and child."

"It would be for only a short time . . . to make enough money to bring them over."

"They are trying to have a second child—or adopt one."

"He went away once before . . . for a year." Throwing restraint to the winds, she says bitterly, "To spite me!"

"Esther, will you never tell me what it is between you two?"

The veins in her neck pulsate. "I am writing the Baron de Hirsch Fund to ask for travel papers and steamship tickets."

"Jacob . . . and his family?"

"You said: Jacob won't leave. Then let him remain here."

Papa, looking bewildered and frightened, beseeches the air. "Jacob and Rissa . . . this land and language . . . all lost? The summer songs? What of them? And the birds of spring?"

March 1908

Hunched over his reading board, my father reminded me of a Dutch painting in which a merchant studies the accounts, his graying hair parted down the middle and his black Vandyke beard meticulously trimmed. His eyes, weak from strain, have made him resort to a reading glass.

"Lermontov or Pushkin?" I asked, resting my hand on his shoulder, a gesture that he never extended to me. He seemed afraid of touching another person; or was it that his mother had so pampered him during his life that he expected others always to comfort him, never the reverse? I gathered that in the early years of their marriage, my mother had indulged him; but those days had long disappeared.

Without looking up, he answered, "Shevchenko."

"Fanny and I have been teaching ourselves English." No effect. "America has Jewish communities in which they speak Yiddish."

"The religious Jews are just as bad as the Orthodox."

In the local Jewish community, my father's nationalism—and secularism—were widely known and resented. He wanted an independent Ukraine, free of the czar and the church. A freethinker, he wouldn't wear a yarmulke, nor keep his sidelocks long, nor observe the Shabbos and the festivals, regarding orthodoxy as a clumsy attempt by the unimaginative to impose order on their lives. He sneered at rules. Although he proudly called himself Jewish, and knew more about the history of the Jews than the rabbi, he decried all religious doctrines and contended that more people had died from religious strife than from disease and malnutrition. "It's a pernicious form of tribalism," he said, "that has ruined more lives than it's saved."

My father had been schooled in Paris and Berlin. His wealthy family wanted him to study law, but he fancied fiction. When his father died, his mother sold their tavern on the Odessa road and bought a small distillery that she turned into the largest and most successful in the state of Chernigov. A beautiful woman, she knew how to charm the local officials into giving her leases and warrants. What she gave in return, my father never discussed and my mother only whispered. She prospered until the czar replaced the governor. The new one immediately declared distilling a function of the government and not of an individual, and especially not of Jews. My grandmother knew better. She knew that independent distillers were to be found all over Russia. So she tried to bribe the governor.

Insulted, he confiscated her business without recompense. My father had written hundreds of letters pleading for the restoration of the distillery or at least payment for what had been lost. He received one letter in reply that briefly said, "The czarist government has the fullest confidence in the governor of Chernigov."

I went to the window and watched the silent snow covering the earth, mentally picturing how I could capture it in miniature. "Are you afraid of being smothered in America by a new language?"

"That's a large part of it. Language is our greatest gift. Without it, we are silent. Smothered, as you say. But that's not my only reason for wanting to stay."

"Do you really believe there will be a revolution?"

"Jacob does." He sipped his drink and stared off reflectively. "The thought of going to another country scares me. As bad as Russia is, it's familiar. It's in our pores. In America who knows what we'll find."

I could hear in the distance the woodcutters returning from the swamp, singing.

> Rushes and roars the wide Dnieper,
> Out of the north the fierce winds soar;
> They bend to earth the tall, straight willows,
> Then lift them high to heaven's door.

I knew what my father was thinking: if he left, when would he hear Shevchenko's songs again? "Pop, for Fanny's sake and mine . . . close the book."

He lit a cigarette and inhaled. "There's a Hebrew saying: 'Hold a book in your hand and you're a pilgrim at the gates of a new city.'"

March 1908

Mama asks me my feelings about leaving for America. Her question hides a hope: that I share her optimism. Ben and I talk incessantly and agree that to emigrate is like waking up a different person. Which is just what Mama wants. Still young enough to turn some heads, and strong enough to make her way, Mama is made of sterner stuff than Papa. And simpler. Her parents, wandering needleworkers, turned her over to an educated aunt, who paid a private tutor to perfect Mama's knowledge of Russian, Ukrainian, and Yiddish. But not Hebrew, German, and French, like Papa, who also has a smattering of other languages. Polish. Italian. Spanish. Mama can also write. Quite gracefully actually. She keeps a diary in which, according to her, she records "the secrets of the heart." Her admiration for learning is genuine, eclipsed only by her respect for perseverance, perhaps because she prevailed in her pursuit of Papa even though his mother opposed the marriage. Openly and vociferously. She was poor and knew hunger. He came from money and dined at a table of plenty. They met in a tea shop. Mama, in a starched white apron, served him coffee, his favorite Turkish blend. Although struck by her dark almond-shaped eyes and fetching smile—Mama's story!—he dared not marry her without his mother's approval. Eventually her beauty and courage slew his fear. And evermore it remained so: when Mama set her mind on some purchase she rarely failed. She once confided in Ben and me that if her wedding—which took place when she was sixteen—had lacked music, it would have resembled a funeral. And so I learned early that she kept her marriage going by gorging on hope.

From all we hear, the trip will be hard. Maybe even dangerous. Russian border guards and customs agents extort money and steal personal belongings. When dissatisfied with their booty, they send people back to their villages. Although Ben is only fifteen, he is tall for his age. By the time we leave, he'll be older. Heavier. His beard thicker. The military will say we bought forged passports and expect us to bribe them for letting Ben leave the country.

I tell Ben I am scared. Also exhilarated. It is easy for him to learn English. Not so for me. We study together. An hour each night. Someone once told me that after the age of eighteen, people find it hard to speak a new language fluently. But I am willing to risk being called a "greenhorn" if I can earn enough money to buy clothing and still help the family. From the hands-wanted ads in the Kiev newspapers, I know that American factories need needleworkers. Skilled ones. I feel certain that I can keep up with the best. With a little savings, I'll open my own shop. Do delicate stitchery. America is the land of opportunity. Everyone says so.

Maybe I can even find a Jewish husband willing to follow my family to Carmel. I am twenty years old. Most of my friends have already said vows. Stood under the chupah and broken the wine glass. The girls in Bobrovitz say, if you're single at thirty, you're no longer "purty." I have ten years to go and already I see in the mirror crow's-feet. Rouge and mascara can disguise only so much. Mama says I shouldn't be so particular. The rabbi twice now has tried to arrange a marriage; the first had a badly pock-marked face, from smallpox, and the second was older than Papa. Never, I told the rabbi. Some girls marry in desperation. I will from love. Mama asks where I get such notions. Tolstoy and Turgenev. That's a laugh, she says. Life is not a book.

Then what is it? Papa says books are about life. Without the dross. I believe him. Madame Bovary married just to be married. And she paid with her life. I don't want to spend the rest of mine yoked. The thought of it! Tied to a man I wish to be free of. A young man, Alex, lives in the same town as Jacob. Whenever I visit my brother, I seem to run into him. Always he looks at me approvingly. He is muscular and handsome, with blonde hair, probably a descendant of the Scandinavians who settled this part of Russia. If I could get to know him . . . unless of course he is Orthodox. Would I actually marry out of the faith? I don't think so. Ben would disagree. He says I'm a romantic and would elope. Maybe, if I cared enough for the man.

At thirteen, my unbraided hair hung to my waist. Ben, eight, would say, if your hair reached the floor, would you cut it? I always replied the same: let's wait to see. I suppose he's still waiting.

Papa seems to be in the same state. Waiting. Will he leave or stay? Not until he boards the train will I believe he's decided. And even then I won't be sure. Unlike Mama, who never changes her mind once it's made up, Papa ponders the subtleties. Some would say he's indecisive. Except about the distillery. I think he's just cautious. And fair. I admire his willingness to say, "Maybe I'm wrong and I ought to reconsider that idea." Mama thinks he's bluffing when he says that if he goes to America and doesn't like it, he'll return. I don't doubt him. Ben doesn't either.

What Mama fails to weigh is the closeness between Papa and Jacob. The scales in our family somehow got tipped. Only Mama seems to know how. Of course she won't say a word. I'm almost certain who's behind it. Rissa. Shortly before she and Jacob planned to get married, he disappeared for half a year. It was all very mysterious. Rissa nearly died of grief. When he returned, the rabbi married them. Since that joyous day, neither one comes to our house. Papa goes to them. Never Mama. Ben says the problem is religion, that Rissa's grandfather was forcibly converted to Catholicism and, when he had a chance to revert, refused. But I think Ben's all wrong. My guess is there was another man in the picture. Maybe someone in Irkutsk. Both Rissa and Jacob travel in revolutionary circles. That's how they met. Occasionally, some of their comrades are arrested and sent to Siberia. Maybe she had a fellow the government exiled to Lake Baikal. An important person in the socialist movement.

Politics seems the only motive strong enough to keep them apart. They would both sacrifice personal happiness for the good of the country. I can imagine Rissa having been in love with another socialist, a handsome fellow arrested by the government. In his absence, she agrees to marry Jacob. Then gets to feeling guilty. Jacob goes to Irkutsk to seek forgiveness from the man, a comrade. (The comrades are that way.) But like always the czarist government makes family and friends wait months. Eventually he talks to the man and receives his blessing. It all makes sense to me, but as Ben says, I can turn a riot into a romance.

"Jewish Perfidy," *Ukrainskaia Gazeta,*
December 1908

As the celebration of our Lord's birth approaches, let us not forget that just a few years ago the vigilant czarist police unearthed a conspiracy against Russia and the Christian world, "The Protocols of the Learned Elders of Zion," the dastardly Jewish plot to attain world domination. Now, with Christmas not far off, is the time to act and, as our beloved Czar Nicholas II has said, remove every last one of these perfidious people to the Pale of Settlement. Otherwise how are we to protect true believers from Jewish subversion?

The Protocols reveal how the Jews work through Masonic lodges and puppet governments and secret alliances to confuse the people, blackmail elected officials, and weaken laws through liberal interpretations. By controlling the press and making common cause with radicals and revolutionaries, the Jews use liberalism to weaken church and state, and undermine the traditional educational curriculum and religious instruction of our schools. They write scurrilous literature to encourage immorality among Christian youth and try to make us believe that Russia is backward and in need of change. As our adored czar has made clear: Jews intend to create an emergency that will provide them with an excuse to suspend civil liberties, and then make the measures permanent. Now is the time to drive them out!

The Editors

March 1908

Living in this godforsaken village has dulled my senses and made me doubt my faith. When I married Meyer, he promised we would move to Moscow. But he would not leave his mother. For all his talk about concerts and museums and culture, he remains rooted in the provinces. When his mother died, he had another excuse: the distillery. But what the czar takes can never be recovered. Now he uses Jacob as a stick to beat me. What does he know about the love of a mother for her firstborn?

I lie awake at night, seeing it over and over again. And always I come to the same conclusion. My intentions were pure. When I try to put myself in his shoes, I say, Mother had my best interests at heart. What more can a mother do? If I have offended God, as Jacob seems to think, I offended Him for love of my son. Only women and God understand a mother's affections. Were he a murderer—God forbid!—I should feel no less.

Although we don't speak, he's actually more like me than Meyer, who cares only for abstractions. His mother distilled the spirit and soul from him with his fancy education. Ideas are his element, not flesh and blood. I foolishly believed that a beautiful woman—yes, I was once a beauty—could excite his passions. But as soon as the novelty wore off, our bed grew cold; mind you, not that it was ever steamy. He bought me pretty dresses. A waste of money in a town of ignorant peasants. So rarely do we see the opera or ballet that my wardrobe is dusty from disuse. The theatre performs lighthearted plays as well as Chekhov, but Meyer prefers the serious. I swear only revolutionaries watch *The Cherry Orchard* and *Uncle Vanya*. Meyer says these plays are the very soul of Russia. If so, then all the more reason to flee this nihilistic country.

All we have here is a country store. Thank God I saved enough from the good days to buy the bodega, or the family would have starved. Even on a market day, I hardly earn enough to keep the family clothed and the house heated. Long gone are the days when the Cohen family held court for all the Jewish families in the area, and the shtetl women all wished to live and dress as well as Esther Cohen. Now they think they honor me by buying a licorice twist.

Unlike those illiterate shtetl women, with their shaved heads and wigs, I can read and write. I can do numbers. I can speak Russian and Ukrainian, not just Yiddish. The only people stupider are the peasants. Just two days ago, I asked Pavel the woodcutter to take me to Kiev in his wagon. He said he had a load of logs to sell and had no room. I offered to buy the wood for whatever price he was asking—if he would drive me. How much, he wanted to know, would I pay him for his trouble? Trouble, I said, I am making the trip easier for you and your horse. You can leave the wood with me and then your wagon will be empty. He pondered my offer and concluded that he could not give me a lift without receiving a fee. You can't cheat me, he murmured, and the horse tugged its load down the icy road.

Last summer, Mrs. Fedorov, the richest woman in the area, watched as her ten-year-old son, Christopher, swam in the local lake. Fanny and I were picking berries on the bluff above the water. Suddenly, her son cramped and cried for help. Three peasant boys stood just a few feet from her, all of them older than Christopher and strong swimmers. Mrs. Fedorov pleaded, "I can't swim. I'll give you each a penny if you save my son." The three boys turned and walked away. Her son thrashed around in the water for a minute or two and then disappeared from sight. The next day his body washed up on shore.

When I asked Peter Ilyich, the father of one of the boys, how such a tragedy could have happened, he said that the Fedorov family drove around in horse-drawn coaches and wore Parisian clothes, while paying only a pittance to the villagers who maintained their elegant home and tended their fields. When the villagers complained, they were told to find work elsewhere. "That's how it happened," said Peter.

To no avail did I explain that the child should have been held blameless for the parents' sins. Did the Fedorovs, I asked, increase your wages after this tragedy? Peter shook his head no. And Meyer doesn't understand why I hate this place.

March 1908

Once infected with an idea, Esther distempers the family. She plagues us with her harangues. The motley masses crowding into teeming New York tenements, albeit many of them Jews, have nothing in common with me. From all reports, they arrive illiterate and burdened by superstition. Bobrovitz is bad enough. I want the kind of companions who know Villon and Voltaire, Burke and Berkeley. Once the life of the mind atrophies, life is not worth the living.

I fear that like a child I will have to be led through my paces as I try to learn a new language. Esther simply replies, "You're an intelligent man. You speak several languages. What's one more?"

"Esther," I plead, "I want to live among people who speak Russian with confidence and beauty."

"Russian: the language of prejudice, pogroms, prison."

"America is a babel of tongues, a cacophony of hopes, but for the ignored and unheard, a place of silence."

"Meyer, you're like a baby; you're so easily discouraged. I promise, you'll like America—and quickly learn English."

"And some day I'll be able to board a train and ask the porter with perfect intonation: 'Can you please direct me to the toilet?'"

"Meyer, wherever you lived, you'd complain," she said losing patience. "When you sit with the royalists in the parks, you are a royalist, and lament the loss of the old culture. When you talk with the revolutionary students at the bookstalls, you swear your undying hatred of the bourgeoisie and wish for revolution. Meyer, you are none of these things. You are the spoiled child of a rich mother, and I have kept you spoiled—at the cost of my health."

Since that discussion, my days are spent without hope.

December 1910

You would think that we had asked for the crown jewels, so hard was it to obtain passports and travel papers. When the blessed day arrived, Pavel took us and our luggage to Kiev in his wagon. He insisted that the additional weight was bad for his horse and charged extra. At the train station, I could see tears in Meyer's eyes. The children seemed excited. On the platform, we paid for cups of steaming chai and supplemented what I had not packed in two large food hampers. To my surprise, I found our accommodations comfortable and clean, but I soon discovered that linens were not changed and plates were reused without being washed. All went smoothly till we reached the Ukrayina-Russian border, where armed guards boarded the train looking for men of military age.

Ben's passport accurately listed his birth date as 1893, but Ben's six feet made the guards suspicious. They asked the four of us to follow them. In a vestibule, a stone-faced uniformed official sat at an improvised table splashed with papers. At his right elbow rested our freedom: an ink pad and stamp. He studied our papers and questioned Meyer and me about Ben's age. These Baron de Hirsch people lie, he said, to help their co-religionists. Is that how you obtained these documents? Before I could answer he ordered the soldiers to accompany us back to our compartment to search our luggage, all the while keeping our papers.

Ben and Fanny had been silent throughout the questioning, but as we threaded our way back through the train, she whispered to her brother. At the compartment, she turned her most fetching smile on the men and offered them each a modest bribe if they would not confiscate what she called the family's most precious possession: a watercolor on vellum by Nicholas Hilliard, Court Miniaturist to Queen Elizabeth I of England. One of the soldiers wondered aloud if such a rare object should be allowed to leave the country. As Ben produced the miniature, which I knew to be a copy that he had drawn, Fanny added: Hill-Hill-iard has p---ainted the l-l-likes of Sir Fran---cis Drake, Sir Walter Ra-Ra-Raleigh, and Sir Ph-Ph-Philip Si---dney.

Whether or not these famous names meant anything to the soldiers, they studied the miniature, pocketed our bribes, and left. A few minutes later they returned to inform us that our papers would be returned to us officially stamped once we relinquished the miniature. Reluctantly Ben handed them the vellum watercolor, entitled "A Youth Leaning Against a Tree Among Roses." Shortly, one of the soldiers returned our documents, reporting that his superior was very pleased and hoped that we had a safe and pleasant journey.

At Brody and on the German side of the border, the customs officials carefully checked our papers and luggage, including the lining of our valises, questioning but not confiscating the miniatures in Ben's bags. Although courteous and proper, they did turn back a number of people for irregularities. I noticed that a few families bribed officials not to inspect their luggage.

As we approached Hamburg, I kept in mind the Baron de Hirsch agent warning us about fraudulent lodging-house owners and emigration agencies. Advised to seek help from the Jewish community or proceed directly to the Hamburg-Amerikanische Packetfahrt-Actiengesellschaft (HAPAG), which had built a refuge for emigrants in the port area in Veddel, we decided on the latter. After a fourteen-day quarantine, we boarded the steamship Kaiserin Auguste Victoria. A large boat, it carried 2,996 passengers, 652 in first-class, 286 in second, and 2,058 in third, steerage, for which we held tickets. I shall not describe the bunk beds, the insufficient lavatories, the body smells, the gross behavior. One couple . . . I can't even say it. Fanny and Ben spent as much time on deck as possible—and still they contracted bedbugs and lice. Whatever I may think of Germans, I always associated them with cleanliness. Not anymore.

December 1910

To the shipping company we represent nothing more than self-loading cargo. In the lower decks, more than two thousand people cram into narrow compartments divided into separate dormitories for single men, single women, and families. My parents and I sleep in three-stacked bunks against one wall, Ben in a lower. Six other people share the compartment. The whirring sound of the engines is broken only by the babel of tongues. And the retching that accompanies rough seas. One stormy day, as Ben rises unsteadily from his bed, a man in the bunk above him vomits on his head. Through the thinly partitioned walls I can hear love moans. Jammed as tightly as bottled pickles and smelling like rancid herring, we soon become a part of the constant stench of spoiled food, seasickness, unwashed bodies, garlic, tobacco, and disinfectants. The greasy steamship food is served from huge kettles right into our dinner pails. Mostly stringy beef and dried pork with potato soup and stale bread. Mama refuses to eat, calling it *traif*, fit only for goyim. Fortunately, just before we boarded the ship, a pushcart dealer had sold us a wheel of cheese and hard-boiled eggs. Also fresh vegetables and fruit. Mama says that if not for the peddler, she would have become a skeleton and would likely have died. As it is, she has been bedridden most of the trip from headaches and nausea. Papa says each meal is his last, but eats three times a day. Grudgingly, he contends.

Lying sick in her bunk, Mama says, has one advantage. She doesn't have to see the ladies from first and second class strutting in their finery on the upper decks. But far worse than the social pretensions are the unhygienic conditions. The women's lavatory resembles a long porcelain coffin. Each side of the pinched room has five faucets of cold salt water and five sinks, also used as basins for greasy pots, laundry tubs for soiled clothing and hankies, and receptacles for seasickness. The toilets, filthy and dependent on shredded newspapers, are never once cleaned during our journey. Not surprisingly, they clog and exhibit disgusting stains. Nearly every surface of steerage feels sticky. To escape this fetid hole, we sprawl on the steerage deck, which is chairless. Measles and whooping cough spread. Several people contract scarlet fever. The steerage air, a fog of illness and tobacco smoke, nearly kills us. The men think that cigars and pipes will kill the germs. Papa, of course, adds to the fumes.

Ben and I quickly meet others our age, like the Polish boy Henryk Nawrocki, who is traveling to America alone. Together we explore the ship. Even the engine room, which looks like a furnace from hell. One of the kids says we are lucky to be sailing on a German boat. The others are worse. Impossible!

When our heads begin to itch with lice, Mama discovers she too is infected. Only Papa's baldness keeps him free of the vermin. Evil-smelling bedbugs also torture us. The ship's staff distribute turpentine to kill the mites. Mama cuts off my beautiful golden locks and shears Ben's blonde hair, then lavishly applies the escharotic to our scalps. Her own waist-length brown hair she can't bear to cut, so it takes her longer to be rid of the disgusting creatures. By the time the Statue of Liberty comes into sight, she is again wearing her hair in a pretty bun. And attracting stares from many of the men.

January 1911

Fanny and I stayed up all night just to glimpse the flickering lights of lower Manhattan. But before entering the Upper Bay, the steamship dropped anchor to allow immigration officials and doctors from the Hudson River Quarantine Station to board. They checked the documents of first- and second-class passengers, who were then ferried to shore, leaving the rest of us to wait for the Ellis Island ordeal. Disembarking on the Hudson River piers, we felt underfoot the ground of America for only a brief spell before we boarded ferries, really open-air barges. The harbor, choked with steamships waiting to discharge thousands of passengers, looked like an armada representing all the nations of the world. At last our ferry shuttled us to the gingerbread castle with the enclosed walkway that led to the front door of the main building. Ellis Island, the hope of millions! As we passed through the glass cage, we felt weary but overjoyed to at last be entering the gates of the golden world.

Inside the massive hall, metal railings resembling cattle pens led the immigrants past the examiners, who looked over the flocks as one might peruse a stockyard for sick animals. The hall smelled of sweat and garlic and urine and vomit and all the attars wrought by poverty. As in Homburg, where people with eye infections were denied passage on the steamships, examiners were turning back immigrants with trachoma—also immigrants with a limp, a wheeze, or even a prominent sore. Some tried to hide their infirmities from the doctors. But whenever a person aroused suspicion, the examiners isolated him and marked his coat lapel or shirt with colored chalk. Not until later did I discover what the letters signified: H, heart; K, hernia; Sc, scalp; X, mental defects. When we reached the examiner on the tall stool behind the high writing stand, he scrutinized our passports and stamped them. But our hope of being "processed" quickly foundered when the examiner asked my father, "Political memberships?"

To Mom's chagrin, Pop said foolishly, "Socialist."

The examiner lowered his eyeglasses and looked at us as though we had some virulent disease. He then summoned a man who led us off to rooms upstairs, where we had to undergo further questioning, as well as mental tests. By this time the authorities had gone through our luggage and turned up a pamphlet that Pop had packed among his belongings: "The Four Freedoms."

As our inquisitor studied the document, we sat restlessly exchanging worried glances. At last, he raised his head and repeated: "'Freedom from forced conversion. Freedom from impressment. Freedom to criticize the government. Freedom to be taught in one's own language.' I can appreciate the first two, Mr. Cohen, but what about three and four?"

Pop explained that to live in Russia under the Romanovs was tantamount to living in a prison, and that the destruction of cheders ran into the thousands.

"America has good relations with Russia, Mr. Cohen, and as for the razing of religious schools, they often breed fanaticism. You have come to a secular country."

"I quite agree," said Pop, "but good relations do not mean that the czarist government rules without fault. It has engaged in many cruelties, especially toward minorities." He paused. "Do you mind if I smoke?" The examiner asked him not to, and Mom smiled approvingly. "As to the fourth liberty, though Jews think that shuls should have the right to teach Hebrew, the authors particularly had in mind the right of Ukrainians to use their own language, in schools, in government, in official documents and the like."

The official pondered Pop's response before he replied, "To avoid America becoming a Tower of Babel, we must insist on English as the official language. Your children will be taught in that tongue. Do you understand?"

"Yes, but America will miss the beauty of hearing many tongues."

"If you find fault with this country even before you have set foot on the mainland, what can we expect if we admit you to America?"

"You can expect to have among your immigrants one family that will always believe in freedom of speech and assembly."

The examiner shook his head, but I could not tell what it meant until he said, "I see you know the U.S. Constitution."

"By heart," replied Pop.

"Good."

He then asked Fanny and me to draw a triangle and two intersecting lines on a piece of paper, a task that any child could dispatch with ease. Handing us a peg board with square and round holes, he directed us to remove small sticks from a box and make them fit the board. I began to wonder about the mental capacities of the people being admitted to America. Writing something down in a leather-bound ledger, he turned to Mom and inquired:

"How do you wash steps, from the top down or bottom up?"

She snapped, "I didn't come to America to scrub stairs."

The examiner guffawed, which led me to believe that he wasn't such a bad sort after all. Before he could return us to the main hall, Pop asked:

"All this because I believe in socialism?"

"Feel lucky, Mr. Cohen. In a great many cases we send the father back to the country of origin and admit only his wife and children."

"Just for political reasons?"

"Can you think of a greater danger?"

"Yes, religion."

The examiner stared at Pop for only a few seconds, but it felt like a thousand years.

Returning to the main hall to collect our luggage, we had one more obstacle to clear, a medical examination. A man with a hook lifted eyelids to look for signs of trachoma. He didn't bother to sterilize the instrument after each person, apparently not realizing that he himself could be spreading the disease; and when Mom requested that he dip the hook into the bottle of alcohol next to him, he seemed amazed at her suggestion.

The ferry ride to Manhattan, as I recall, took only a few minutes.

January 1911

At the dock, Mama and Papa look for cousin Max. Who is nowhere to be seen. I cling to Ben's arm. Battery Park is thronged. Hawkers, charlatans, pimps, thieves, and religious zealots are everywhere. They try to sell us herring, rent us rooms, steal our money, induce me to model for a magazine. Different religious agencies advertise themselves. A Bible zealot tries to get Papa to renounce Judaism for Methodism. I laugh. Not a word does Papa understand. Men and women stand around with placards. Hawking hotel rooms and hostels and horse-drawn cabs and restaurants for the lost and forlorn. A bearded man in a black coat, resembling an orthodox Jew, sits behind a card table with a sign: Baron de Hirsch Fund. We push through the hordes of people and introduce ourselves. He checks his manifest. Circles our names. "Thank God for the telegraph!" says Mother. In Yiddish, the agent introduces himself. Mr. Isaac Kagan. He directs us to take the horse trolley uptown to an apartment on Riley Street. Reserved for us. Our Carmel farmhouse is still under construction.

"It shouldn't be more than a few weeks," he says. "By the way, I have a letter here for you from a Max Duberman."

From a disordered pile of papers, he finds the envelope. It has been opened. He says the officials were trying to determine the intended recipients of the letter. It reads:

Dear Esther,
I have gone to California. If I strike it rich, I will send you and the family tickets to San Francisco. The people from the Baron de Hirsch Fund will look after you. Carmel is a nice place. I've been there. It's just that I couldn't resist the temptation to start my own business. I can hear Meyer now: the road to easy riches is paved in pain. Maybe he's right. We'll see. Love, Max

"From the first letter I knew he was unstable. But no, he's ambitious and enterprising, you said. So here we are in New York, and Max? Lost somewhere in California. What a *meshugana* family!"

The agent removes a soiled handkerchief. He wipes his profusely sweating forehead and mechanically repeats what sounds like a rehearsed speech.

"The land is in the country, on twenty-three acres. There's a river running through the trees. Soil's real good . . . for some things. You can put the water in a jug and a year later it will still be the same."

Papa, querulous, grumbles, "That's what Max said. Do you all sing the same song?" The man pulls at his unruly beard and turns his bloodshot eyes on Papa, but fails to reply. "What else is there to do besides farming?"

At that moment, a pushcart vendor bellows. Like an answer from heaven to Papa's question. "Eating keeps starvation from the door. Try my herring and potato latkes."

"Mr. Cohen," says the agent dully, sounding as if reciting from rote, "to till the soil is to participate in the divine, to place one's hand in the process of creation."

The pushcart man. "Just the thing to fill your *gotkis*."

Papa glances at the Battery grounds and says, "Where are the trees? Everywhere, garbage."

Mr. Kagan sighs, "All the more reason to make a new life in the country. Lovely summer evenings. Fireflies making soft spots of light in the darkness." Papa waves his hand dismissively, and the agent abruptly changes his tone from sympathy to annoyance, saying pointedly, "Let me remind you, Mr. Cohen, what this is all about—the disrupted lives, the cost, the pain—it is not about you and me, but our children. Measure your success in them, in the fulfillment of *their* dreams. That's how immigrants measure success in America."

"In other words, we—"

Knowing exactly what Papa has in mind, Mr. Kagan interrupts, "Yes, we are buying our children's future with our own."

Papa turns up his nose and changes the subject. "The place smells. Even here next to the water."

A frustrated Mr. Kagan shrugs. "A city's a city. What do you expect: there should be a garden of Eden at the dock? Wait, you'll see. Forty miles from Philadelphia, villages and farms, where Jews from different countries work side by side, devoted to building a new life through agriculture."

"Mr. Kagan," Papa asks skeptically, "what did you do before you worked for the Baron de Hirsch Fund?"

"Advertising . . . for a Yiddish daily."

"Figures," says Papa.

Schlepping our luggage for a city block to a trolley stand, we wait in line. At last we board. The horse clip-clops along the cobblestones, kicking up dust on the dirt streets strewn with rubbish and excrement. Ragamuffin children in rags run to and fro. Some grab hold of the back of the trolley to get a free lift. Pushcarts and peddlers, thick as maggots, crowd the curbs. A man with an undernourished child at his side holds a plate for contributions. He plays the accordion and in Yiddish hoarsely sings:

When nighttime falls on New York streets,
All you smell are oily eats.
Jewish songs fill the summer air;
Cooking odors are everywhere.

Those guys with garlic on their breath
Could very nearly be your death.
There's herring and homemade noodles,
Honey cakes and apple strudels.

Everybody coughs and sneezes,
Like a bunch of dirty greasers.
All you see is pushcart dealers,
When nighttime falls on New York streets.

January 1911

Even the Baron de Hirsch agent sounded like a snake oil salesman. This was not the impression that I wanted America to make on Meyer. One look at his discouraged face told me he was already wishing for a return passage home. I tried to cheer him up by pointing out that at least we'd be living for a while in America's greatest city, with theatres, museums, bookstores, and newspapers. But having to haul our bags, like overburdened donkeys, from the trolley to our apartment did not improve his temper. The brown brick building with four apartments looked bleak. Inside, the hallway smelled dank, and when we opened the door to our furnished apartment, the odor of mold nearly bowled us over. No one had taken the time to clean for our arrival. The toilet needed to be scrubbed, the dishes and silverware sterilized in boiling water, the stove dismantled and the parts soaked in kerosene, the walls and floors washed, and the kitchen cleared of cockroaches and rats. The job would be bad enough without Meyer's complaints, so I sent him and Ben to get a feel for the neighborhood. Meanwhile, Fanny and I began with the windows so we could at least see out, which proved a mixed blessing. Behind the house stood a concrete courtyard surrounded by dilapidated buildings. In front of the house, the street teemed with gamins who apparently had nowhere else to play.

An hour later, when Meyer returned, he announced that the golden world did not begin on Riley Street or on any other in the area. I asked about stores, and he told me about Mr. Shapiro's grocery at the corner, a drugstore with a soda fountain, a kosher bakery, and a small shul on the next street, the Young Israel.

A few days later, I introduced myself to the rabbi and explained that I and my children would like to attend services. He greeted me warmly and explained that since so many families had left their relatives and friends behind in the old country, when it came time for a bar mitzvah or bris or wedding or, God forbid, funeral service, the neighborhood congregation crowded the shul and became as one big family, all speaking Yiddish. He said, You need never be alone. I thanked him, and he asked me had I lost my husband. I could have said yes and not been telling a lie. But I knew that one day he would see us walking together in the neighborhood and inquire. So I told him, My husband reveres Jewish culture and history but has little taste for religion. He said, Skepticism is the lifeblood of Judaism.

January 1911

At the top of Riley Street, Papa patronizes a stand selling the *Forward*. In the section called the "Bintel Brief," he finds letters from immigrants, most of them decrying their hardships in America. He exploits the letters to nurse his grievances against Mama. Every evening he buys the paper, sits on the curb, and reads to Ben and me. He then goes inside to belabor Mama.

Thank God for my rudimentary English. Spare as it is, I manage to buy things and get from one place to another. Within a week of our arrival, I find a job. As a sewing machine operator at New York's biggest maker of blouses, the Triangle Shirtwaist Factory. A building on the corner of Washington Place and Greene Street in Greenwich Village. Because of my experience, I receive fifteen dollars a week! Ben gets hired by a cosmetics factory. The Cosin Company. He works in the shipping room putting gum tape on boxes. So artful is he that the department stores compliment Mr. Cosin on the skill of his shipping clerk. For his labors he soon earns twelve dollars a week, having begun at ten.

Papa looks in the paper for jobs, but sees nothing to his liking. No surprise! Mama has gone to work for a local grocer. Keeping his books. She makes ten dollars a week. But the grocer gives her free fruits and vegetables. And sometimes a little more.

Although we worked long hours, Fanny and I made time for the stage shows and the nickelodeons, where Fanny first saw Sarah Bernhardt, whom she adored. Fanny's room, a shrine to the "Divine Sarah," over-flowed with postcards, sculptures, cabinet cards, press notices, cigarette cards, character portraits, posters—any scrap bearing the great actress.

One evening after work I stopped at Marty's Pool Hall on Broadway to see for myself this game that so many immigrant boys played. A Jewish fellow, ten or twelve years older than me, was shooting pool with an Irish kid. They had been playing for hours, or so the boys around the table said. I stood mesmerized at their skill and cool nerves. A small bundle of cash lay on a table: winner take all. The crowd, divided between the "Paddy" and the "Yid," was making side bets on almost every shot. Absorbed in the action, I lost track of time, forgetting about dinner. Around me, boys and men guzzled beer, keeping the owner of the pool hall jumping.

I couldn't help but notice that, even though the drinks were on the house for the two players, the Paddy drank but not the Yid, a fact that might explain the outcome, which took place well after midnight, when the Irish kid missed, and the Jewish guy ran the table. His adoring fans and those who had been betting on him cheered, "Way to go, A. R." Speaking Yiddish, he thanked his supporters. When I pumped his hand and said, "Mazel tov," he replied, "Arnold Rothstein."

He clapped me on the back and said in Yiddish, "You new around here? Haven't seen you before. What's your name?"

"Ben Cohen. My family recently moved to the neighborhood."

"How's your English."

"I'm learning."

"Everything else jake?"

"What's that mean?"

"Listen, kid, you don't look like the rest of the bums around here. Stick with me and I'll turn you from a greenhorn into a regular. Come back tomorrow night. If you need dough, just ask me."

February 1911

Already weeks ago my angels found work to keep us in food. Me, too! When I walked into Mr. Shapiro's grocery down the street, I told him how nice and clean he kept the shelves. He said he wished his ledgers were so clean. So? I said and hitched up my skirt above the ankle pretending to tie my shoelace. Let me have a look. Maybe I can help. The next thing I knew he offered me the job of bookkeeper, with a high stool at a slanted writing desk. A pretty leg never hurts!

Fanny, who has magic in her hands and can stitch a wedding dress in less than a week, spoke to Mr. Harris at the Triangle Shirtwaist Company, and he hired her to sew blouses. Why shirtwaists, I asked, when you could be working for an uptown dress store making evening clothes? Don't b-b-be old---fashioned, she said. N---early all w-w-women wear shirt-shirt-waists now---adays with a skirt . . . above the an---kle. She went into her room and brought a magazine with pictures. There, she said, s-s-see for-your-yourself. Well, I answered, if you make stylish blouses like this one, you should have a lot of mazel on the job.

Nu! She wasn't on the job two weeks before she talked about the girls at Triangle striking the factory for higher wages, extra safety precautions, and better working conditions. She said the year before the girls had walked out and, as a result, conditions improved. I told her she was mad. Jobs were not so plentiful. For every sewing machine operator, a dozen stood ready to take her place. She fumed, We g-g-girls can have on---ly one b-b-brief ab---sence from our w-w-w-work to use the la-la-vatory. The air on the n-n-ninth floor suff-suff-ocates us with dust and cloth par---ticles. One of the t-t-two el-el-evators is al---ways b-b-breaking down. The se---curity people lock the d-d-doors at four for-for-ty five to pre-pre-vent the theft of shirt---waists, forcing us to w-w-wait in line for the one o-o-perating ele---vator. It's un---safe.

I told her that for too long she'd been listening to her father's socialist ideas. America, I said, does not throw its workers on the garbage heap, like in Russia. Wait, you'll see. Just write a letter to the owners. They'll correct the wrongs.

Ben had no complaints, thank God, and yet I thought he could do better. Cosmetics, I told him, were for frivolous women. He agreed, saying that if they spent as much time preparing their minds as they did their faces, they'd be geniuses. But since cosmetics sold well, he figured he had a future with the company. So I told myself, you can't live your children's lives; and if you do, who will live yours?

Of course, there's Meyer. He stays at home reading and smoking. I hate to say it, but he should have remained behind with Jacob.

The three wage earners brought home enough for us to leave Riley Street, but the free rent thanks to the Baron de Hirsch Fund made me stay, even though I was unhappy with Mrs. Shirley in the apartment below. She ran a brothel with three girls. Her clientele came from the seedier classes and were often drunk. I feared for Fanny's physical safety and Ben's morals. He seemed attracted to Mrs. Shirley's place and in particular a girl he met a day or two after we moved in. Cherry. I asked him what kind of girl would have a name like that? He said she came from the Cherokee Indian tribe. Some explanation, I said, and dropped the matter, telling myself that if Ben took up with this Miss Cherry, I could always call the police to close the bordello. In the months to come I used that threat more than once to keep Ben from bad ways.

Once, I went downstairs and told Mrs. Shirley that I didn't want Ben seeing her girls. It's only one he fancies, she said, as if I'd failed to make my point. One, two, or three, I said, I won't have it. She shrugged and said, What can I do? You can bar the door, I said, he's only seventeen. How old were you when you first . . . ? she asked me. Sixteen, but I was married! You want I should tell them to get married? she said. I nearly choked. He can't afford tarts. She said, Not even for nothing? For a moment I missed her meaning. You're not telling me . . . she interrupted. That's exactly what I'm telling you. She likes him and in her off hours, for free, well, you understand. I hardly knew what to say and found myself repeating, But he's only seventeen. She laughed and said her father had two children by that age and walked away.

When I brought up the subject with Ben he asked, Would it be better for Cherry to work in a paint factory and die of lead poisoning or a hat factory and die of mercury poisoning or a sweatshop and die of tuberculosis? Enough, I said, with these horrible examples. There are other kinds of work. Look at me! I walked into Shapiro's and walked out with a job. Not everyone's so lucky, he said. I have a friend who lives on the Lower East Side. I can show you people crowded into tenements eating and sleeping without privacy, in rooms that double as workshops. Here women and small children, side by side, sew, make tassels for dance cards, roll cigars and cigarettes, tat lace, string beads for moccasins and handbags, sort human hair for wigs, pick the meat from tens of thousands of nuts, assemble brushes. Is that what the girls downstairs should do? My son had never spoken to me this way, and I felt the sting, but I am no fool. I see, I replied, better they should die of syphilis and gonorrhea, but before they die infect dozens, maybe hundreds, of men. How do you know whether at this very moment you're not sick with one of those dreadful curses? Personally, I would rather be poisoned in a factory than go mad from a venereal disease. The girls are careful, he said. Now that's a laugh, I told him. What does careful mean? A sad look came into his face, and it was then I knew I was having the better of the argument. He said, They take precautions. Does a doctor come in every week? I asked. How do you know what germs those disgusting, drunken men carry? He said nothing. I could see the fight draining out of him. From now on, I said, you'll avoid that Cherry girl—and see a doctor tomorrow.

A few days later, on a Sunday, Ben took Cherry to a dance hall. He swore they would only swirl to the music and not come back to snuggle at Mrs. Shirley's. What could I say? And the song he sang for days after, what did it mean?

> Ev'ry little movement has a meaning all its own.
> Ev'ry thought and feeling by some posture can be shown.
> And ev'ry love thought that comes a-stealing o'er your being,
> Must be revealing all its sweetness
> In some appealing little gesture all its own.

Fanny had no suitors, thank God, and amused herself with Sarah Bernhardt memorabilia and Broadway shows like *Madame Sherry*. Meyer haunted the Yiddish vaudeville houses and twice dragged me along. The last time, on the way home, Meyer said, "Where were you Americans born?" repeating a joke from the comedian. "Russia," he laughed. "Then you're naturalized Americans?" I shook my head, anticipating the silliness. "Naturalized nothin'. We're pickled or petrified."

Although I wholeheartedly agreed with the sentiment, I couldn't get over what had happened to Meyer—and so quickly—since our coming to America. In Russia, French farces earned his contempt; only Chekhov was worth his time. The more I thought about it, the more I realized that Ben too had changed, and that only Fanny and I remained untouched.

March 1911

Living at home, subject to my parents' scrutiny, led me to make another life away from Riley Street. I befriended other fellows with whom I'd sometimes have a drink or see a burlesque. But most of all I liked hanging out with A. R. at Marty's Pool Hall or at a baseball game. He always had a talent for mischief—and money. Twelve years older than I, he had connections in the gangs and had earned a name for himself as a smart cookie. I had no desire to break the law, except in harmless little ways like bagging dough from A. R.'s Harlem numbers operation, or passing him information about his opponents' hands during poker games. Madame Sylvia, as the boys called her, had a house in midtown, not far from Broadway. In one room she hosted card games, in another she ran a small roulette wheel. She made her dough from charging the players a "rental" fee for her premises and from drinks. Pretty girls provided the players with cigars, drinks, new decks of cards; they also served as croupiers. I would hide in the room above the poker players, positioned to see the action below through several pinholes drilled in the floor. When A. R. found himself in a high-stakes game and needed some help, he would ask Madame Sylvia for a glass of ice tea, the signal for her to come upstairs and learn from me what hands the other players held. She'd bring him the tea on a small tray with a napkin, inside of which she had scribbled the information. A. R. paid me not in gelt but in favors. In particular, he let me use a two-room apartment that he kept on Second Avenue for friends on the lam. Here Cherry and I met for lovemaking and, on more than one occasion, ran into seedy characters in trouble with the law.

A pretty girl with bronzed skin and heavy black hair reaching to her waist, Cherry wore bright-colored dresses and striking turquoise broaches. Her sharp nose, small mouth, and thin face made her look gaunt, but she had the personality of a jovial butterball. At fifteen, she decided that life on the Oklahoma reservation had little to offer her, so she made her way to Ada and rode the rails from there to New York City, where she found work as a scaler in the Fulton fish market. One day, Mrs. Shirley showed up and remarked that if Cherry wanted employment without chafed and bloody hands, she could arrange it—and at higher pay. But Mrs. Shirley discovered Cherry's age only after she had hired her. She knew that using a girl of fifteen could land her in jail, so she kept Cherry on for several years as a housekeeper, running errands, serving drinks, cleaning up, cooking. From the other girls, Cherry learned the trade: how to tell the difference between the sexually hungry men and the mean ones, the shy and the bold, the big spenders and the pikers. Just in case of an emergency, she kept a shaving razor in her room, which she had to resort to on only two occasions, once when a man pulled a knife, and once when a drunk tried to rob her. Among her clientele she counted a few of the cops on the beat and a city councilman. But she claimed none of her men ever meant anything to her until I came along. Why that should have been, I can only guess. Perhaps she liked my reading poetry to her in Russian or appreciated the miniatures I gave her, or maybe my living in the same building had the feel of family. The reason certainly had nothing to do with my sexual skills. She taught me how to love a woman: how to fondle, how to kiss, not wolfishly but suggestively, where to run my fingers, and the many ways to bring her to an orgasm.

Without intending to fall for Cherry, I found that the more time I spent in her presence, the more I wanted. Her exoticism haunted me. I had no idea what it meant to love a woman. From what I'd seen in Russia and America, most marriages seemed based on convenience or some mutual arrangement: you look after the kids and cook and sew, and I'll bring home the paycheck. In the novels that I'd read, lovers swooned or sensed the earth shaking beneath their feet or felt lightheaded or broke into a sweat or became tongue-tied or suffered from insomnia. They couldn't concentrate for thinking of the other or experienced palpitations or the stirrings of the heart—whatever that means—or wrote passionate letters daily to each other or dissected each word for some hidden meaning or weighed each virtue and defect to determine if this person was really, as they dreamed, the person they would want to spend their life with. None of this conduct rang true to me. What I felt in Cherry's presence was the exhilaration of discovering a new world, and the animal magnetism of her bed. If such matters are the stuff of romance, then I suppose I was lovestruck.

Cherry liked going to the theatre or the dance halls. The stage featured a number of plays about fallen women and the double standard, for example, *Anti-Matrimony, Her Husband's Wife,* and *As a Man Thinks.* Cherry and I talked about the double standard and agreed that the men and women in these plays inhabited a society apart from ours. They had money and homes and status; they had time to gallivant and worry about where their wives and husbands spent their afternoons; they weren't dying of tuberculosis and praying for enough money to put food on the table. The vaudeville houses, with their sardonic humor, came closer to the truth.

Our favorite outing, and the cheapest, found us walking in Central Park. Once we rented skates and joined a group of rich kids on the frozen pond. Cherry spent more time down than up, "I'm used to being on my back," she quipped. Having often skated during Russian winters, I played ice tag or hockey as Cherry watched.

One night, we pooled our money and took a bus to Rector's, a snazzy restaurant on Broadway and 48th Street. No sooner had we sat down than A. R. walked in, alone as usual. Seeing us, he came over to say hello. I didn't want him to join us, but Cherry, who had often heard me talk about A. R., invited him to pull up a chair. Right from the start, the two of them hit if off. Who could have guessed that Cherry would put him in touch with Mrs. Shirley, a contact that led him, Owney Madden, and the madam to open several houses. In all my life I never met a more enterprising goniff. A. R. could smell a moneymaking scheme from two blocks away. I suspect his love of the green stuff grew out of his need for it. He compulsively gambled, making and losing large sums. Eventually he opened his own gambling den and bankrolled others, putting himself on the side of management and letting the bettors take the risks.

Before the waiter handed us menus, A. R. asked us if we liked oysters, offering to buy a bucket.

"They're not kosher," I said with a straight face.

"Get serious, kid."

"I never had them, but I'm game," said Cherry.

"Count me in also."

A. R. placed the order and immediately began asking about the bordello: the life of the girls, the money they made, the cut for the madam, rent, heating, lighting, laundry bills, and other expenses. I could see his mind churning, adding up percentages. When he learned that some prominent men came to the house, he wanted to know if they too received a cut.

"Just the favor of the ladies."

"I suppose they keep the girls from being arrested."

"Sometimes the cops run us in, but one call from Mrs. Shirley to her friends usually gets us out in under an hour."

A. R. smiled. "Then you have no special love for the law?"

"Not if they keep me from making a living."

His next statement didn't please me.

"I could use someone like you."

"Doing what?"

I remembered hearing that A. R. ran a sideline in strike-breaking, employing spies, usually women, inside the unions, and hiring young toughs to break up picket lines. And I knew who paid the bill.

"Ever hear of the Triangle Shirtwaist Company?" he asked her.

Interrupting, I said, "Yeah, my sister works there."

"I didn't know," he mumbled, just as the waiter brought the oysters. "Forget it."

"Fanny's been talking about the union walking out for better working conditions and pay. What do you know about it?"

"Like I said, nix it."

"You work for the owners, don't you?"

Cherry's eyes darted from me to A. R. and back.

"I've met with them. Nothing more."

"My sister belongs to the union. She'll be on the picket line if they go out."

A. R. studied his plate of Maryland oysters as if he had suddenly taken a scholarly interest in crustaceans. Eventually he muttered, "There won't be no rough stuff."

I put a hand on his arm and said, "A. R., you don't need that job. The bosses are bastards. Find another."

He may have been weighing the competing claims of friendship and money, because he kept shaking his head and biting his upper lip. Finally, he turned directly on me his heavy-lidded eyes, which during moments of strain often seemed half closed. "Tell her to stay home when I tell you to."

"I can't do that, A. R."

"Why not?"

"Because I believe in the workers' cause."

Cherry laughed with such force that the oyster in her mouth sailed across the table and landed on the floor, where I tried discreetly to scoop it up with my linen napkin.

Grinning at Cherry, A. R. said, "My feelings exactly."

She didn't reply, but I knew from her expression that A. R. had misunderstood; in fact she was reveling in the position I'd taken.

"You know the Triangle bosses?" I asked.

"Yeah, they're a couple of putzes."

"That's what Fanny says."

"Well?"

"Well, what? Would you rather I took money off nice guys or shmucks?"

I think for the first time, I noticed A. R.'s lizard leer and milky skin. He lived more in the night than in the day, rising in the afternoon and not retiring until almost morning. I suppose working in the shadows agreed with his enterprises.

"Some of the gangs," I said, "protect the unions."

"The owners pay more."

"So just once take less and do the right thing."

He poked a toothpick in his mouth and came out with the most remarkable aphorism. "A stiff penis has no conscience, and neither does money."

My thoughts migrated to Cherry's lean hard body, the firmness of her small breasts, the radiance of her skin, the whiteness of her teeth, and the herbal scents with which she laved herself. At this very moment, I could smell a hint of sage. In the worst way, I wanted the dinner to end so that Cherry and I could leave and return to the apartment where I knew we could never die.

On the sidewalk, we parted with A. R., but not before Cherry said, "Thanks for thinking of me, Mr. Rothstein."

I added puckishly, "She's a Eugene Debs man."

March 25, 1911

Such a noise, I thought. At first it sounded like a cat being tortured, a favorite sport of urchins. But then I realized the cry was human. Leaning out my front window into a mild springlike afternoon, I saw a woman pulling her hair and rending her clothes, crying, My Clara, my Clara! I called to her, What is it? She cried, My God! Mrs. Cohen, come quick! A fire in the Asch Building . . . the top floors. Then she put her hands to her cheeks and howled lamentations that no living person should ever feel such pain to make. I looked at the clock on the mantel, 5:01, took a light coat, and left the building. An hour later I reached the Triangle Shirtwaist Factory and saw before me a vision of hell. The streets glistened with blood, the air smelled of death. Dozens of broken bodies lay on the sidewalk with numbered tags attached to them. Thousands of people stood milling aimlessly in Washington Square. Fire trucks and their crews surrounded the building. Policemen darted in and out of the lower floors. On the roof of New York University, next door, students huddled stonefaced. I heard muffled cries and voices all around me, then an occasional shriek. I caught shreds of conversation. You could feel the heat on the street. Witnesses were saying the ladders had extended only as far as the sixth floor, and the safety nets were torn apart by the falling bodies. Water hoses couldn't reach the fire. The eighth and tenth floors mostly escaped. The ninth is where they mostly died. They jumped from the window ledges, hand in hand. One couple kissed and embraced before they leaped. You could still hear cries for help in Yiddish and other languages. Mostly Jewish girls and some Italians, a few men, but not many.

As I approached the corpses, a policeman stopped me and wouldn't let me pass until I explained that my precious Fanny had been working on the ninth floor. The dead now lay in rows. I looked at their faces: scared, pained, burned, some surprisingly serene. In my heart I prayed that if Fanny didn't make it out alive, then Dear Lord, let her be among these, not up there. Though I looked repeatedly, I couldn't find her body on the street, and the police forbade anyone to enter the building. As if by some pull of nature, families coalesced in Washington Park, forming a large circle. We consoled those who already knew their daughters had died; we offered hope to those who had yet to hear. Some parents wanted to lift their dead from the pavement and carry them home in a blanket or sheet. But the officials insisted that all the bodies be removed to Charities Pier.

About an hour after I arrived, I saw Ben passing along the row of dead and called to him. She's not there, he said. Maybe she survived. I couldn't answer, but my tears bespoke my fears. He held me a moment and then advanced toward the building. I followed. The police barred his way. He yelled, My sister worked on the ninth floor. I have to reach her. The officer said all the survivors had been evacuated and only the dead remained. Ben grabbed the officer by the arm and demanded to know who was responsible. There will be an investigation, said the policeman. Ben turned to me and whispered, I know men with guns, people who won't let the guilty escape. Guns, I said. Hoodlums have guns . . . the Italians, the Irish. Ben said, Also the Jews. I know where to find such men. Don't! I begged.

By the light of lanterns and torches, we watched carriages take away the dead from the street, and then, after the firemen brought all the bodies from the top floors, watched them trucked to the makeshift morgue. Ben and I followed on foot, but most of the bodies were burned beyond recognition. With no way of reaching Meyer, we returned to Riley Street, where we found him sitting in a parlor chair, his head in his hands, doing something I had not seen him do in years, davening. Rocking back and forth, he sobbed and repeated the Hebrew prayer for the dead, *Yis-ga-dal v'yis-ka-dash sh'may ra-bo. . . .*

I never asked him how he heard. It seemed pointless. We all sat up that night reminiscing about Fanny. The thoughts of return that Meyer harbored, he saved for later. This night belonged to Fanny. Meyer remembered her precociousness, and how she would pretend to fall asleep and after everyone else had dozed off, she would sit up in bed and read by candlelight Russian translations of Jane Austen and George Eliot. Ben reminded us of the time she dressed up like a man and sat downstairs in the synagogue among the men rather than upstairs with the women. I recalled the time a peasant, who had often dropped his loaf of bread in our honey barrel claiming it was an accident, came into our store and went immediately for the honey. Smiling at me, he reached back, removed the lid, and, when I looked away, dropped his bread. But Fanny had switched the honey barrel with the brine.

"141 Men and Girls Die in Waist Factory Fire; Trapped High Up in Washington Place Building; Street Strewn with Bodies; Piles of Dead Inside"

—New York Times, March 26, 1911 (p. 1)

Three stories of a ten-floor building at the corner of Greene Street and Washington Place caught fire, and while it raged 141 young men and women, at least 125 of them mere girls, were burned to death or killed by jumping to the pavement below.

All Over in Half an Hour

The victims who are now lying at the Morgue waiting for someone to identify them by a tooth or the remains of a burned shoe were mostly girls from 16 to 23 years of age. They were employed at making shirtwaists by the Triangle Waist Company, the principal owners of which are Isaac Harris and Max Blanck. Most of them could barely speak English. Many of them came from Brooklyn. Almost all were the main support of their hard-working families.

There is just one fire escape in the building. That one is an interior fire escape. In Greene Street, where the terrified unfortunates crowded before they began to make their mad leaps to death, the whole big front of the building is without one. Nor is there a fire escape in the back.

The Triangle Waist Company was the only sufferer by the disaster. There are other concerns in the building, but it was Saturday and the other companies had let their people go home.

Found Alive After the Fire

The first living victim, Hyman Meshel of 322 East Fifteenth Street, was taken from the ruins four hours after the fire was discovered. He was found paralyzed with fear and whimpering like a wounded animal in the basement, immersed in water to his neck, crouched on the top of a cable drum and with his head just below the floor of the elevator.

Meantime the remains of the dead, it is hardly possible to call them bodies, because that would suggest something human, and there was nothing human about most of these, were being taken in a steady stream to the Morgue for identification.

"It's the worst thing I ever saw," said one old policeman.

Chief Croker said it was an outrage. He spoke bitterly of the way in which the Manufacturers' Association had called a meeting in Wall Street to take measures against his proposal for enforcing better methods of protection for employees in cases of fire.

No Chance to Save Victims

Last night District Attorney Whitman started an investigation not of this disaster alone but of the whole condition which makes it possible for a firetrap of such a kind to exist. Mr. Whitman's intention is to find out if the present laws cover such cases, and if they do not to frame laws that will.

March 27, 1911

Where is God, I kept asking myself. The day of the fire and the day after, Ben and I could not identify among the dead my gorgeous Fanny. Meyer held me tightly and shook convulsively. He finally summoned enough strength to join Ben and me when we returned a third time. Walking between us, he looked like a straw man carried along by his family. We made our way to the subway and then on foot to where Twenty-sixth Street meets the East River, Charities Pier, which people called Misery Lane. The bodies lay in wooden coffins, open to public scrutiny. Those who had leaped from the building could be readily identified; those who died in the fire could not. The day after the blaze, a hundred thousand people—relatives and friends and gawkers and thrill seekers and rabbis and priests—had stood outside the morgue waiting to see the rows of dead. When we saw some of the disreputable persons in the line, we had gone back home. That day I agreed with Meyer: dignity and decency were more important than the Jewish custom that the dead must be buried within twenty-four hours. Large crowds still gathered two days later, on March 27; from their somber and reflective mood, I knew why they had come. These were families who had been unable to identify their loved ones during the first two days and had returned to try again, looking for a familiar piece of jewelry or amulet, a unique mend in a piece of clothing, a shoe, a scar, a gold tooth, a strand of hair, a distinctive finger or crushed thumbnail, perhaps injured in a childhood accident. As we made our way up and down the rows of unidentified dead, I could hear the babble of strange tongues, but mostly I heard Yiddish because mostly Jewish girls had perished. The sulfurs hanging from the rafters cast scant light on the scene below, requiring policemen to stand about a yard apart holding lanterns. I could hear the sound of gulls and the river tide among the pilings. Rain began to pelt the shed. A cold chill pervaded this death house. Occasionally a shriek pierced the silence as a mother found a shred of evidence. More than once, distraught parents tried to leap from the pier into the river, only to be restrained by the police.

I knew that Ben and Meyer would never see the one clue that would make it possible for us to identify our blessed Fanny. Of course, all of us prayed that we would be like the few who had searched and found children absent from work that day. Perhaps, Meyer said, she took sick and went to stay with a friend. Or perhaps she got out alive and in her fright ran away. Or perhaps . . . I told him to stop. The day of the fire, Fanny had worn a pair of shoes with worn heels, so worn that she had nearly broken through the shell of the shoe. But many of the women here had no shoes. While Ben and Meyer circled the caskets, I asked a policeman whether any shoes had been recovered separately, and he led me to a display. Among them I found Fanny's. Holding them to my breast, I stumbled to the open end of the shed and vomited into the river. Had I not consoled myself with the thought that maybe I could match the shoes with a body, I might have jumped. But we came away from Charities Pier knowing that we would have to say kaddish over an empty coffin, Fanny's burial place known only to God. Bitterly, Meyer said, as we walked back through the rain, For this we had to come to America! Then he suddenly halted in the middle of the street, sank to his knees, and silently wept with a wordless grief.

March 28, 1911

As I sat trying to write a eulogy for my darling daughter, a young man came to the door. Esther and Ben were at the shul making funeral arrangements. He identified himself as Allan Barbarosh, an NYU student who claimed to have helped several women escape from the roof of the burning Asch building—an apt name, I bitterly thought. Speaking to me in Yiddish, he told me that among the survivors whom the students pulled to safety was a shoeless, blonde, curly-haired woman, mute from shock.

"Why do you torment me with this news?" I fulminated. "Are you one of those jackals who read the names of the dead in the newspapers and then come to prey on the families with stories of false hope? How much are you asking for information about Fanny? That's how it works, isn't it?"

Mr. Barbarosh seemed puzzled. "May I come in?" he asked. We had been standing at the door. I reluctantly led him to a chair and repeated my accusation, "How much will it cost?" He handed me a folded piece of paper. Inside was written, "The bearer of this note can bring you to me. Fanny."

"Why is it typed, and why doesn't it say, 'Love, Fanny?'"

Mr. Barbarosh, who couldn't have been older than twenty, looked perplexed. "I know what you're thinking . . ."

"Of course you do. I just told you."

He nervously pushed a hand through his hair and said pleadingly, "Her hands were burned, her right one rather badly. We took her to the temporary clinic NYU opened in the basement . . . for triage. She stared but wouldn't speak. Not until this morning did she communicate. We gave her a pad. She wrote a few words: her address, her name. I made up the rest of the note."

Impetuously taking Mr. Barbarosh by the arm, I breathlessly ran him around the corner to the shul . . . I hadn't run so fast in years . . . collected Ben and Esther, hailed a cab, and let Mr. Barbarosh give the directions. The driver made directly for the Village. No one dared speak of our prodigious hope. At the college, I paid the driver and we followed Mr. Barbarosh into the clinic, to a corner of the room that had been curtained off from the rest of the ward. Our unspoken fear—that the person lying behind the curtain was not our beloved Fanny—kept us from entering the enclosure. Mr. Barbarosh looked at us with astonishment.

"Don't you want to see your daughter?"

In truth, a part of me feared that what I would see would not be the beautiful Fanny that I had been so proud of. Finally, Mr. Barbarosh slid back the curtain to reveal my daughter, her hair burned back to her scalp, with just a few clumps of blonde hair sprouting from her head, like patches of weed. I could see that the burns on her face were superficial, even though they had coated her skin with silver nitrate. The real damage, Mr. Barbarosh had said, was to her right hand, and in particular her thumb. Of course, we could not see her hand, swathed in bandages dipped in witch hazel. At that instant, I thanked our lucky stars she was left-handed. She recognized us immediately and smiled weakly. In a moment Ben was gently—and tearfully—embracing his sister. Esther pulled up a chair and stroked Fanny's arms, applying the kind of tickling motion that parents use when they play their fingers over children's backs. I stood and stared down at her. Dressed in a white gown, lying on a mattress of gray ticking, covered to her waist with a white sheet, she brought to mind my mother in her winding-sheet.

Esther tried to elicit a word or two from her, but Fanny simply stared. Mr. Barbarosh had said that once or twice she had tried to speak, but nothing came out. So I reached down and patted her leg. "We thought you had died. By giving this young man your name and where you lived, you saved us from kaddish." I meant the word "saved" as a joke; but when Esther immediately shot me a censorious look, I knew why. Mr. Barbarosh excused himself, clearly uncomfortable with family signs he was unable to read. I thought to myself: so few of us know what we are seeing; how can people juggle a life while dark to its imports?

Fanny opened her mouth—and only a death rattle sounded.

Ben assured her that she'd recover and that the two of them would, as soon as she wished, visit the nickelodeon or the theatre. But Fanny faintly shook her head no, signifying what I couldn't tell.

❧

We made arrangements to take her home the next day. She lay on the couch as our neighbors, upon hearing the miraculous news, poured into the apartment to wish her good luck, a speedy recovery, *nachis*.

They arrived at our door with dishes of food and fresh fruit. People whom we knew only casually cooked pasta and bread and cookies; they shared their meals; they brought olive oil and vinegar; they gave us crucifixes and mezuzhas. Even Mrs. Shirley and her girls stopped in to express their happiness for Fanny's good fortune. With each display of generosity Fanny cried unashamedly, but never spoke. Smiled, yes, but her language had fled. For the sake of our guests, Esther shared family daguerreotypes, explaining where they were taken and on what occasion.

In Fanny's presence, they said, "Such a wonderful smile. She looks like a silent movie star. What an angelic face. You mustn't cry, Mrs. Cohen, she'll recover completely." Then they would touch Fanny's bandages as if they were sacred relics, telling her that God in His goodness would heal her. She need only pray. I wanted to lock myself in our bedroom and never come out, but when I whispered as much to Ben, he took my arm and stood at my side for moral support.

In the midst of the celebrations, a florist delivered a six-foot-high horseshoe of roses. At first, Esther and I thought that they had come from Ben, until we saw the card: "My heart kvells for you. Sincerely, A. R."

"Who," Esther asked, "is this Mr. A. R.?"

Ben shrugged and said, "A guy."

Esther noodged, "He must be more than *that*!"

Ben mumbled, "A *nice* guy."

Papa spends days at my bedside. Ben sleeps on the living-room couch. I occupy myself rereading every magazine story Papa can find about Sarah Bernhardt. I have always suspected that for all his silences and distance, he dearly loves his children. With a special fondness for me. Maybe because I alone, of all the family, never reproach him for his wastrel ways. We also enjoy that special bond shared by readers. We often talk about novels. Papa notes subtle points that might have escaped my notice. I remember him explaining that the title of Jane Austen's novel *Emma* omitted her second name because, in large part, the point of the book was whether Emma would remain single, and thus keep her maiden name of Woodhouse, or marry and become Emma Churchill—or Emma Elton—or Emma Knightley. He always used to tease me about how many offers I'd have.

Of all the neighbors who visit, I like Cherry best. She never urges me to talk. Instead, she talks to me. "It's still in the papers," she says, "how some girls got out. The Greene Street door led to the roof. And some Bernstein guy led the way. The reporters said women tried to wrap their faces and hair in shawls or coats or cloth laying around. I guess you couldn't find any stuff, I mean, judging from what happened to your head."

I nod to indicate that Cherry is right.

"They say the stairs to the roof filled with fire. That it came through the windows and up the air shafts, like a tornado. I suppose that's how you and the others got your faces burned . . . and hands, trying to stamp out the flames from your burning clothes—and hair."

My eyes tear as I remember the pain. In front of my sewing machine, as if by magic, a collection bin with shirtwaists bursts into flames from a spark that seems to come out of the floor. I reach into the bin to remove the flaming fabric. The moment I do, the whole thing explodes. The flame shoots into my throat, which seconds before I had sprayed with a moisturizer. Could the mixture have been flammable? Then comes the rush for the elevator and stairs. Thank God, Mr. Levy pushes me toward the Greene Street door. Going up the stairs is like passing through a fiery ring of hell. The roof, where we hope to be saved, only increases our fear. We are trapped. On two sides, nothing, just the street ten stories below. On the north and west sides of the Asch building, two adjoining buildings. But they tower above us. I crouch shaking from shock, waiting for the flames to reach the roof. It seems like a year until ladders appear, lowered by young men from the roofs and windows of the next door buildings. In relays they haul us to safety. On reaching the roof next door, the NYU Law School, I collapse. Lungs scorched, right hand flayed, hair incinerated. I remember two boys lifting me up. Then a bed. My first thought is, who removed my clothes and, vain me, what did they think of what they saw?

On this day, I notice that Cherry is wearing a black babushka trimmed in white. The very scarf that I know Ben has given her. She suddenly stops talking about the Triangle fire. Her eyes become misty. She tells me about a fire in Oklahoma. From the little she says, I imagine that she had once been in love with a boy who was scarred when he fell against a kerosene lamp. I'll bet she really liked him, because his burns didn't seem to matter. That means their parents must have kept them apart. He was probably older and wanted to go to college—and promised he'd wait for her. My hunch is they met secretly. Then gossip started. So her family shipped her to New York. Out of despair she finally became a whore.

After Cherry leaves, Mama comes into the room with a long face. She doesn't like Cherry. Thinks she's a bad influence on Ben and me.

"What does the tart talk about? Not her business downstairs, I hope. If I ever catch her saying a word—"

I take Mama's hand and shake my head no.

"Sometimes I wonder what goes on in that silent head of yours."

Then Papa peeks around the door. Mama turns and says, "Her silence. How does one explain it? One doctor says shock, another, injured vocal cords." She sighs heavily, "Who am I to ask? God's will is inscrutable."

Papa mordantly replies, "Then why do all the world's religions lay claim to knowing it?" On that critical note, Mama leaves. Papa is carrying a book. Shakespeare's sonnets. The book he often resorts to when trying to make sense of life's woes.

"I've written to Jacob to tell him the wonderful news." He pauses and looks toward the window. "I've also told him that I'll be returning shortly to Russia." He turns back to face me. "I'm hoping you'll go with me."

I take the slate and chalk from the nightstand next to my bed and write, "Not now, Papa, we can't leave now."

"Can you think of a better time?"

I scribble, "I need you."

He awkwardly strokes my head and says, "Thank you for saying so, but it's not true."

The size of A. R.'s floral wreath, I suspected, was in lieu of his failure to visit our family. No matter. He and I would be doing business shortly, if I could find him. Max Blanck and Isaac Harris, the owners of the Triangle Shirtwaist Company, would have to pay for the death of all those young women—and my sister's injuries.

With everyone in bed, I grabbed my overcoat, hat, and gloves and went looking for the night owl. He was not at Marty's but at Katz's deli, stuffing himself with a slice of chocolate cake as large as his head. At his elbow stood a glass of milk.

"Pull up a chair."

He was sitting with a hoodlum who looked no older than eighteen or nineteen. I tried with nods and body language to indicate that I wanted to see A. R. alone, but he refused to take the hints. Finally, I was forced to say, "Can I see you alone, A. R.?" The young punk gave me a murderous look and before A. R. could object got up and left.

"Not smart, kid. D'ya know who that was?"

"Listen, A. R., thanks for the roses, but I need more than flowers. Your old employers at Triangle . . . I want them killed."

"I guess you don't care that the guy you just high-hatted was Owney the killer Madden."

"Who the hell cares?"

"You might if you knew how dangerous he is."

I grabbed the salt and pepper shakers in each hand, as if grasping A. R.'s shoulders, bent over the table, and whispered, "You once said the big job costs a hundred bucks. I'll give you two hundred to rub out two guys."

A. R. turned his reptilian smile on me and said, "Madden, who just left, that's his line of work. But you foolishly got on the wrong side of him."

"And you?"

"I'm no trigger man, Ben. I break the law, as you know, but I avoid rough stuff. That's for other guys."

"But you *could* arrange it?"

A. R. took the saltcellar from my hand and tossed some of it over his left shoulder. "*Men ken makhn dem kholem gresser vi di nakht,*" he said. "One can blow up a dream to be bigger than the night." We often conversed in Yiddish, especially when we wanted to make a point. The hatred in my heart, I told him, weighed heavier than the night.

For several minutes neither of us spoke. I listened to the clatter of dishes and the sounds of eating utensils scraping on plates. The smells of different foods came in waves: pastrami, pickles, chopped liver, sauerkraut, strudel, minced pie. A. R. called to the waiter and ordered apple pie and three chocolate éclairs. I glanced at the clock: 2:10 a.m. He often began a meal with dessert and then moved on to the main course.

"Killing is never sweet," he said. "Can't you just make a deal?"

"No."

He waited silently for the apple pie and then, between bites, asked, "Ben, d'ya know what you're saying?"

"Max Blanck and Isaac Harris. Dead!"

"I'm still on their payroll."

"Then get off."

"Listen, kid, I know how you feel. But let the law take care of those guys. They'll be dragged into court and have the book thrown at 'em. Believe me, they're facing ten years at least on the rock pile."

I knew that the families of the dead girls would sue. At Charities Pier I had heard talk of lawyers and fines and prison sentences. But I knew that the rich in America, just as in Russia, usually escaped punishment.

"They'll get a smart lawyer and maybe even pay off the jurors. I know how these things work."

It didn't take a genius to see that the courts belonged to the rich, and that the poor exacted justice with violence.

A. R. rubbed his clean-shaven chin with a thumb, looked at me, away, and then back. "What good will them being dead do you? When a killer fries in Sing Sing, the victims' families say they're glad the guy's dead, but it can't cure the pain. Trust me on this one. Better to get even with Blanck and Harris by asking for big bucks. Maybe the dough can make something good happen."

"If I do it your way, will you help?"

He took a few seconds to respond. "Do you mind working with Owney?"

"You said I rubbed him the wrong way."

"With a good word from me and a cut, he'll forget that you didn't pay him the proper respect."

"Then ask him."

"Do you want to be involved?"

"It depends on the details."

"I'll set up an appointment for you and Owney to meet . . . say in a few days. That suit you?"

"To a T."

April 13, 1911

After such pain, God owes us healing, not tsoris. Since hearing the doctor say that Fanny's laryngeal nerve on the left side was paralyzed and that she would never speak again, Meyer has taken to disappearing. He leaves the house and doesn't return until dark. Sick with worry, I look for him in the neighborhood and down by the Hudson, but can't find him. When he returns, I ask where he's been. Just walking, he says. I began to fear that he might injure himself, so yesterday morning I followed him. He never looked back and walked all the way from the Bronx to the Village. In Washington Square he sat on a bench looking east, staring at the Asch building, the top three floors stained from smoke, grime, and water.

It was an overcast day with an occasional streak of sunlight piercing the grayness. I could smell in the air the threat of rain, and I had come without an umbrella. Meyer huddled on the bench, his overcoat pulled around him, his hat shoved down over his ears. He looked like a vagrant, but so forlorn that even other homeless men avoided him. I stood at a distance and tried to collect my thoughts. I glanced around. To the north of the Square stood handsome homes; to the south, tenements. Unruly children ran through the park, some of school age—why hadn't their parents enrolled them in class? They yelled at each other in several languages. I listened for Yiddish but happily didn't hear any.

To one side stood a vendor selling peanuts. He had a stand with a small charcoal-burning brazier. I bought a bag. Warm your hands, he said, you look cold. I removed my gloves and spread my fingers over the coals. The heat felt good.

Sitting down next to Meyer, I wordlessly handed him the bag of peanuts. He took them as if they had dropped out of heaven and landed in his lap, seemingly unable to connect the bag and the donor. Such a look of bewilderment crossed his face. Slowly he realized he wasn't alone and the person next to him was his wife. You . . . here . . . how? he said. I explained that I'd followed him, fearing for his safety. How good of you, he murmured, and took my gloved hand in his. The bag fell to the ground. I bought them for you, I said. Give them to the pigeons, he replied, I can't eat. We sat for a long time without exchanging a word. Tell me, Meyer! Tears clouded his eyes and, as he spoke, rolled down his cheeks. I know she's alive, but still can't get over what's happened to her.

It's all so unnecessary, he grieved, so senseless. Locked doors. Ladders that couldn't reach beyond the sixth floor. Safety nets no better than cobwebs. Those poor dear girls, children really. Death is so final. There's no reprieve, no making up for it with something else, like losing a leg and using crutches. I squeezed his hand and let him continue talking. At the apartment he had said almost nothing. That he wanted to unburden himself I thought was a good sign. He said, I feel her hurt. It is terrible. My head teems with memories: her youthful games and dances, her teaching her brother to read, her conversations, her reading aloud, her speaking in different languages, her—. He broke off and cried bitterly, his body racked with sobs. It is unnatural, he sobbed, for a human being to lose the power of language. It is a violation of nature.

We will make a new life in the country, I said. Wild laurel and the smell of lilacs will ease your pain. When you were younger, you loved to walk in the woods. Fanny can join you. She'll have the time, since it's unlikely she'll ever be able to sew again.

This admission pained me deeply, but it was the truth.

No man will have her, he said, as if he hadn't heard me, that's what my head is full of—and burning flesh. I smell it everywhere, in the soggy ashes from across the street, in the gutters, among the cobblestones, in the garbage piled up at curbs, on the breath of men and women, even kids. I smell it in the cold wind, in the steaminess of horses and their droppings, on people's clothing, especially the rich, in the open windows of tenements, in our own apartment where Fanny's favorite scents have turned to offal, outside of shops, in the food of vendors, but most of all in cooking oil, as if body fat was being used to fry a . . . He broke off.

You're smelling morbid thoughts, I said, that's what you smell. Nothing more. Think of Fanny's perfumes and her favorite Parisian soap. Just think of how much pleasure they give her. Every city has its odors—Kiev, Hamburg, New York—and though they may all differ some, they smell of life. What you are inhaling is the city's breath.

No, Esther, I'm not mistaken. I never told you everything about the time our distillery business took me to a village that had only days before experienced a pogrom. All the dead, according to the law, were buried, but the town smelled of burning flesh: in the smoking chimneys, in the earth, in the hair of those I came in contact with. The old writers identify the angel of death with the smell of decay; even when the angel can't be seen, his smell makes him corporeal. Do you understand what I'm saying? Fire is palpable.

Perhaps, Meyer, you should see a doctor. I'm sure the Baron de Hirsch Fund can suggest a good one. People who have visions belong in hospitals. They occupy park benches throughout New York. Are you one of them? My own Meyer Cohen, with his education, his beautiful words?

I can read and understand, he said; I can hear exquisite music and appreciate it. I can touch objects and tell whether they are hot or cold. My taste buds know sweet from bitter. I still have my senses. But since the fire always in my nose I smell burning flesh. Just sit here with me for a few minutes. It will come, and when it does, I'll point it out.

What could I say? So I said nothing. We sat staring at the building that had heard and seen the last terrible minutes of so many young lives. The rawness of the afternoon crept into my bones. I heard a tingling bell. A vendor pushing a cart came by selling fried onions. The smell of oil made me gag.

Meyer began to speak again, saying, Each day that we live, from the moment of birth, we draw closer to death. Strange that the three-score years and ten promised us should begin at birth, when we are hardly sentient human beings. It should start in adulthood, when we have some comprehension of what a life means. All those girls—their lives cut short by forty and fifty years. If what happened to them is an act of God, then God should never show his face—for shame. If there is no God, then who is responsible for this horrible thing? Who will exact justice? In this country fairness has been shoved into the gutter by the power of money. *A likhtike velt, nor vi far vemen.* A radiant world—but, oh, for whom?

Come, I said, let us start to walk home. If you are tired, we can take a trolley. He rose like a zombie and I led him by the arm to the avenue. His mind, as it often did, wandered to books. I have lived, he said, in the world and I have lived through literature, and I prefer the latter. Good, I said, then let us stop at the Yiddish bookstore and see if maybe you can't find there an author you would like to read. We walked slowly and said little. As we approached the bookstore, he remarked, Chekhov knew about sinister smells. Captain Solyony regularly applies perfume to his hands to dispel the odor of death. Such a brilliant touch on Chekhov's part. The captain deals in death: where he stands stands nihilism. Meyer stopped in the middle of the sidewalk and, for the first time since I'd found him in the park, looked into my face. As the pedestrians walked around us, he explained, People say that the Russian intelligentsia are nihilists. If they are, they have been made that way by the absence of hope. But let me tell you, in America the workers are being driven to nihilism. The human decencies are sacrificed on the altar of profit and greed, and the incense that rises is the scent of burning flesh.

April 20, 1911

Owney Madden and I met in a dingy cafe on Eighth Avenue not far from the Village. I arrived first and sat nursing a cup of hot chocolate. Lost in thoughts of revenge, I never saw Madden until he seated himself across from me. He wore a dark overcoat and black fedora. Placing his palms on the table and, without removing his coat or hat, he said:

"A. R. told me the deal."

Owney and I seemed about the same age, but in fact he was two years older. When I had seen him in the company of A. R., I hadn't really looked closely. Neither he nor Rothstein had the face of a gangster. Owney's slight figure and sad eyes and thin face and prominent nose brought to mind a banty rooster. I could see how his looks would win over the girls. But behind the innocent front lay a bloodthirsty mind.

"Well?"

"I checked into it. Here's what I can tell ya. Blanck likes to parade around like a big shot. Harris stays in the background. Blanck wears a diamond watch fob, two diamond pinky rings, has a well-dressed wife and kids and a chauffeur-driven car. Lives in a swank place with half a dozen live-in staff on West End Avenue, around the corner from Harris."

"What's *he* like?"

"A weasel. Sharp eyes, always peering over his shoulder. The Triangle survivors say he's cunning. He lives at West One Hundred First Street with his wife, two kids, and four servants. I caught up with the laundress on her way out of the house. For a fin she told me he's a penny pincher and worries a lot."

"Good. Let's make him worry some more."

"The bad news, kid, is since a few days ago these two guys have been indicted for manslaughter, first and second degree. It will be the trial of the century, so it won't be easy to get to 'em."

A waitress came to our table and asked Owney if he wanted to order. She glanced at me with contempt, as if my chocolate had hardly been worth her time.

He said, "A cup of java and a slice of lemon pie."

Owney slipped off his coat and hat and ran a comb through his dark hair. Except for his English accent, he could have passed for any one of the million drummers in New York selling lotions or *shmattas*.

"What brought you to America?"

"I had no future in Liverpool."

A. R. had told me that Owney's preferred weapon was a pipe wrapped in newspaper, but that he had no reluctance to use a gun, blackjack, or brass knuckles.

"Now that everyone has them in their sights, Blanck and Harris will probably get some personal bodyguards. Maybe I could grab one of their children, but kidnapping gets sloppy. You have to mess around with ransom notes and places to hide the kids. You have to feed the brats and have someone stand guard all the time. By the time you're done, you've involved too many witnesses. The more people the more chances someone will talk. I prefer just sending the bosses a threatening letter and telling 'em where to leave the cash."

As much as I wanted to see the two men dead, I remembered what A. R. had said. Why not squeeze them for what you can get?

The waitress brought Owney his coffee and pie. I paid.

"How much do you intend to ask for?"

Owney spooned a slice into his mouth. "They're crying they're broke. I don't believe it, but that's what we'll hear—unless we ask for a sum that won't break the bank."

"Like?"

"A grand from each guy."

"Two thousand dollars for more than two hundred lives? Not a chance. I want ten times that amount. I want it to support my sister and some others into old age."

Owney ate and drank silently. When he had finished, he oozed into his coat, took his hat, and thanked me for the nosh.

"Where the hell you goin'?"

"You better get someone else for this job. I'm not your man."

"How come?"

"The price ain't right."

My temples pounded and my gorge nearly choked me. But knowing that I could not do the job myself—what choice did I have?—I said, "All right, do it your way. Get what you can."

Bad enough I have to worry about Meyer and Fanny. Today, what do I see in the hallway? Cherry had just come back from church, and Ben pinched her cheek and *potched* her tuchis. It's what I don't see that worries me. In the afternoon, when I went to work at Shapiro's, I told him about my Ben and the shiksa. So long as he doesn't get her in trouble, said Mr. Shapiro, your son will be fine. How's that? I asked. The moment he meets an Ashkenazi beauty, he'll want to get married in a shul and have sons and a bris. It's easy enough for you to say that, I shot back, but I know the look that comes into a young man's eye. Not for nothing did I get married at sixteen. My Meyer had such a look. He may seem bent over now, but he wasn't always that way. Mr. Shapiro, always generous, said, Meyer is a fine man, married to a fine woman.

I wanted to ask what's with all this *fine*? A lot you know. How could I tell him about my hopes for the future and why I wanted to come to America? Overcome by emotion, I retreated to my desk in the back room of the store and sat remembering. Since the day that Jacob left the house and I stood in the middle of the road watching his horse-drawn cart take him away from me, I have lived with a pressure around my heart. To hear my firstborn call me wicked was more than I could bear. The worst I did I did for love. When I tried to explain my feelings, he said just because you feel a certain way doesn't make what you do right. Like his father, a philosopher!

If not for my children, why am I here? In my *hartz*—and is there any truth greater than that which comes from the heart?—I felt that life in Russia, even in the Pale with other Jews, would suffocate a good mind. All my children, thank God, were born with *sachel*. But you can't thrive on good sense alone when those in power hate you. When I thought of why the Jews were first driven from Moscow—the gentile merchants couldn't compete with them—I knew that given an even chance, my children would succeed. In America, for all its obstacles, its quota systems, and prejudice, a Jew is not barred outright from opening a business or owning land. I knew that on an equal footing, my children would one day rise to the top.

How can Ben fail, unless that whore kills him with some disease or gives him an appetite for . . . I've seen young men who learned early about those pleasures and could never do an hour's work without thinking of *that.* Not for my boy. Enjoy it in marriage, not in stolen hours with a slut. I know the old adage. What's taken freely is paid for dearly. He has a long life in front of him, and I won't have him wasting it on an Indian trollop. When I told him that I didn't want him carrying on downstairs, he began leaving the house at all hours of the night. Where? The one day of the week that Cherry tart has free, Monday, Ben always comes home from work late. It's our busy day, he says, but I'm tempted to call his boss and ask. I'd bet a nickel against a pickle that he's meeting that strumpet in some love nest.

Before retiring, I asked Ben if we could have a talk, just mother and son. He was sitting on the couch with a drawing board on his lap. Through the window, I could barely see the street for a misting fog. It will probably rain, I said. He put aside his drawing and, before I could bring up the subject, said, It's about Cherry, right? He smiled lovingly and added, You think that if I continue to see Cherry, I'll regret it. His admission that he was still seeing her made me want to run into my bedroom and give Meyer a good shake and say, See, like I told you, he's still *shtooping* that squaw. Nu, you told me to mind my own business and stop imagining things. Well, now I have proof!

You could become a big farmer, I told Ben. You might even end up in the granary business, like Mr. Karlovsky in Kiev, with a fine house and a beautiful wife and brilliant children. I feel it in my heart. You have a wonderful future in store for you, maybe even as a painter, if you don't let youthful passions go to your head. In Carmel, we'll work hard and make a good profit. On Sundays, we'll take a picnic basket to the river and sit on a blanket telling stories to each other of old Russia. According to Max, there are hayrides and lectures and concerts. We'll even plant a little garden in back of the house, and Fanny can grow sunflowers, her favorite. We'll also plant lilacs. You remember how she used to put a spray in her hair?

April 30, 1911

Tomorrow is May Day. Ben urges me to leave the apartment and take a morning walk along the Hudson. He says I can wear a cap to hide my bristly hair. He bought me a pair of white gloves so my burned hand won't show. I write on my slate that I need more time. He says that when we leave for southern New Jersey, I will have to go outside and board a train and now is as good a time as ever to get used to being among other people. But tomorrow will be a special day. As a child I used to swing around the maypole and put lilac sprigs in my hair. I want to be alone with my memories.

Muteness, in itself, doesn't scare me. Perhaps because I was always so ashamed of stuttering. But how will others look at me? Must I be cut off—because they think I am? Can I ever marry? Rear children? What work is there for me? My hand is slowly healing, and I no longer stay in bed. Now I sit in the parlor chair and look out the living-room window, watching the hurly-burly on the street. My slate is always at my side, as well as my *Moving Picture World* magazines, which Ben brings home regularly.

Mother has been talking to me about Cherry. Again! She's afraid that something is going on between her and Ben. Do I know anything? Ben doesn't confide in me about his personal life, but I can guess certain things. If Mama didn't make Cherry feel unwanted, Cherry might come upstairs more often. Then I might learn something, because of Cherry's garrulousness.

Yesterday, as soon as Mama went out, Cherry appeared. We sit side by side, like two old friends. Giggling and gossiping. I think Cherry knows Mama's hours at Mr. Shapiro's store. Clever of her. Cherry begins by telling me that she has been reading a book about Russia. Mentioning the cities and rivers and dress of the people. I can tell she is working her way into talking about Ben. When she says that Kiev sounds lovely, I know what's coming next. She hands me my slate and chalk.

"Put down a check for yes and an X for no."

Before she can ask a question, I write, "Ben is discreet."

Looking perplexed, she repeats the word.

I write, "Secretive and silent about personal matters."

She smiles and says, "He told me it would be good for you to get outside. If you go out, d'ya mind if I tag along?"

"I'm staying here," I scribble.

"Sure wish you would 'cause we could have such a good time, just the three of us." Taking my right hand in hers, she gently strokes the scars. "It really ain't bad, Fanny. Besides, you can wear your gloves." Pausing, she picks up a copy of *Moving Picture World* with an article on Sarah Bernhardt. "Why, look at her. She hurt her knee real bad and still goes on stage. She didn't let a fall stop her. You gotta grit your teeth, I always say, and move full steam ahead."

Tosca, I recall. Year: 1905. On tour in South America. In the last scene, Tosca leaps to her death from a parapet. The stagehands have badly positioned the mattresses while trying to hide them from the audience's view. Sarah lands on her knee on the bare boards. Although hardly able to walk, she finishes the run of the play. Despite her terrible pain.

"Did'ya hear she's making a film called *Camille?*"

Yes, I had heard. The moving picture, based on the Dumas *fils* novel *La Dame aux Camélias*, will include the handsome Lou Tellegen as Armand.

"And did'ya know it's gonna be out by the end of the year?"

So delighted am I to hear that it will be in the nickelodeons soon, I swing my arms wide in imitation of Bernhardt's acting.

"Yeah, I read all about it. Naturally, Ben and me came to mind. The prostitute with tuberculosis who leaves her lover 'cause his father asks her to. But then she returns to die in her lover's arms. Don't it sound like the movie was made about Ben and me? Camille and I both love a man above our station in life. And your mother will stop at nothing to part us. Maybe I would even sicken and die, though not from TB. Heartbreak. But do people actually kick the bucket for love? They must. Every day in the newspapers I read of wives who arrive in this country, find their husbands with other women, and kill themselves. Really, Fanny, isn't it eerie? They say it's gonna be quite a picture."

Cherry exits saying, "Keep your chin up, honey."

No sooner has the door closed than I realize why she thinks the movie relates to her and Ben. It's not because she and Camille are prostitutes or because a parent protests. It's about failed love! I'll bet Armand is a fine talker, just like Ben. But as the moving pictures teach us, people communicate better through looks and gestures, hands and eyes, than through words. So when Ben looks at Cherry or she touches him, they are conveying feelings unfiltered by language. Silence speaks louder than words. Which is what makes the moving pictures so wonderful. They allow us to understood what people are *really* saying. I miss the nickelodeons.

May 1, 1911

I can guess what Pop is thinking. Workers all over the world are marching today, everywhere but in America. The bosses say it is a Monday, only Sundays do the hands have off. Maybe Pop is right: that it is here that Jacob and his friends should come to make a revolution. In the shipping room by myself—Bill Cline, my Negro partner, had to make a delivery—I can't help but think of Mom's opposition to Cherry. She's always going on about it. If only Pop would just once come to my defense . . . but Fanny's muteness has defeated him utterly.

Today is Cherry's and my playday, the name we have given our Monday escapes. She will be at the apartment waiting for me and, as always, will have a hot meal on the stove. When I enter she will be wearing an apron, which she will slowly untie from behind and lift over her head. She will let it fall to the floor as she throws her arms around me and kisses me with such feeling that I will rise immediately and she will laugh and say not till later.

We will have a glass of wine in the small sitting room with its Murphy bed and look out the window at Second Avenue. This fashion or that one will catch her eye. A horse will occasionally stumble and the cart driver will swear and climb down from his seat to adjust the halter or examine a hoof or berate and beat the animal. She will lapse into memory and recall a family picnic along the river, with her father fishing and skewering fat worms on the end of his hook. She will reminisce about the rattlesnakes that would slither across their path or hide in their garden. She informs me that Oklahoma is snake country, at least where she came from. It's also socialist country—and for good reason. The pay is paltry and the conditions in the fields abysmal: no break from the heat or the cold, no toilets, no fresh water, no limit to the working hours, no compensation for injury, even if it's the fault of the boss. It is from this kind of life that she fled.

I can see us taking a second glass of wine and slipping into a conversation about the future. She will ask, as she often does, whether I've heard anything further about the move to New Jersey. I will tell her that planting season is already over and that unless the Baron de Hirsch people have sown the fields for us, I see no point in taking up residence on a farm where the land hasn't been seeded.

She will smile serenely and lean back in her chair and turn the glass in her hand. I can imagine what would happen if I broached the question of my mother's resistance.

"Once she knows me better," she would say, "I think she'll be happy."

"But to know you better would imply that we are remaining together. That's not what she wants."

"Because I'm not Jewish? I'll convert."

Reluctant to tell her the truth, I will say, "Religion certainly plays a part, but she has definite views concerning her son and the woman he marries."

"A loving wife, a good mother, a hard worker . . . these are not things she would want in a daughter-in-law?"

"She values them all."

"Then what's the problem?"

How do you tell a woman you love that in some way she is unworthy, particularly when that "way" seems to her harmless enough?

"How you make your money."

She will look at me confused and say, "But once we are married I will no longer be a prostitute."

"My mother has certain ideas . . . about probity."

"What's that?"

I will regret using that word because it is so hard to define, and yet so useful. "Uprightness . . . what is proper and good."

"A great many good girls are prostitutes, including Jewish ones."

"True. But my mother would object equally if my girlfriend were Jewish and were . . ."

Cherry will regard the pause, which I intend as a gentle omission, as an occasion to say, "a whore."

"She's always polite to me on the stairs."

What Cherry means is that perhaps I am wrong and that I am misreading my mother's objections. "She would never be rude. She prides herself on her good manners."

"Well, then maybe she would be willing to give me a chance to prove how good a wife I could be to you. If she had a grandchild—"

"Don't even think it. She would call the child a momzer, a bastard."

"Even if we were married?"

"I'm afraid so."

"But you just said she had good manners."

"She would draw a line."

"And you, would you ever marry without her permission?"

"Yes, but I would prefer to have her blessing."

"Would you marry without it? Or maybe you just don't think of me that way."

Why am I imagining this conversation when I know full well how it must end? In tears, pain, and recriminations. But I am not yet prepared to give Cherry up. Does that make me selfish, a gigolo? I suppose so. Although I tell myself that at least I take her to dinners and stage shows and museums and for walks in the park, I know what my principal interest has been. How awful it is to have to tell a woman that you desire her only to satisfy your desire. She will immediately think: has he not noticed my gentle ways, my kindness, my caring, my sacrifices? What's wrong with me: am I not clever enough, not pretty enough, not compliant enough . . . too loud, too soft, too crass, too retiring? What did I do wrong, and when? Why did he give me no indication of his displeasure, no hints? How could I have been so terribly wrong?

To hurt Cherry in this way will torture me, but to marry her just to spare her this pain will lead only to subsequent problems. So how does one extricate himself when, in fact, he doesn't want to be free of the girl, at least for the moment? To keep leading her on will only make it harder to separate later. Perhaps I can say to Cherry that neither of us is in a position to marry, and at this point in our lives it is better not to talk about love. Then I can tell my mother that Cherry is merely a temporary girlfriend and doesn't figure in my future plans. Maybe that will satisfy them both.

As I leave Cosin's factory and make my way to the Second Avenue apartment, I have already rehearsed what I will do and say.

Putting a finger to her lips, I will whisper, "I still haven't heard about the farm. Let's not think ahead but enjoy this moment."

May 9, 1911

Dear Lord, forgive me my sins.

Yesterday, I did a contemptible thing: I followed my son from his place of work to a building on Second Avenue. Across the street, in an Italian restaurant, I sipped cups of strong coffee and waited. Eventually I had to order a meal, spaghetti and tomato sauce. At a little after ten o'clock, Ben and Cherry left the building, arm in arm, and took a northbound trolley. When I reached the apartment on Riley Street, Fanny was in bed, and Ben was already in his pajamas, brushing his teeth in the kitchen sink. I threw down my coat and without answering Meyer, who wanted to know where I'd been, said, Preparing for bed, are you? Ben washed out his mouth and replied, Yes. Crossing my arms on my chest, I chided, I should think you had enough bed already. Or maybe it's that you're worn out. Ben wiped his mouth on a towel and said, Mom, what are you talking about? I harrumphed. You know very well what I'm referring to. But before he could reply, I let the cat out of the bag, just in case he had any intention of giving me some cock-and-bull story. You ever hear of the Roma restaurant? He looked at me as though I had just spoken a foreign language. It sounds familiar, he said, why? Why? I repeated, because I sat there from 6:45 to 10:05 waiting for you to come out of that building on Second Avenue. That's why. It's across the street from where you were shtooping the Cherry tart. The moment I used that word, I wished I hadn't. But my anger got the better of me. Never before had I used such language with any of my children. But there was no going back. Now you know I know! I thought I told you I would call the police about Mrs. Shirley's unless you stayed away from that girl. If you think I don't mean what I say, just ask your father.

Meyer stood in the archway between the kitchen and the living room, looking as if someone had shot him. He held one hand to his heart and the other he rested against the doorjamb. His breath sounded labored, and when he dropped into a chair I thought maybe his heart was giving out. What kind of words am I hearing? he said, staring at me and then Ben. Since when, Esther, do you use such words with your son? You would make it sound like loving another human being is a sin. A whore! I added, losing all self-control. The Bible, he said, is full of whores. I replied, And since when do *you* believe in the Bible, you who have always declared that it's all a lot of meshugas? Meyer shook his head and looked at me in that despairing way of his, as if he had married a handmaiden to stupidity. Well, I may be a lot of things, but I'm no fool. So I told him, I will not treat a whore like a lady. And only a lady is the kind of woman good enough for my son. Do you hear me? A lady, not a Cherry tart! Meyer clutched at his shirt and said, Where's your compassion? I shot back, My heart is as large as yours, larger, because I am willing to lose the love of my son in order to save him. You simply seek the road of least resistance. Path, he corrected. What are you talking about? Meyer replied, The *path* of least resistance. Then I really got mad and told him to behave like a father and provide his son with some moral direction.

Mom, let's talk about it tomorrow, Ben pleaded, not tonight. I have to be at the factory early. Ha, then you should have come right home from work, I said, instead of. . . . Completing my thought, Ben nearly knocked me over. Instead of spilling my seed into that shtoop, is that it? Once I caught my breath, I said, Yes that's it exactly!

If you'd give her a chance, maybe invite her to dinner, you'd see—I interrupted. See what? That she's not one of us. That she's much too old for you and much too . . . used.

Meyer sat shaking his head. Ben chewed his lip and then said, You know, Mom, it's possible to love your children beyond reason. *Genug.* I'm seventeen. It's about time to let go. At my age you were already married. He's right, Meyer said. Just because he has a girlfriend doesn't mean the world is coming to an end.

I listened and thought, how did I marry a smart man with such an impractical *kup*? All right, I said, I'm unreasonable. Isn't that what you said, Ben? He sighed, Not exactly. Well, it was close. Now let me tell the two of you a few things. How often is a young person's life undermined by marrying too early or the wrong person? Marry in haste, repent at leisure. That's the proverb. Ben cut me short. Who's getting married? I pointed to the window. Go, look! See how many young couples are schlepping around kids. The mothers, still in their teens, look like old ladies, and the boys, maybe one or two years older, seem like graybeards. Whether they know it or not, their lives are over. All right, Ben is not married—yet. But already he's talking about having that woman upstairs to sit at our table. I know what he has in mind: I want you to get to know her. Why? He wants me to see how nice she is. After all, you don't dine with strangers to distance them, but rather to join them.

From Ben's silence I knew that I had made my point. Meyer simply continued to sigh. I told Ben a mother has to go to extremes. That's what she's for: to protect her children, even at the cost of her own life—or their love. Even before she feels a stirring in her womb, she begins to plan for her child's future. An education, a profession, respect, a devoted family, an honorable place in the congregation . . . are these so terrible? If they are, then correct me and tell me what I should want for my son. Why did we come to America? For me? No, for you and Fanny. Meyer interrupted and said to leave him out of the discussion. All right, I take the full blame. It was my doing we traveled this enormous distance, and I will not permit my son to cause doors to be shut in his face.

Although it wasn't yet closing time, I told Mr. Cosin that I was expected for a Friday night dinner with my family—"You know how my mother feels about Shabbos"—and left work to meet Owney at the same rundown cafe. He had composed a threatening letter that he planned to send to Max Blanck and Isaac Harris.

"I'm not guaranteeing anything," he said, "because as you know dozens of families are suing, and them bastards are crying poverty."

"The papers say they're going to make plenty from the insurance."

Owney lit a cigarette and drew in the smoke, which seemed to disappear, until suddenly plumes rushed from his nose and his mouth. "You know, Bennie, it might make more sense to cut a deal with the insurance companies. They stand to lose hundreds of thousands. With the shirtwaist kings dead, they'd probably get off paying a lot less."

I looked at the letter, which I could never have written myself because of my imperfect English. It read: "To Mr. Blanck and Mr. Harris. I am one of those who has a family member burned in the great Triangle fire. From the newspapers, I see that you have hired a smart lawyer, Mr. Max D. Steuer. He may get you off the manslaughter charges, but he can't protect you from me. The only way you can save your lives and make sure that your wives and kids are not hurt is by paying for your crime. I want two thousand dollars in ten dollar bills. You can leave the money with the Chink cleaners, Yoo San, two blocks east of you. If you call the cops, it will cost you more than money. It will cost you your lives. One last thing: you are being watched day and night. You have one week to pay."

"Well?" Owney asked with a satisfied smile.

"I like it, but what if they call our bluff?"

"That's the risk we gotta take."

Since Owney had told me the addresses of the shirtwaist kings, I had entertained the possibility of haunting their neighborhood until I could catch them off guard. Jacob had once described a train bombing in which he had participated. They used bottles filled with kerosene and rag wicks, thrown into the coal tenders. When I asked him if anyone died, he said they had taken great pains to avoid any personal injuries. But I noted that he never really answered me. I knew now how he felt: destroying material property was one thing, killing people quite another. Nothing stood in my way of throwing a kerosene bomb through the windows of Blanck's and Harris's houses, except that I had no way of assuring that only the house would burn down. And what if Blanck and Harris weren't home—but their children and servants were? Although death by fire appealed to me as poetic justice, I gradually convinced myself that extorting money from these merchants of murder would give me more satisfaction—maybe even give them more pain—than torching their homes. However, the question still remained, what would I do if they refused to pay?

Owney ordered a bowl of chile and a cup of coffee. I requested hot chocolate. The same waitress as before waited on us, and just like last time she looked down her nose at me for my paltry order. While we waited for A. R., who had requested this meeting to talk about some important business, Owney asked:

"You like the dames?"

"I've got a nice one."

"What's her name?"

"Cherry."

"I like that. Did you take hers?"

"Yeah, dozens of times."

"A real wisenheimer."

"I'm learning. A. R. says you're pretty quick on your feet."

Owney laughed. "He means dancing. That's how I like to spend my evenings. When the dance halls close, I take my girl to a bar and then later to a hotel. It's a great life if you don't wear out."

The waitress brought us our orders, and this time Owney insisted on paying. He gave the waitress six bits and told her to keep the change. I thought she would die from ecstasy; she even smiled at me.

"To tell you the truth, I got several girlfriends. One ain't enough to keep me interested."

"I heard about the trolley car incident."

Owney shot me a murderous look that slowly softened as he recounted the incident. "This goddamn clerk in the lotions department of a store. My girl winks at him, he falls for her, she agrees to go to the movies. I shoulda shot her instead of him. I nearly ended up in Sing Sing 'cause of that dame. I got off scot-free, which I must say made quite an impression on my gal. It was damn lucky that A. R. made a few telephone calls for me. I owe him big."

Rothstein was running late, so Owney ordered a slice of lemon pie and a refill on the coffee. Insisting I eat something, he told the waitress to bring me a hot salted pretzel.

"Why that?" I asked.

"The last time we talked, I watched you for a few minutes after you left the restaurant. Just a habit of mine: bein' doubly sure. You bought a salted pretzel from a street vendor."

Before I could say anything further, a dapper A. R. entered, dressed to the nines.

"Sorry to be late," said A. R., "I just came from shul."

For a moment I thought he was joking. But then I remembered him saying something about his father's piety.

"I do it to keep peace in the family. If I missed a Friday night service, the sun would grow cold and the earth would fly apart, or so my old man believes."

"Tough break," Owney quipped.

"Here's the deal," said A. R., snapping his fingers for the waitress and ordering a piece of lemon pie with chocolate ice cream. "I need to relocate one of my brothels. The old place is going to be shut down by the cops. A friend of mine in the precinct called to warn me." He slid a big paw across the table and laid it on my hand. "I hate to tell you, kid, but you're involved—indirectly—so I expect you to make it up to me."

Owney scowled as if toting up his losses.

I shook my head in denial and blurted, "What are you talking about?"

"Your mother got a lot of signatures from neighbors, including a rabbi, and called the cops to complain that Mrs. Shirley was running a whorehouse in a respectable street."

May 27, 1911

As we are packing to leave for south Jersey, Ben hands me a note. It's from Cherry. She says she must see me. Alone. I still haven't left the apartment. With all the bustling around, where can I find a place to see her away from the family? At the thought of even stepping into the hall, I feel a rush of panic. Using Ben as a go-between, I send Cherry a note telling her I can't get away. She replies that I should lock my bedroom door at 4:30 in the afternoon and she will come to me. At first, I wonder how. Then I remember the fire escape. For her to climb those rickety, rusty stairs, it must really be important.

Just before 4:30, I plead exhaustion. I go to my room and lock the door. I sit next to the window and wait. Sure enough, a few minutes later I can see Cherry on the fire escape. I open the window. She comes in. Whispers, "I have to talk to you." We huddle next to the window in case she has to get away quickly. Her hands are coated with rust. She looks at them and comments, "Better to wear out than rust out."

I know she is pretending indifference. A second later she proves it, burying her head in her hands and sobbing. When she looks up, her face has orange streaks. I embrace her. She puts her arms around my neck. Her breathing is like that of a child who can't catch his breath. More like hiccups. My white shirtwaist has oxide stains. On the shoulders and front. I use a handkerchief to wipe her face and try to clean my blouse. Better to change it so Mama won't notice. Which I do, as Cherry calms down. She carefully folds the handkerchief—to wash it, she says —and to my astonishment removes from inside her clothing a man's shaving razor.

"Here, take it!" she commands. "Otherwise . . . I may hurt someone. I can see you think I must be mad and maybe I am. Look, I keep the thing in the stand next to my bed for protection and once in a while grab it to show the customers I mean it when I say no rough stuff."

She pauses and opens the blade. Running it along her arm, she removes all the hairs with one swipe. I guess to show me its sharpness. Folding the blade, she again thrusts it toward me.

"Take it . . . for your brother's sake. The last few nights I've had a dream and it's always the same. Ben is laying on my bed with his head in my lap. I ask him not to leave me behind and he rattles on about the family and some farm in south Jersey. My patience finally gives out and I hold the razor just under his chin and say, 'please let's stay together,' and then I press the razor to his throat and he feels the steel, but he still refuses and so I slit his windpipe."

At that instant I take the folded razor and slide it inside my large handbag between the lining and the shell.

"Am I crazy, honey? I always wake up screaming, at least that's what the other girls say. I spit three times, like they tell you to do to banish bad dreams, but it doesn't help. I'm afraid to go to bed and I can't rest because I'm sure I'll dream it again. But the worst part is that I keep thinking about the dream even when I'm awake, and the moment I catch sight of Ben I think about how it would feel . . . I can't get the idea out of my head. I had to give you the razor so when we say good-bye I won't use it. I ain't told anyone else about this. Be a peach and swear you'll never tell. You and me, we've become friends. So will you swear?"

I nodded yes. She hugged me and, before climbing back out on the fire escape, kissed my forehead. I closed the window and sat on my bed. Just thinking. What could it all mean?

After a while I finally figured it out. According to the Vienna doctors, people are like icebergs. The part that is seen is really quite small. Most of our lives take place underwater, in the subconscious. Mama angrily tells me that you can't trust Germans or Austrians. And besides they have filthy minds. But I've read enough to know that Cherry's dream has deeper meanings. Oh, not that she wants to cut away Ben's manhood. No, she wants to keep him intact. Them intact. Together. In her dream she wants to cut his throat. Why? Because she wants to stop him from talking. He keeps saying he cannot include her in the family's exodus to Carmel. What better way to stop a person from saying what you don't want to hear than to cut his windpipe? She wants to silence Ben. Make him as mute as me. Then he can't hurt her further.

June 3, 1911

The last time I saw Ben, he told me what his mother had done and how she felt about me. He offered to help Mrs. Shirley and me and two other girls move to our new house in the Bronx . . . yesterday we moved so we could get set up over the weekend . . . but Mrs. Shirley was furious about having to change her location and didn't want to have anything to do with Ben and told me to avoid him also. The look on his face reminded me of when I left Oklahoma and said good-bye to my father. Mother and me jawed over what we had to say in the house. Once she said I'd miss the big land and the sky, she turned away and went into her bedroom and closed the door. My father walked me to the road. While we waited for the bus, he had told me not to forget my people, saying an Indian in the white city was like a ghost child wandering the earth in search of its family, with no body and no humanness. When I boarded, he leaned his forehead against the doors and pounded them with clenched fists. From my window seat I could see his tears and the slow way he shook his head during hard times.

I told Ben these things and said he would be lost without me and only with me could he be whole. We had gone to his friend's apartment on Second Avenue and were on the bed, which he had pulled down from the wall, clasped in each other's arms. Between lovemaking he whispered promises I knew he would forget once he and his family went to that farm he kept talking about but which I really don't think he wanted to move to. He didn't actually cry . . . my father had really shed tears . . . but he looked the same way, like someone had pulled the sun and moon out of his sky. I think this is why he wanted to remain in me as long as he could and refused to come, because he wanted to stay attached. There are other ways to stay connected, I told him, through friendship and love, but he wouldn't let go.

I really think he would have continued to meet me and make love if his mother hadn't decided they would move to a place called Vineland and wait there until their farm was ready. He said he would take the train and come back to visit me often, but once the seasons change so does the weather. I know he wanted to buy me a gift but didn't have enough money, because later that night we walked to the factory where he works. He used his key to open the door and invited me to take any of the cosmetics in stock. Powder puffs and mascara and nail polish and jewelry boxes and perfumes and lotions and salves and something called facial unguents. He took me into the main office and stood me in front of the showcase, insisting I point to anything I wanted. Then he went into the storeroom and packed it all up in a box that he carried back to my house and handed me at the front door—with one other thing, a miniature painting.

But before we left the factory, he spread on the cutting table a sheet of lamb's wool, the stuff they cut powder puffs from, and we climbed up on it and made love several times. He acted crazy, as if the world were coming to an end, and I kept telling him that tender was better. When it was time to go, he cried.

He asked me to tell him how *I* felt. So I told him that losing him made me feel like losing my child. At the word "child," he sat up and crossed his legs on the table and leaned over and put his hands on my cheeks, where they must have stayed for at least a minute. He wanted to know if I meant a real child or some other kind. I told him I meant a real one. In my business, I explained, accidents happen. More than once I had to have an abortion, which I got from a Dr. Posner three streets away and which Mrs. Shirley always paid for. She took good care of her girls, all of us. She and Dr. Posner were friends. I guess she had gone to him several times herself. Well, anyway, one time I didn't know I was that way because my periods kept coming. When they finally quit, it was too late for Dr. Posner to do anything, so Mrs. Shirley and I decided I should have the baby. I did and it was a girl and a pretty one and I gave it to some agency that placed kids of that kind. Pointing to a slight stretch mark above my hip, I said I got it from giving birth. Ben touched the mark and looked at me like he had never seen me before and was trying to locate the old Cherry in this person sitting in front of him. I'm twenty-nine, I told him, and have been in this business a long time. These things happen. I also told him how much I wanted to marry and live somewhere else, maybe near my parents in Oklahoma. Of course, he guessed I was thinking of him and he said he couldn't leave his family in the east while he lived in the west. I knew from what he had told me about his mother he respected her and would never go against her wishes, but I did wonder when he would ever grow up and told him he had to live his own life. He guessed he wouldn't like doing farm work and was convinced his father would hate it and therefore he would probably return to the city in a very short time and if I was still here we could become lovers again. But like I said, seasons change.

Instead of taking the trolley, we walked all the way back to the Bronx, talking the whole time, him with his arm around me, every once and a while giving me a nice squeeze. Of all the things I want in this world, I said, it's a home, my own house, with or without a fence. Just my own place. I dream of a nice bungalow with a patch of ground in the back to grow cucumbers and tomatoes and peas and squash and lettuce. The house would have a flush toilet, none of this going out in the yard stuff. And it would have radiators. I'm tired of freezing to death in the winter, crouching in front of a small heater to take the chill out of my blood. The walls would have bright colors, red and green and blue. The icebox would be the real thing with electricity. And the stove would cook with gas, not wood. If I could get a house like that I'd marry damn near any man.

Ben asked did I really mean "any man"? So long as he didn't drink or beat me. I knew what Ben was thinking. What about love? Listen, honey, I said, I loved you and it got me nothing except I did like hearing you read poetry and having you touch me. Your sweetness actually made me think maybe you and me had a future, and didn't I say before that the two of us make one whole? Actually I knew you'd say no. Mrs. Shirley put me right. She's Jewish, too, and knows about mothers like yours. At first I wondered what's wrong with me, why couldn't I make him happy? But like I said, the moment Mrs. Shirley explained, I knew your dream and mine were headed in opposite directions. You're a sweet boy and I wish you only the best and I know some day you'll make it big. All I ask is once in a while remember Cherry and maybe say a prayer that one day I'll marry a guy with more in his pants than just a hard-on and we'll move out west and have some kids and live in a really swell house.

June 16, 1911

On the New York to Bridgeton train, Fanny as always was silent, and Mom and I exchanged not a word. We had hardly spoken since the evening A. R. had told me about the police planning to close down Mrs. Shirley's place. Not having me as an intermediary between her and my father, Mom had spent the last two weeks retreating to her bedroom to escape his complaints. Vineland, he maintained, would be no better than Bobrovitz, since we would have to support ourselves, albeit temporarily, clerking in a general store and living upstairs, an arrangement worked out by the Baron de Hirsch Fund. At least in Bobrovitz, we spoke the language, knew the Jewish community as well as a great many in the gentile part of town, lived close to Kiev, and could occasionally see Jacob.

I sat watching the forest of pines. In the occasional clearing, tobacco advertisements covered the sides and roofs of barns, as well as boards mounted in fields: Fonseca Cuban cigars, Sir Walter Raleigh pipe tobacco, Ettan Swedish snuff, R. J. Reynolds chewing tobacco, Philip Morris hand-rolled Turkish cigarettes, and a new brand of "little cigar," Chesterfield, "They satisfy." Cigarettes, popular in Russia, were just taking hold in America, where a great many men still regarded them as effeminate.

My thoughts turned to the last time I'd met with Owney at Marty's Pool Hall. I had arrived a few minutes late and found Owney sitting in the back watching A. R. wax some smart aleck who thought he had a way with the cue stick. The light was bad from the clouds of tobacco smoke. A. R., who hated the weed, kept waving his hat to clear the air, and Owney, in deference to him, chose not to light up, though he did lip an unlit cigarette. We sat on wooden saloon chairs tipped back against the wall. Owney's fedora, which he wore pushed forward, made it difficult to see his eyes, which provided the best indication of his mood. They could move from doleful to dangerous over a perceived slight or careless word. The few times I dealt with him I made it a point to check them out before hazarding an opinion. Not being able to see his eyes put me at a disadvantage. So I played it safe and asked:

"How did it go?"

"We're here, ain't we?"

I took that to mean Owney had been successful.

"Glad to hear it."

He continued to lip his cigarette and follow the game. I tried to interpret his silence, but decided not to interrupt it. At least ten minutes passed, the only sounds the click of pool balls and the occasional expletive from a frustrated player.

"Kid, give it up," said Owney to the punk. "I got business with the man, and you ain't worth shit."

The punk, angry at having been taken to the cleaners by A. R., turned on Owney and brandished his pool cue.

"Don't do anything stupid, kid," said Owney, reaching into his jacket and removing a pair of brass knuckles.

The kid threw some bills on the green felt, grabbed his jacket and hat, and left. Only then did Owney stand up. Pushing back his hat, he shuffled over to A. R. at the far end of the table and handed him an envelope. A. R. opened it and removed several bills, which he slid over the green felt and added to the loser's money.

"That's for you, Ben, courtesy of Mr. Blanck and Mr. Harris."

I looked at Owney quizzically.

"A. R. helped arrange things."

Leaning over the table, I scooped up the dough. It came to twenty-five hundred dollars. "Can I ask you something, A. R.?"

"Don't, 'cause I never reveal how I work. Right, Owney?"

"As long as I've known you, A. R., mum's the word."

On my way back to Riley Street, I decided not to tell my family about the money, but to use it judiciously. I had seen my father's imagination run riot when he thought the distillery would be returned and he would again have money at his disposal. He talked of supporting the arts, of contributing to philanthropic groups, of adding hundreds of volumes to the city library. My mother, far less idealistic, was nonetheless capable of spending money with abandon. Her own particular weakness was kitchenware: iceboxes, stoves, porcelain sinks, silvered faucets. I knew that if they got wind of the twenty-five hundred dollars, they'd have it all spent by the time we reached Carmel. Besides, I had some ideas for the money myself. Although I had said nothing to my parents, I knew that one day I would leave Carmel for the city, either Philadelphia or New York. With the experience I had gained working in Cosin's cosmetic factory, I hoped to open my own place and specialize in cosmetic cases. Every woman in America had or wanted one. Well, I would offer them in all price ranges and from a variety of sources, including Russia, which crafted some that could pass for real works of art. I knew that if I worked hard and invested wisely, I'd eventually make a bundle. I had to laugh. Here I was thinking this way after just a few months in America. Already the dream had infected me.

Dear Jacob,

I write from the heart, as only a grieving father can. The only word we have had from you is your telegram expressing your happiness that Fanny survived and asking about her ordeal. No, doctors can't help her. The fire destroyed her voice box. Every day I hope for a miracle: that she will speak again, even stutter. But I know, as Turgenev says, a miracle is the hope that two and two will equal five.

We have finally left the city and moved to southern New Jersey. Our new address is on the back of the envelope. Knowing little about your activities, I cannot comment intelligently on your life. How I miss our talks about politics and social conditions. Let me take solace in telling you about our hegira to southern New Jersey.

The packing was all very chaotic, but eventually we arrived at the station clutching our tickets for Bridgeton. You would be appalled at the primitiveness of American trains. We sat on wooden seats and the uneven tracks nearly shook loose our kishkas. Quickly the city flew by and for hours we saw nothing but pasturelands. After many stops at small towns, none of them worth recounting, we entered a forest landscape that brought to mind the woods near our old house. But unlike those in Bobrovitz, the trees here are mostly pine. Only occasionally do you see a break in the woods where some hardy pioneer, undoubtedly at great effort, has cleared a small piece of land, leaving behind hundreds of tree stumps, and built a tar-paper shack. Can you imagine living in a hovel and removing tree stumps for the rest of your life? We had been warned that the thin, sandy earth would not yield vast grain harvests, as in the Ukraine, but lent itself to vineyards, fruit orchards, and truck farming, especially tomatoes, peppers, strawberries, and corn. The Baron de Hirsch people also suggested chicken raising, dairying, and cranberry bogging. Near Bridgeton, we passed through a wild and desolate stretch of oaks, and I wondered if logging wouldn't earn more money than those other endeavors. As the train approached the station, I got a good look at the small stores lining the streets. I can think of nothing worse than spending a life waiting for the bell over my shop door to jangle. Of course, it is mean-spirited of me to criticize what supported us after I lost the distillery. But rightly or wrongly, I believe that labor should ennoble. I just hope that we aren't reduced to the backbreaking work of tilling fields and harvesting crops to pay for our daily bread. In all honesty, I have no idea what I am good for, disliking equally manual labor and clerking. After sixty years, my skin still doesn't fit me.

At the station, we hired a young boy to help with our bags. He loaded us into a rickety cart, pulled by a horse that he led on foot. We passed some houses dating back to the American Revolution, but sadly they were few, and the ones that had been built alongside of them paled in comparison. A river runs through Bridgeton, the Cohansey. On a bluff overlooking it, we stopped at a shabby lodging house, booked rooms, and asked the proprietor where we could find a livery. He directed us to Tendrick's Stable and Forge. The family agreed that in the morning we should drive to Carmel to survey the property that had been set aside for us, and then continue on to Vineland—and Brotman's general store, the source of our temporary employment and housing.

Mr. Tendrick stood at an anvil hammering a red-hot horseshoe with arms like telegraph poles. Crimson-faced from the heat of the forge, he wore a black leather apron and gloves, just like Max the farrier in Bobrovitz. Bald on top with long side hairs that covered his ears, he sweated profusely. With each stroke, sparks flew from the steel, and in the bell-like sound I could hear John Donne's advice about death. We waited till Mr. Tendrick had plunged the shoe into a barrel of water and the hissing had died away before Ben asked him about renting a conveyance to take us to Carmel and Vineland. Looking at us skeptically, he pumped the bellows and stirred the coals.

"Perhaps you didn't hear me," Ben ventured.

Eventually, he deigned to speak. What transpired between him and Ben, I learned only later.

"You got an accent."

"Russian."

"A lotta Russian Jews been movin' into this area, 'specially to

Carmel. They're mostly socialists, which is just another name for troublemakers. What's your name?"

Ben knew that Cohen would not do, so he replied, "Metternich. Perhaps you're familiar with the name."

"Can't say that I am. You ain't one of those who practice that strange kind of Catholicism, are you?"

"Lutherans. We come from the German settlements around Moscow."

He smiled and wiped his face with the back of his glove. "My family hails from Cologne. I'm second generation."

"Glad to meet a fellow German. Now about that rental. . . ."

"It'll cost ya 'cause I have to send my boy along to bring back the horse and wagon. But I won't charge ya for his time, seein' as you're one of us."

"We'll arrive about nine, if that suits you."

"It'll be waitin'."

"By the way, what's your boy's name?"

"Hardy . . . and he is."

As we all started to leave, Ben said, "Mr. Tendrick, I was just wondering: why do you think so many Russian-Jews are socialists?"

"It's in their blood."

"What," asked Ben, "the desire to improve working conditions or to make trouble?"

"They're one and the same, to my way of thinking."

"Some people say there's no progress without struggle."

Mr. Tendrick spat. "Remember, cash on the barrelhead."

My first look at the Carmel house gave me heartburn, but I held my tongue. The inside offered no surprises: downstairs, a sitting room, kitchen, and pantry; upstairs, two bedrooms. No indoor plumbing. I could see immediately that life would be hard, carrying water from the pump to the kitchen and having to heat the stove with a wood fire. Just walking around the shell of the house, I could feel the lingering heat from the summer weather and could well imagine the cold gathering in the winter. We had been promised that before long all the farms on the road would be equipped with sewage lines and tanks, which of course would require regular bailing. I saw no electrical lines. Your mother tried to comfort me by saying that we had given up a grander style of living in return for a freer one. But why not work instead to liberate Russia? What good is freedom if all one does with it is worship cash on the barrelhead?

Journeying on to Vineland through the pine forests along a dirt road, we passed a few wagons with tired horses clumping along hauling hay or some other load. The farmers looked weary and all touched their caps as we passed to acknowledge our presence, just like Russian peasants. Instead of the forest providing relief from the heat, the pines seemed to generate it. The trees certainly incubated millions of insects, particularly mosquitoes. Hardy seemed unaffected, as if he had some magical immunity; but we spent most of the trip trying to wave them off and swatting those seeking our blood.

"Even the insects are anti-Semites," I said. "They ignore the goyisha boychick and attack us." Fanny laughed.

On the approach to Vineland, I took special note of the names of the farms and vineyards. Most of them were owned by Italians, with a scattering of Scandinavians, Germans, and French. Jewish names could be seen affixed to the signs of clothiers, shoemakers, carriage manufacturers, and a small shop advertising pearl buttons. Of course, Brotman's General Store was owned by a Jewish family. Mr. B., as he's called, helped us unload our belongings and carry them upstairs above the store. The living arrangements, though spare, offer more amenities than the bungalow in Carmel. We have an attic, two bedrooms, an indoor bathroom, and an alcove with an electric hot plate and a few cooking utensils, including some dishes and silverware. When we returned downstairs, Mr. B. introduced us to the dry goods owner next door, Mrs. Kasper—I gathered that once in America she had dropped the "ski"—and her four beautiful daughters, ten, fourteen, fifteen, and eighteen, each one blonder than the other. Their skin resembled alabaster. Mrs. Kasper and I spoke in Polish. She told me her family had come to Vineland from a small town, where she said they had lived like animals. She wore a simple housedress and had fashioned her hair in intricate loops and braids. The only part of her person I didn't like was the large crucifix around her neck. But why should I care what superstition she espouses?

Like many immigrants, she extolled her new land, glad to have been delivered from a hovel to a house, from no heat to a wood-burning stove. She insisted that we would love Vineland and the countryside around it, even though, she readily admitted, the area lacked adequate roads, reliable transportation—horses and wagons were hard to come by—and steady work. Her husband, she said, picked strawberries and cranberries for local growers at a few pennies per bucketful and felt himself lucky; a great many men, often with wives and children in tow, had to walk miles in search of farms needing pickers. She wanted me to tell Esther that seamstresses could earn more money than field hands. I thanked her for the tip, but explained we'd soon be moving into our own farmhouse and supporting ourselves from the land.

Ben, who's usually chatty and friendly, said nothing. Then I discovered the reason. His eyes were focused rapturously on Mrs. Kasper's oldest daughter, Irina. Already your brother is smitten.

I beg you to write about yourself and Rissa and the children. We yearn for news of your family.

Lovingly,
Your father

June 18, 1911

My heart sank when I saw Carmel. I knew that Meyer would never agree to live in this one-street town unless Ben asked him to try it. A dirt road divided the homes and businesses. On one side stood small bungalows and farmhouses with corn and vegetable patches, as well as some enclosures for poultry and cattle, and on the other side a kosher butcher, a shul, a needlework factory, a smithy, and a meeting place, Columbia Hall, housing a library.

Where's the town? Meyer asked.

Following the map the Baron de Hirsch people had sent us, I directed Hardy to take the road marked to Vineland, which passed the Carmel cemetery and led to our property. But before leaving Carmel, I had Hardy stop so Ben could read a notice posted on a Hands-Wanted board in front of a two-story brick building housing a manufacturer of nurses' uniforms. The moment we halted, swarms of mosquitoes attacked us, leaving Ben barely enough time to translate the advertisements. The factory wanted seamstresses. Fanny shook her head no.

A few minutes later, as we passed the cemetery, Meyer said, Esther, did you notice how nice they keep the graveyard? He of course was trying to provoke me. I can guess why, he said. Because it's so often in use. People come here to die. Ben, ask the boy if he knows how many times a day they have funerals in Carmel.

Meyer, I cried, genug, enough! So strident was my outburst that Hardy reined in the horses. Fortunately we were talking in Yiddish, and the boy had no idea of what had been said. Ben reassured him in English that our property lay just ahead. When we arrived at the bungalow, still under construction, I could see that although several acres had been cleared in a V-shape spreading out from the house, hundreds of stumps covered the ground. All of them would have to be cleared. I thought of burial stones, with their remains underground.

Vey iz mir! Meyer exclaimed. *This* is it? He held a hand to his head and looked as though the land he saw before him was beyond redemption. Ben, you can just tell the boy to turn around and take us back to the train. I nudged Ben with an elbow. Pop, have a little patience and give Carmel a chance. You, too? he muttered. I thought you had more sense than to want to be interred in foreign earth.

We left the wagon and, waving off the mosquitoes, followed the ground stakes to the end of our property, which terminated a few feet in the woods at a meandering stream. I suppose we'll have to schlep water from here to the kitchen, Meyer said. Not so, I replied, I saw a pump behind the house. Meyer snorted, Did you also see the privy? I did! The plans for the house, I replied, include an indoor bathroom.

Before Meyer could mock me, our attention, thank God, was drawn to a stag that materialized on the other side of the stream. He shook his great antlers, sipped from the gurgling water, and trotted on, utterly oblivious to our presence. That interruption led Meyer into a reverie about nature and, of course, the beauties of the Ukrainian countryside. Ben, bless his heart, exploited the moment. Pop, we'll take long walks together, just like in Bobrovitz, you, me, and Fanny.

If the mosquitoes don't kill us, Meyer said.

At least he hadn't said no, hadn't complained that the countryside here wasn't worth the walking. I knew then that I stood a chance of bringing Meyer round to my point of view, at least until he had to roll up his sleeves, remove stumps, and actually farm.

June 20, 1911

With no transportation to see the countryside, particularly Union Lake and Maurice River, which Mr. Brotman recommended, Mom and I surveyed Vineland, street by street. Among the rows of houses, we saw no doctor's shingle. Having lost a baby boy because the doc lived so far away, Mom had hoped for a physician within hailing distance.

Almost immediately, Mom and I began clerking in the store, and Fanny found a job minding a seven-year-old deaf and dumb girl, Alexandra Gavrilov. Her father, Vasily, a defrocked Greek-Orthodox priest, lived on the Zeffin farm, where he worked as a handyman. Pop, as I expected, remained in his room, sitting next to an open screened window, reading and smoking, "acclimating himself," he explained. Until midafternoon, the day proceeded uneventfully, except for my having to translate for Mom what the English-speaking customers said. Fortunately, many of them spoke Yiddish, which always made her feel at home among landsmen. By three o'clock, I told her to join Pop upstairs and I'd tend to our few customers. Mr. B. sat in a back room reading opera librettos and humming the tunes.

Although I had seen Negroes in Vineland, I was taken aback when one walked through the door. He said little, seemed to know exactly what he wanted and where in the store it was shelved, removed a wad of bills, paid, and left. I watched him put his purchases in the back of a horse-drawn wagon and depart without once looking around. A minute or two later, Irina, she of the white-blonde hair and perfect skin, entered the store and, without so much as a hello or what's new, said:

"That Negro is coming once into town each week. He shops here always and is buying sometimes from Mama. His name's Crenshaw, I know from stable man, Mr. Bly, but nobody is being sure of his employer. Now ain't that strange?"

Lost in her blue eyes, I had to force myself to respond. "Yeah, really strange." Suddenly I had the maddest desire to ask her to marry me, a sensation that I had never felt before and have never felt since. Overcome by her innocent beauty, I had no voluptuous thoughts, only adoration. That summer afternoon was the closest I have ever come to a religious experience. I wanted to worship her. Such overwrought language normally embarrasses me, but not in this instance. I had been struck by what my Sicilian friends in New York called "the thunderbolt," and Americans call "love at first sight." It certainly could not have been love at first hearing, because she had virtually no schooling as a child in Poland and hardly any in Vineland. Although she could speak English, she spoke it far worse than I. But at that moment I didn't care if she never spoke again, so long as she merely stood in front of me with her shining hair, her radiant skin, her thin wrists and long fingers, and her tiny feet pointed slightly outward, like a dancer's. Though her dress hung to her ankles, I knew that she had the legs of a ballerina. I could hear Tchaikovsky's *Swan Lake* in my head and wanted to be the apologetic prince and whisk her away not to a grim ending but to a happy one, where lovers could live in unending wordless bliss.

Except for weekends, I saw her every day—and always had the same tingling reaction. One morning, after Mr. Crenshaw had come and gone, Irina entered the store.

"Would you like that we are making some excitement?" she said.

Would I, I thought. But on reflection, I realized that her poor English had led her into an unintended meaning.

"What kind of excitement, Irina?"

"We next time are following to see where Mr. Crenshaw goes."

I agreed to the lark, though I guessed that if he wished to keep his movements private, he would make every effort to lose us. As we plotted, Irina saw out the window her father returning early from work. Predicting trouble at home, she excused herself, remarking:

"It can be meaning one thing only. His boss quit some workers."

Around seven that evening, just before closing, I could hear screams and curses issuing from the Kasper Dry Goods Store. Not until later that night, when Irina came to our door, did I learn that her father had indeed been laid off from work and, in drunken despair, had been beating his wife.

Distraught and shaking with fear, she asked me if I would accompany her on a walk down Landis Avenue, the main thoroughfare. My mother shot me a look rife with resonance: I don't approve of young unchaperoned women, particularly Catholics, inviting men out, especially Jews. My father paid no attention, except to say that if her mother needed any assistance, we would of course help. I smiled at his generosity knowing full well that he would never intervene in a family quarrel, but would have no reluctance to volunteer me.

"I'll be back by ten," I said.

"Make it nine," Mother countermanded.

Irina and I strolled down the street and actually said very little. I gathered she wanted a silent companion as she sorted through her mind the brutish images. Never having been privy to domestic violence—altercations, yes—I couldn't imagine a man beating a woman. How often had I heard my father disparage the peasants by quoting Swift's lines, "I saw a woman flayed the other day. You have no idea how it altered her appearance for the worse"? We must have walked at least twenty minutes, past the modest shops struggling to survive, past the grain lot, before Irina spoke.

"I am hating him!"

What can one say to such a declaration, don't hate him? Filial love, I mused, initially comes for free and then, when the child becomes sensible, has to be earned.

Hearing a crying sound in the distance, we turned down a side street in search of its source. At first, it resembled a child's cry, but then we saw three young boys wrestling a cat into the hole of a privy. Seeing us, the boys fled. We found a dead tree branch and, holding one end, I lowered it into the stinking stew. A minute later, a black cat emerged, covered in excrement, but saved from drowning in that reeking offal. Taking the cat by the scruff of the neck, I carried it to an outdoor pump a few feet from the privy and held it firmly while Irina drew up a steady stream of water to generously bathe the poor, writhing creature. Fortunately, the night was warm and the cat slunk off into the high grass to shake itself dry. On the way home, we exchanged some cursory comments about the cruelty of humans; by the time we reached her house, the cat, whom I immediately named Cato, had joined our company but decamped the next day, apparently preferring a stoic life to the Kaspers' volcanic one.

That night I lay awake, unable to sleep. In New York, the city dwellers thought nothing of dumping their garbage from windows onto the sidewalks and streets. Horses defecated in the roadways, and tenement dwellers relieved themselves in the two- and three-holers behind their buildings. Outside of wealthy homes on the East Side, discarded items that looked practically new attracted scavengers, who greedily scooped up these barely used furnishings and clothes and children's toys.

Toward morning I dozed and dreamed that I was back on the Kaiserin Auguste Victoria steamship. From the top deck to the bottom, women were jumping overboard. When I asked them why, they paused in their descent and made numerous replies: "My husband has mumbled the sacred Jewish words and now we're divorced"; "my husband breeds me like a cow"; "my husband says I'm his property"; "my husband beats me"; "my husband tells me that if I want a new garment I can just pick through the garbage cans of New York." Suddenly my brother Jacob appeared, urging me to detonate bridges and derail trains to undermine the Romanov government, but I told him that I was needed to tell the dispossessed of America that they, too, had recourse to revolution.

June 30, 1911

The short time we've been in America has already created divisions in our family. The old versus the new ways. Our parents are like the pitch pines that monotonously cover so much of the Barrens. The most successful pines are those whose cones open only after being badly burned, shedding their seeds. They are the most hardy. Like Ben and me. The death of the old pines increases the light. The overhead canopy no longer prevents the growth of new plants. We will thrive with the other immigrant children who have exchanged the old for the new. My only fear is how do we live from the soil, which is right for pitch pines and oaks, but not for planting. Who buys cheaply pays dearly. Why did the Baron de Hirsch Fund choose this area without first testing the ground?

Never mind. Mama is determined to succeed, even if Papa is not. She wants to transplant her Russian energy in American earth. Papa, poor papa, he wants the social utopia that exists in his dreams. But nowhere else. Mama, on the other hand, is convinced that by our having survived the feverish fires of pogroms, she and Papa have created for Ben and me the possibility of a sunny future. Of late all my thoughts are steeped in the figures of fire. The ancient fear. Probably burned into our brains millions of years ago. Fire, which not only destroys but also cleanses—for those who survive.

If our family makes a lot of money, I wouldn't mind living in a big house in the middle of Manhattan. With Tiffany glass and crystal chandeliers. I'd join Jacob Riis to help feed the poor. Belle Moskowitz and Robert Moses and Al Smith would dine at our table. Talking about education and parks and politics.

First, though, we have to succeed. And how can I contribute? I am currently tending a deaf child. For pennies. A Vineland rabbi suggests that I attend the Pennsylvania Institution for the Deaf and Dumb in Philadelphia. He says that a Dr. Alston can teach me Gallaudet's method of sign language. Then I can both speak and help deaf children. But can the family spare me? And does work like that eventually pay? Ben tells me I shouldn't worry. He will support me. How? With the help of a friend, he replies. No, I want to be a real wage earner. My right hand, the doctor says, will never again be dexterous enough for me to engage in fine stitchery. I could run a sewing machine, but memories of the factory would haunt me. If I never hear the din of those machines, never again feel a treadle underfoot, I will feel delivered. To teach deaf children to communicate would be a *mitzvah*. A blessing.

When Alexandra naps, I fall into dream. And always I see Mr. Chernovsky, my tutor. His shingled cottage stands at the edge of the village. I have to cross a bridge; I watch the water, which seems to be running the wrong way. Six girls meet with him three times a week in the afternoon for two hours. We sit at double desks, side by side. My companion is Rachel Heber. Her father is a shoemaker. I have been teamed with her because she is the slowest student, I the most advanced. She resents me and tries to show her superiority by wearing for each class different shoes. I think she has seven or eight pairs. Me, two. Though she can sound the Hebrew words, she doesn't understand what she's reading. Mr. Chernovsky calls her predicament an omen. I don't know what he means. He says what good are sounds without meaning—like village gossip.

At one time, the classroom must have served as a dining room. A sideboard holds not dishes but Hebrew textbooks. Looking down from one wall is a photograph of two girls in white cotton dresses with sashes and knee-length white stockings and patent-leather shoes. Rebecca and Rose. Mr. Chernovsky's daughters. A second photograph hangs next to the first. But it is always covered with a black cloth. He lives alone. His wife disappeared. Both his daughters buried during the typhus outbreak. A scholarly man, he is nonetheless superstitious. Hanging from his neck is a garlic bag. When he sneezes, he touches the mezuzah on the doorjamb. The world is aswarm with evil spirits, he says, and demands our constant attention. Signs, we must always be attentive to signs, he insists. Perhaps this explains his belief that left-handedness is a mark of evil. The devil's signature. Mr. Chernovsky ties my left hand behind my back with a belt and makes me compose with my right. Then he takes my slate and holds it up as an example of poor cursive. After school, I beg him not to, saying I am a good student and often answer his questions. But he ignores me. Slowly I grow silent. When I do speak, I stutter.

The other children find my stuttering amusing. They mimic me. Papa, having heard that stutterers speak normally when they sing, tries to help me by having me sing my lessons. My lessons sound like a mournful Hebraic song.

July 26, 1911

Every day I try to improve my English. But my mind still thinks in Polish, where words come more easily, and I don't feel like a fool. At least, thank God, I can speak. Ben's sister went away to learn how to talk with her hands. Such a nice girl. When she is returning, I don't know.

Yesterday, Mr. Crenshaw, like always on Tuesday, came to the general store. In a buckboard I borrowed from Mrs. Slotsky, me and Ben followed at a distance. To get away from our mothers, who would complain about us being together UNCHAPERONED, I told Mother my bleeding was so bad I was dizzy, and he told his he wanted to check their farmhouse.

Ben stayed out of sight, taking the Bridgeton road. South of Carmel one mile he turned into a path that led to Maurice River. I had once been this way on a church ride. He asked if I remembered any houses in the woods, and I said yes, one. Ben left the wagon before the cutoff, and we walked on the pine needles so as not to leave footprints. Every step being bitten by mosquitoes, we came to a clearing with a whitewashed house, a privy, a small barn, two wagons, a few chickens, and a pump and large wooden tub to catch the runoff. When circling the house from our hiding place in the woods, we noticed behind the barn a clapboard hut with a corrugated tin roof. Because of the skitas we soon hurried back to the road. But before we left, Mr. Crenshaw appeared at the back door of the house with a man I immediately recognized as someone with a bad reputation, Nathan Boritski. He and Mr. Crenshaw spoke briefly and then Mr. Crenshaw went in the hut.

"That Boritski house, as the crow flies, isn't far from our Carmel farm," said Ben. "I could probably walk it in twenty minutes."

"If covered with citronella."

"Right," Ben laughed.

"We must leave before he shoot us."

Ben looked at me like I am crazy. I whispered that Mr. Boritski had a reputation for meanness. When we reached the wagon, Ben said: "Now tell me what you know about Mr. Boritski."

I explained that he had once been in jail and still sometimes gets in trouble with the police because he shoots guns at strangers when they come close to his house. No one knows why. Mr. Crenshaw runs errands for him and that sort of thing. Last year some newspaper reporter snuck to his property and wrote an article saying a person the police wanted was staying there. But when they looked, they found nothing. Mr. Boritski sometimes comes into our store to buy men's clothing and spends many dollars. Mother said when she tries to talk to him he only mumbles. Last time he came into the store, it was several months ago, he bought clothes again. Overalls, boots, denim shirts. Always he pays cash and always he has a full wallet.

After our adventure I returned to the store. Father was drinking in the rocking chair, still out of work. Mother was afraid. I told her to go home and I would lock up, praying that Father would stay with me. But in a few minutes he left. An hour later I peeked into Brotman's to tell Ben good-bye. He offered to walk me home, just one block away. In Yiddish, Mrs. Cohen complained. I know she doesn't like that he likes me. That's why whenever I go into Brotman's I first take off my silver crucifix. Ben kissed his mother's cheek and we started down the road, with him kicking dirt clogs. Near my house, I heard cries and, guessing what it meant, I told Ben to turn around. But he said no and walked me to the front door. I opened it and saw a terrible scene. My father was beating my mother with a belt. She was cowering, her arms covering her head, pleading in Polish, "Not in the face. People will know."

To my shock, Ben grabbed Papa's arm and swung him around. "Pick on me," he said, but Father, whose English is terrible, did not understand, so Ben shouted, "Irina, translate." I did. Father stood like a paralyzed person. Slowly off he went.

I told Ben he shouldn't have shamed Father because Mother would pay dearly. But he said I should tell Father that if he ever again hits Mother he will horsewhip him. I know it will do no good. Father can't stop his feelings. It is because of the whiskey and him not making a living.

That night he didn't come home. I secretly prayed he would fall into a creek and drown and asked the Virgin Mary to forgive me for thinking such sinful thoughts. Mother sat on the couch whimpering and I kneeled at her feet trying to explain what to men having no work means. She was like a little girl. Married at fourteen and right away having children, she never had a chance to grow up. Her whole life what mattered were her home and family and now the store. Father used her body like you rent a horse for an hour. The doctor told her she couldn't have more children after the fourth and performed some kind of operation which made her "safe." Hoping for a son, father was enraged and went to the local priest, wanting the doctor arrested. But the priest knew about the

Kasper house and told him to go home and cherish his four beautiful God-given daughters.

Mother whispered in Polish, "You like Ben Cohen?"

At first, I resisted telling the truth. Then I told.

"It's impossible," she said.

"Why?"

"Because he is Jewish and you, Catholic."

My mother's faith, learned by tradition, was boundless and blind. I knew if I talked to her about God wishing for his children only the best, she would not understand. So I said what I knew would affect her the most.

"Jewish husbands don't beat their wives."

Her silence and the lack of light in the room made me think of a grave. After what seemed like a lifetime, she resurrected herself. "You know this for sure?"

I told her what Ben had said, that on the head of the man who mistreats his wife great shame falls. Of course there were some bad men, but not hitting women was part of their religion. Once she heard Judaism condemned wife beating she decided to help me by speaking to Mrs. Cohen. I thanked her and said, "Don't make wedding plans yet. I've known him only a short time and his feelings are a mystery."

"Maybe bake him a cake or knit him a sweater. Show him how good you are with your hands."

"Mother—"

She interrupted. "Do what he says. An obedient wife is what men like. Show him you know your duty."

"Yes, Mother." I saw there was nothing to gain from arguing. "When the time comes, and IF it comes, I will tell you."

"How could he not notice a beautiful girl like you, and so pure?"

"Thank you, Mother. But what will come only God knows."

"Sometimes these things need a little push."

I smiled at her generosity and wondered if her life had happened differently what she might have been.

"There is one thing . . ." she warned. "A rich Jewish family has moved into Carmel, the Aprils, and they have a pretty daughter. She came into our shop. She might catch his eye."

"Aprils?"

I remembered something Ben told me about Russian revolutionaries. "Better, I think, the Aprils should be called Decembrists."

July 31, 1911

Today we began moving into our Carmel house and have already started arranging for the coming year. All those nights above the store, planning our new life, and now, at long last, the time is upon us. For the next several weeks, Ben and I will be gone from Brotman's to clean and paint the bungalow, which still smells of wood shavings. Fanny has moved to Mt. Airy, a suburb of Philadelphia, to learn how to teach some sort of finger language to deaf and dumb children. When I asked how she could support herself, Ben said he had made all the arrangements. What does that mean? But he was as silent as Fanny.

To support ourselves until the crops have been planted and harvested, we will have to divide our time between the store and the farm, at least for a while. Already several itinerant farmers have agreed for two dollars a day to clear the fields of stumps and weeds and prepare the soil for planting. Since I know Meyer won't pick up a hoe and Ben seems daily less interested in farming, I told the men that they could start work just as soon as we moved all our belongings from Vineland to Carmel.

The Fund has given us some money and of course the house, but if not for Mr. B., we would be as poor as the pickers. No, I exaggerate. Whenever we are down to our last nickel, Ben goes to the Vineland bank and returns with some cash. His explanation—Mr. Cosin wires him the money—doesn't ring true. How will he pay him back? But since he wouldn't tell me about his arranging things for Fanny I don't question him about his golden goose. I did ask him, though, how he could afford to take Mrs. Kasper and her daughters to Philadelphia. Last week, they went on the train and spent the day. What they did there is anybody's guess. You would think Ben is a secret agent. He tells me nothing.

In my chest I feel a burning—I know it's a warning—telling me that Ben is spending too much time with that Polish towhead. If he's not careful, her drunken father will be coming after him with a shotgun. I know these Poles from the old country. They hate Jews and love the Pope. They would rather eat uncooked potatoes than not give to the Church. That's all I need, a grandson with Polish-Catholic blood in his veins. It would kill me. But since I know it's no use to bring up the subject, I intend to tell Ben about my meeting Mrs. April in the butcher shop. Such a nice Jewish lady, and rich. We talked about our children. It warmed my heart. She came into Yonny's to buy a *broost*. I told her the sirloin was better.

Really, she said, acting like she was surprised I could afford a steak. But not wanting her to think us poor, I told her we often ate meat. At least three times a week, I said. She no doubt thought that like the other Carmelites we mostly ate fish or chicken. So I winked at Yonny and repeated, Even maybe four times a week. Right, Yonny?

His fat face, which never has any color, turned red. *Altz is kosher v'yosher*. Everything is on the level.

I see your husband bought that old building covered with ivy. The sign out in front says he's going to make dresses. Proud as a peacock, she replied, It's his second factory. He owns another in Atlanta. That one his brother runs. How nice, Mrs. April. God should always bless you. Have you any children? Three, a son and two daughters. So how old would these wonderful children be? Erika, my oldest, is seventeen. That's her middle name. She prefers it to her first, Âme. Our family originally came from France. Her sister, Ruth, is fifteen, but looks twenty, and her brother, Morris, is twelve. What a blessing, Mrs. April. And you Mrs. Cohen?

Two sons, one still in Russia. My daughter, God bless her pure soul, helps deaf children in Philadelphia. The boy with me here in this country, Ben, he is like your Erika, nearly the same age. Mrs. April smiled. Really? It would be nice they should meet. How could I not agree? So I said, I would love it. Such a courteous lady, like you, your daughter can only be perfect. She asked me, You like classical music? I lied for Ben's sake. What's better? She took her package from Yonny. Tonight, Harold Bauer, you know, the pianist, will be playing at Columbia Hall. But I'm sure you already have tickets. I nodded. Yes, my Meyer bought them. I look forward to seeing you there. She made a kind smile and said, I'll introduce you to my family. I answered, It will be such a pleasure. Your son's name again? she asked. Ben. He's a good worker and likes to paint. She frowned. Houses? No, miniatures. This evening you'll meet him. She said, Well, shalom. I replied, You should always have nachis.

When she left the butcher shop, I thanked Yonny for not telling her that I had just bought a chicken, our usual fare, and quickly walked down the road to tell Meyer and Ben what had happened and how we all had to go to the concert.

I thought you preferred a different kind of music, Meyer said. What made you change your mind? Annoyed, I snapped, So you don't want to hear Bauer? Of course I do. But who knows at this late time if they still have some tickets. At that moment, I could see my plans ruined. Meyer just shrugged. We're going! I said. There's someone I want Ben should meet. Meyer asked, even if we have to stand through the concert? You're always complaining about your varicose veins.

When Ben suggested he bring Irina, I nearly died. A Mrs. April wants us to know her family. New in Carmel. Irina, she's a sweet girl, but she wouldn't fit in. For me, just this once, don't argue.

We dressed in our best summer clothes and stood in the back of the auditorium. I hardly listened. Scanning the room for the Aprils, I saw them sitting up front, the five of them. It took me a minute to sort out the two girls, so young did Erika look. At the intermission, I took Ben by the arm and led him to the Aprils, who were standing on the front porch of the building. To escape the heat, Mrs. April said, introducing her family. The moment I laid eyes on Erika, I thought *oy gevalt*! What will Ben think. She had a port wine stain on the right side of her face. But he never blinked, behaving like a perfect gentleman. The two of them spoke politely, even taking a few steps away from the families to talk. What they said, who knows? But I did see them smile and laugh, and when we returned to the concert, I noticed that Erika turned around twice.

The next day at Brotman's, I waited until the customers had all gone and then remarked to Ben how beautiful Erika was. I expected him to mention the stain, but he never uttered a word about it. She's also very young, he said. Seventeen! I pointed out. Ben gave me one of his looks. And childlike, he answered. You want at seventeen she should be an old woman? We'll see, he mumbled, how things go. What does that mean? Ben replied, I'll stop at her house. I sputtered, And? He sighed, And what? I wanted to give him a good shaking. And you'll ask for permission to see her. If her parents approve, I'll invite the family to dinner. Sirloin. How does that sound?

August 10, 1911

Ever since Mama mentioned the April girl I have been watching for her. Yesterday it was so hot I had a hard time breathing. My chest hurt worse when I saw this girl and her mother come out of the blacksmith's shed. I crossed the road to Mr. Bly and asked who they were. He said "the Aprils from Carmel." I thought maybe they had come to buy a carriage but he said they wanted a large eagle for the water cap on their Franklin automobile. Then I lied saying I had once met the daughter but couldn't remember her name. "Erika," he said.

She was dressed like she lived in New York instead of Carmel, which has poor farmers mostly. The way she took her mother's arm, you would think she needed help to get down the road. And she walked like she was stepping around cow pies. In one hand she carried a pink umbrella which she opened outside the forge even though there wasn't a cloud in the sky. Olga told me later it's called a parasol but with the weather so good and the sun so bright I saw no reason for it. Rich people I guess just mind sweating more than the poor.

To get a better look I followed them down main street until they stopped to stare through the shoemaker's window. I nearly tripped over Erika as I pretended to look into the same store. She turned to me. Then my heart sank because in a delicate way I saw she was really pretty, except for a mark running from her hairline, across part of her forehead and cheekbone and half her eyelid. To hide it, she combed her hair forward and held a hand up to her face. I could tell that from the minute she was born she never worked hard for ONE DAY. Moments later they walked off, both of them in fine clothes and wearing soft leather shoes.

August 13, 1911

My mother's real motive for wishing to unite Erika April and me was because of Irina. Having lived as a child in the borderlands between Russia and Poland, Mom had seen the Polish peasants drunk on vodka and religion, an incendiary mixture that fed their wrath against Jews and their patrons, those nobles who, a hundred years before, had invited Jewish merchants and intellectuals into the country. In other words, Erika represented a diversionary tactic. My mother had often said no man ought to marry before the age of twenty-one, and, given her need to have me on hand, I knew she would oppose my marrying early. Once Irina had been set aside, if she approved of Erika, she would make sure that our courtship ran into years. Her stratagems, familiar to my father, had come clear to me only when she had launched her plan to leave Russia.

To please my mother at no cost to me, I left a note at Erika's house asking her parents if I might call. The family invited me to lunch, warmly greeting me on my arrival. Mrs. April led me through the handsomely furnished house to an oval gazebo in the back garden. Screened to keep out the insects, it had a glass-topped table set with fine china, linen napkins, and silverware bearing an English emblem. I gathered that the family intended to impress me. On my part, I gave them a small pencil drawing, which elicited oohs and ahhs. After the usual gossip, we found our name cards and sat, with Erika at my right. A Negro woman dressed all in white served a first dish of melon, and then blue fish, string beans, fresh baked bread, and a tomato salad. For dessert we had apple pie. Erika wore a pink summer dress with puff sleeves and a matching bow in her hair. I noticed her white shoes and small feet, a feature in people that my father often observed, quick to disparage those who had feet "as big as rowboats."

I hoped that the dinner-table conversation would escape the usual loop of languid talk and touch upon a subject worth mentioning. But I had no such luck. We traversed from the weather to the neighbors to the goyim to the new arrivals in Carmel to the background of my family and theirs and back to the weather.

"Did you like the concert?" I asked in hopes of pointing the discussion to music.

Mr. April, who I gathered cared less about culture than his wife, replied, "I was hoping Bauer would play more familiar tunes and not so much of the . . . unfamiliar."

Liszt's *Ballade No. 1 in D flat major*, unfamiliar? I dared not object, and studied my plate. Mrs. April remarked that Liszt, a composer Mr. April found less congenial than Mozart, encouraged younger colleagues and promoted others' music.

"Do you play?" I asked Mrs. April, hoping to turn the subject of music lessons toward Erika. Mrs. April made the bridge.

"I don't, but Erika does."

"Really?" I said, moving my chair so that I could face her.

"I'm not very good, but I *do* practice."

Her comment struck me as peculiar because it cut two ways. On the one hand, she was ingratiating herself with her parents by saying she practiced; on the other, she seemed to be saying that she was so lacking in talent that practice didn't help.

"Perhaps with a first-rate teacher," I said, "you'd improve."

She smiled sweetly and studied her hands, but didn't reply. Staring at her silly bow, I noticed that it held in check a profusion of black curls. Her slim pedestal neck supported a pretty face. She had a tiny mouth with thin lips, almond-shaped dark eyes, pale skin, high cheekbones, and a finely shaped nose. Her every gesture, word, opinion had been forged in the crucible of her class. From her music lessons to her choice of forks, she exuded good manners. I didn't need to ask; I knew that she had attended one of those southern academies that taught rich American immigrant children how to behave like nineteenth-century ladies. I had to smile at the distance between us. Irina, like me, was salt of the earth, though we came from different faiths. Erika seemed fragile, similar to a swooning Dumas fils heroine in the final throes of consumption.

Mr. Isaac April, having polished off two portions of dessert, leaned back in his chair, rested his thumbs in his cotton vest pockets, and began the catechism. "I trust you have big plans for that farm of yours. What do you plan to raise?"

"Corn and peppers and tomatoes."

"The future's in eggs. You'd be better off with a chicken farm."

"To tell you the truth, Mr. April, I have no aptitude for farm life and would prefer something else."

"Namely?"

"Starting my own business . . . in cosmetics."

"I like an enterprising lad. Maybe I can help you get started."

Thinking of the dough that had come from Madden and A. R., I replied, "I may have enough to swing it on my own."

"Well, if you need some additional cash, let's talk."

With the exception of Erika, who remained seated, the family migrated into the house, leaving the two of us at table. Her shyness manifested itself in a series of blushes that turned her colorless face crimson. We babbled aimlessly, like a brook carrying a leaf or twig to some unknown destination. To terminate this purposeless chatter, I asked, "How do you normally spend your days?"

Her reply took me by surprise. "I stay at home and keep the account books for my father."

"You're a bookkeeper?"

"The school I attended . . . all the girls were taught how to type and take shorthand and do some accountancy."

"Useful skills," I replied, intending no irony. But she looked at me as if I had.

"As a matter of fact, I do think they are useful. A girl never knows when she may have to support herself."

I admired her spunk, though her self-defense was not at all necessary. "Don't misunderstand me," I said, touching her hand, "I absolutely agree with you. If I knew accountancy, I wouldn't have to clerk in a store."

"Would you like to learn?"

"Bookkeeping?"

"Yes."

"Well, I had never thought of it."

"I'll gladly teach you."

Whether she genuinely had my education in mind or just wanted to create an occasion for us to meet regularly, I couldn't say, but I decided that nothing ventured, nothing gained.

"Do you have any hobbies?" she asked excitedly, as if any doubts she had harbored about me were resolved.

"Other than painting miniatures, no."

"I collect postcards. Let me show you my collection."

While I waited on the porch, she went to her room and returned carrying a shoe box with cards from all over the world.

"Whenever my friends travel, I make them promise to write me a card. Someday I hope to take the Grand Tour. Wouldn't that be just the most wonderful way to spend a year?"

"If you could afford it."

"Daddy says that if I work for him a whole year, he'll let me go with a friend."

"What if by then you were married?"

Her face flushed, going from crimson to scarlet to carmine.

August 15, 1911

Dearest Diary, Two days after I invited Ben to learn accountancy he showed up at our house just as we were finishing evening dessert. He joined us in the sun-room for whipped cream and fresh strawberries. The atmosphere was much more relaxed than when I met him at the concert or the day before yesterday for lunch. Then I felt my parents watching me, waiting for some sign that I thought *he* was the one. This time, the scent of new mown grass, the fireflies, a crescent moon . . . it was like a wonderful play. I suddenly knew how I would capture the moment. At Miss Pritchard's Academy, our English teacher had said that an elegant diary, one that we would wish to read in the future, should transcend summaries and confessions and read like a play. Her advice took shape naturally. Just as if a dramatist had written our parts, we talked smoothly and let the stage directions govern our behavior. When we had finished our dessert and the others had gone, Ben and I conversed, not about accountancy, as we had planned, but about us.

—May I call you by your first name?

—Please do.

—I understand, Erika, you came to New Jersey from Georgia. What was it like in the South?

—Atlanta had about it a slow elegance. Lovely homes with great porches. Papa's friends all seemed to have a lot of money, even though it appeared they never worked. I couldn't understand where the wealth came from. And friendly . . . they would stop in the street to say hello. We had a grand piano in the living room and a dining room large enough to dance in. And your town?

—I remember best the orchards and reed fences. Orchards of cherry and apple and plum trees. Most of the houses had straw-covered thatch roofs. The peasants kept beehives and grew gooseberry bushes. The moment the weather was warm enough, we'd all go barefoot.

—Atlanta was really quite wonderful. In the summer, Papa would roll up the rugs, and we'd invite all the neighborhood boys who were home from college. We lived in the lap of luxury . . . that's not very original, I know, but we did.

—You must have had a flock of suitors.

(I decided there would never be a better time than now to introduce the birthmark.)

—One boy in particular seemed very interested. He came from a wealthy German-Jewish family in Atlanta. When I finally met his parents, they were very formal and distant. The next day, the boy ended our friendship, explaining that his family felt I had the mark of Cain.

—I hadn't noticed.

—Papa says that we appreciate beauty all the more for its slight imperfections.

—The Renaissance painters would have agreed. They always managed to insinuate into their work a slight blemish, to heighten the beauty. Your father's right. He's a wise man.

(From the living room came the sound of waltz music. Papa had put a disc on the gramophone. I nearly laughed because he was so obvious. Ben reached out a hand and asked me to dance. So we swept around the sun-room.)

—You dance wonderfully, Ben. Where did you learn?

—A girl in New York taught me. Why do you ask?

—You don't seem the type.

—You misjudge me.

—It's just that you're not like the college boys.

—You are a very beautiful girl, Erika.

(I blushed from head to foot.)

—I've never regarded myself . . . because . . . I mean. . . .

—Have you been to Parvin Lake?

—Never.

—Perhaps you and your family would like to go for a picnic?

—I'd have to ask them, but I'd love to.

(As soon as he left the house, I told Mother about his invitation.)

—You like Mr. Cohen?

—Yes, he's a very nice man.

—Nice? What does nice mean? You like him, you don't like him? Which?

—I hardly know him. He seems like a kind man. I gather he works hard, but I wonder about his future as a clerk in Brotman's.

—Your father can always take care of that.

—He reads a lot.

—Which is all to the good.

—And you know from the concert that he likes good music.

—So when are you going to tell me what's bad?

—He seems a lot older than me, even though we're close in age.

(Papa, who had entered the kitchen unseen, interrupted, obviously having heard what I was saying.)

—It's time you went out with men, not *pishers*. Ben Cohen is a man. And if he's interested in you, I'll make him rich.

—Yes, Papa.

—And from what I can see, he's got pluck, Erika.

—Yes, Papa, yes, but there has to be more than that.

—More? What more is there? You'll like Ben Cohen. He's no pisher.

(Papa shook a finger in the air and strode off. Mama waited a minute before she spoke.)

—Erika, when you're dancing, don't get too close to him.

—Who? Mr. Cohen?

—Anybody.

—Why?

—Never mind why. Just don't get too close to him.

August 19, 1911

Dear Ben,

I haven't seen you in almost three weeks, so I hired the scribe, Herschel Skilowitz, to write this letter. He said I could speak to him in Polish, and he could write in Yiddish. That way my thoughts would be clear to you.

Before you left for Carmel, you said that maybe we would take a trip to New York like the one to Philadelphia. My mother and sisters would love it. We had such a good time visiting Independence Hall and the historical sites, and I'm sure New York would also be interesting. But I don't want you thinking you have to pay. Mother and my sisters and I can save up. It's just that you lived in New York awhile and could show us around. We've never been there.

Business has been slow, and my father is still out of work. But my sisters have been helping out, working as maids. Olga found a job in Carmel with the April family. I told her to look for you and say hello. She still talks about our trip to Philadelphia and says you're just the grandest fellow. So do I.

What did you think of the rain last week? I hated it. Rain makes me feel dreary and sad. Mother says I'm a sunshine girl. Maybe she's right. Rain makes me think of funerals, though I do like the smell of the fields after a good downpour. Did I ever tell you about the time I went swimming in Maurice River after a heavy rain? The water was so high it came over the banks. My father tied a rope between two trees, one on each side of the spot in the river where we like to swim. We started upstream and were carried downstream in the strong current, grabbing the rope in order to stop ourselves. I kept thinking what would happen if we missed the rope or it broke. A person could be swept all the way to Union Lake. My father told us that when it rains hard the timber rattlers come looking for high ground—and those places are just below where he strung the rope!

When you come back to work at Brotman's, I will make us a lunch and we can eat it in the park, unless the mosquitoes are too bad. I'll even buy kosher meat, so you won't have to catch the dickens from your mother. I'm hoping to get to know her better because I think she's a fine woman, and be sure to tell her I said so.

How is your father doing? He seems like a fine person too. I wish, like him, I had read many books. Every time I see him, he has one in his hands. He must be terribly smart. I just hope for his sake he doesn't mind living in Carmel, which is a pretty small place.

My mother said the strangest thing the other day, that Jewish men make good husbands because they don't beat their wives. Think of me sometimes.

Your good friend,
Irina

"Silent, silent, all the time silent. Do you do it to hurt me or have you *too* lost the power of speech?" Esther's complaint is her way of saying that she will make a success of this Babylonian Captivity, like the Talmudists of old, and that I stubbornly hope to return home. How am I to speak in this strange land? I know neither the barbarous tongue nor the Philistine habits. Except for my family, the other immigrants I meet speak Russian and Yiddish badly. To hear beautiful and rich languages misused breaks my heart. Man's greatest gift, our most wonderful symbolic system, language, should be employed to convey subtleties and beauty, not to stumble from one way station to another. The few people who read can hardly understand what the words really mean. At shul, the other day, where I go to keep up my knowledge of Hebrew—they have a small collection of such books—our supposedly learned Rabbi Kolodny had just read *King Lear* and tried to engage me in conversation. "Jewish daughters," he said, "would never treat their fathers like *that*." Poor Shakespeare. He thought he was describing a universal condition; he didn't know the Jews were exempt.

I doubt Rabbi Kolodny has any familiarity with the great American writers. You can hardly find a person in this country who has read Melville or Emerson. James Madison, Alexander Hamilton—merely names. The painters and poets? Americans can't name one. What they know are inventors, like Alexander Graham Bell, and millionaires, Astors and Guggenheims and Morgans and Rockefellers. What will become of such a country?

Yes, I wanted money too, I wanted the family distillery returned, but not in order to build a mansion and hire servants. I wanted the freedom to read and think, the opportunity to help support the Kiev opera, the financial influence to help modernize my own country. Must I die exiled from my own culture and consciousness? Every day I read in the Yiddish papers how many immigrants come to America. What the paper doesn't say is how many return. I hear the number is as high as one-third. And why not? They realize their mistake or make their nest egg and return. Just as soon as this Carmel business is settled, I'll go home.

Two days ago, Ben took me to Bridgeton to see a physician about my constant coughing. I swear I know more than the doctor. His office had one anatomy book, a guide to drugs, and a medical journal seven years out of date. He listened to my chest and said, if I wished, he could arrange for me to have an exploratory operation to determine my thoracic condition. I'm surprised he even knew the word. When he leaned over with his stethoscope, I detected liquor on his breath. I wouldn't be the least bit surprised if he had come straight to his office from the tavern. Frankly, I can hardly blame him. No self-respecting physician would want to practice in a town like this one. He asked Ben, who translated, if I suffered from nerves. What in the world does *that* mean? If he had asked am I melancholy, a good seventeenth-century word whose meaning probably eludes him, we might have gotten somewhere. Cigarettes and melancholia are at the root of my problems, neither one curable by surgery.

But to whom can I explain the soreness in my heart: the rabbi? A provincial. Esther? She's determined to vindicate her decision to emigrate. Fanny? Off in Philadelphia. Ben? He's a handsome, willowy lad, and no doubt his blonde hair and pale blue eyes win him more than feminine smiles. But there's the problem. He would rather romance pretty women than paint miniatures. His art work, his reading, his study of Hebrew, his interest in biology—all lost. He's been in America five minutes and already exhibits the same acquisitive values. For his sake, if for no other, we ought to return to Russia. His brother Jacob could take him under his wing. I am no model for him, neither is Esther. We are old, living out the ragged end of our days. The truth is, Esther wants to keep her children with her till she dies. I ought to know. My mother could have written a treatise on how to use guilt to keep a child at home. I've tried to warn Ben about his mother—Fanny understands—but when he looks at me I know what he sees: a desiccated life, the ruins of great expectations.

August 25, 1911

Dad is apparently a lot sicker than he knows. The doctor stopped me as we left his office. Fortunately Pop couldn't understand.

"His lungs," he said, "have an illness."

So do you, I mused, as I caught a whiff of his breath. "Namely?"

"Probably cancer."

"But you're not sure."

"We see so little of it. Most men smoke pipes and cigars or chew plugs, which lead to throat, mouth, and lip cancers. I'd recommend you take him to Philadelphia to see a specialist."

On the way back to Vineland, in our rented horse and wagon, I mentioned seeing a doctor in the city. Pop dismissed the idea, saying he would wait till he returned to Russia, where he could consult a real expert. Then, after several minutes of silence, he asked:

"How bad is it?"

Some people think that patients should be kept from bad news; I figured that if Dad had only a short time to live, he would want to know. So I told him what the doctor feared.

He looked resigned. "I'm not surprised. Some doctors have been predicting that cigarette smoking would lead to more cases of lung cancer. I think all along I knew it was only a matter of time."

Fanny and I had often whispered that Dad seemed indifferent to an early death, though at sixty-four he was approaching his three score years and ten. I expected him to quote one of his favorite poets about intimations of mortality, but he surprised me by observing:

"If you married the April girl, I'm sure her father would set you up in his business, or in one of your own."

I laughed. "He's already offered."

"See, your old father's no fool."

"That's a label I would never pin on you, Pop."

"How about malingerer or laggard?"

I answered obliquely. "In some communities if you choose to spend your time reading Hebrew texts at the synagogue you're revered."

"With answers like that, you'll soon be a full-fledged rabbi."

Pop lit a cigarette and the smoke disappeared into his vitals, only to appear again when it streamed from his mouth as he spoke.

"Rabbi Kolodny's threatening to bar me from the shul library."

"What do you mean?" I asked incredulously.

"He calls my smoking on the Sabbath an unpardonable sin. Actually, he's disgruntled because I disagreed with his reading of a certain biblical passage, citing the original Hebrew in support of my argument. He felt mortified, even though I corrected him in private."

Scratch off the shul library: one less refuge for my father in a culturally inhospitable country. As his world shrank, he would, I realized, become even more self-centered and disinclined to seek friends in the community. I could even see him, despite his poor health, buying a return steamship ticket to Europe.

I stopped the horse and wagon in front of the Carmel post office, not for my sake but for Pop's. He checked the mail daily hoping to hear from Jacob, whom he religiously wrote once a week, and to collect Fanny's letters, which came regularly. Jacob's silence, Dad reasoned, proceeded from one of two sources: his rupture with Mom or his political activities. If the first, he rightly wondered, why should his elder son snub him as well as her? If the second, political acts against the czar were punishable by internal exile to Siberia. I could certainly understand my father's concern.

Handing Dad the reins, I sprang from the carriage and into the one room over which Mrs. Myshkin held sway. With her dog Bissel at her side, she sorted and distributed the mail. When nature called, she would lock the front door and leave Bissel behind as she attended to her needs in the outhouse. The barking of the dog told anyone wishing to collect his mail that Mrs. Myshkin was temporarily indisposed. No barking meant she was absent from the post office, because the dog was her constant companion.

To my surprise, Mrs. Myshkin handed me two letters. The one I expected was return-addressed "Chesterfield"; the other bore no name of sender. I slipped both into my pocket and returned to the wagon, telling my father that his hoped-for letter had still not arrived.

My mother anxiously asked about my father's health, but he dismissed her concern with the fabrication that he was "strong as a horse." She looked at me, and I rolled my eyes. That evening, when he had stepped outside to look at the fireflies, which he likened to flashing signals from a far-off planet, Mom and I sat down at the kitchen table, the site of all our serious talks. Over a cup of chai, I told her what the doctor had said about Dad seeing a specialist. We both agreed that as soon as I could make the arrangements, I should accompany him to Philadelphia.

Before we had finished our tea, my mother left the kitchen and joined my father, patting his arm affectionately. I knew she was worried; he had grown terribly thin and his appetite had atrophied. The signs were not encouraging.

I then remembered my letters. The first contained a stock certificate acknowledging my purchase of a thousand shares in the Liggett & Meyers tobacco company. The second set me back on my heels.

Dear Benny,

It's from your old friend A. R. I'm not much of a letter writer, but I didn't know how else to reach you. I have a favor to ask. There's a fellow who I'm doing business with staying out near you. His name is Dr. Freedland, and he's trying to clear his name for helping a woman in trouble. Until he can get good legal advice, which I'm trying to arrange, he has to lay low.

The favor is this: Dr. Freedland needs a courier who can carry things between your neck of the woods and Philadelphia. I figured you wouldn't mind helping once you learned that the money you got from Blanck and Harris really came from me. Those bastards refused to pay, but so as not to disappoint you, I put up the dough. In return for this favor and for what happened with Mrs. Shirley, I want one from you.

Dr. Freedland is bunking at Nathan Boritski's place. Ask around. I'm sure someone can tell you where to find it. Nate is expecting you. Don't be surprised if you find a *schvartze* working for him. His name's Al Crenshaw, and he's A-one.

The sooner you get over to Nate's, the sooner the lawyer in Philly can get what he needs. If you want to call me, I'll be at Marty's on Friday night, September 1. The number there is Chelsea 2 5460. I'll tell Marty you might call.

Your pal,
A. R.

August 26, 1911

Dear Family,

Dr. Alston finally received permission from the authorities to teach me sign language. As I told you in my last letter, the school charter requires oral methods. But I was having no success in learning to make sounds. Owing to the paralysis. Dr. Alston says that my progress in signing astounds him. I think Dr. Alston may be writing a scholarly paper about me. He stays after hours to give me extra time and takes a lot of notes. My left hand, of course, is better than my right. He has me doing finger exercises to stretch the scar tissue. Too much and it will tear, so I mustn't overdo it. I cheat a little though. At night, I rub salve into the skin and try to extend my fingers just a little bit farther than before. By the end of next month, I hope to return home. Sharing a small room with two other girls is awkward. Especially when they are being trained to teach speech to deaf children, and I am learning sign language. We are not birds of a feather.

I look forward to helping Alexandra. But I am torn. Maybe she should learn to make sounds and not what I have to teach. The school does have scholarships. Poor children, as young as three, come here, their expenses paid by the state. Mary Garrett, the director, Papa would love. A real socialist, she says she would admit Alexandra even though Alexandra comes from another state.

Now, we must think about how I can contribute to the welfare of the family. I don't want to be a drain on our meager savings. Where Ben found the means to pay for my schooling is beyond me, but this much I know. If I am to teach children it will have to be here or in some other large city. Like New York. Vineland and Rosenhayn and Norma all have a few children who are deaf and dumb, but the families can't afford to pay. Which is a terrible pity because I've learned that such children can be helped. More than helped. They can be made almost normal.

I know Mama would like me to stay close to home, but I've never yet seen a man in Carmel or Vineland who I would want—or who would want me. Dr. Alston teases me and says that countless men would be glad to marry a silent woman. But jokes aside, I will never be able to support myself in southern New Jersey. So

I am reading the advertisement pages. Some schools in New York and Washington, D.C. are just beginning to make provisions for deaf and dumb children, and are even introducing sign language. They want teachers. I intend to apply. Please understand, Mama and Papa, how much I care for you—and how much I don't want to burden you. I've watched Mary Garrett and learned from her what it means to be independent. I so admire her work with children. And her strength to stand up to injustice.

Then too there is Dr. Alston. He says he would like to help me find a good position, and hints that he would rather be at a school that teaches lipreading and sign language than one that struggles with the oral method. I think he may be saying more than he is actually saying. But who knows?

Love,
Fanny

September 1, 1911

When Fanny said she would be returning soon, Esther decided we should have a party and invite all the eligible young men in Carmel. "Esther," I said, "what are you thinking? The men in this hamlet are either married, or worn out, or ignorant, or religious zealots, or indigent." Esther was forced to agree that the boys in this town were from hunger, but said, "That's what marriage brokers are for."

"A shadchan!"

"Why not?"

"It will cost."

"Not much if the first man is the right one. As they say, when the bride and groom kiss, the shadchan can go home."

We made some inquiries and were introduced to a Simon Epstein from Rosenhayn. His stomach preceded him by a foot, and his beard could be read like a menu. Everything he had eaten for the last several days clung to his curly black hairs. He smelled as if he hadn't bathed in a week, and his clothes reeked of mold. If I hadn't known better, I would have thought I'd been carried back to a miserable shtetl in the Pale. The only thing lacking was the fiddler.

Esther agreed with me that Mr. Epstein did not fit the bill. So we dispatched him and agreed to go farther afield to find a cultured woman who would have all the graces. But to travel on dirt roads is not easy, and word of mouth, I reminded Esther, is what brought us Mr. Epstein. For the first time in years, I found us agreeing. I even said, "Something must be wrong. We aren't at odds." She said that maybe she would take the train to New York—and make inquiries.

My letter, like a miracle, brought Ben back. In Vineland after Sunday mass he appeared driving a friend's horse and wagon and invited me and my sisters to Maurice River for a swim. Olga and Anna wanted to go but Mother worried that our being three girls with one man might make the wrong impression. I told her we sisters could look after each other.

Ben took the same road as when we had followed Mr. Crenshaw. He said he had an errand at Mr. Boritski's house. My sisters and I packed a picnic lunch with tuna fish salad and pickles and a pail of ice to keep the cream sodas cold. The day was being blazing hot. When we pulled up, Mr. Boritski came out of his house with a rifle.

Ben shouted, "I'm Ben Cohen!"

"Who are the girls?"

"Friends."

"A. R. said you'd be alone."

Ben asked me to take the reins and ride to the river. He said he would catch up in a few minutes. So ahead we went, finding a nice sandy spot to spread our blanket and put down our basket. While waiting for Ben we played leapfrog and skimmed flat stones across the river. I made one jump five times. Olga came in second but Anna being clumsy couldn't make hers skip. After twenty minutes and no Ben I began to worry. My sisters teased me and said I was in love. Of course I would never tell them the truth—I am! Ten minutes later Ben came carrying a book. Anna asked him what's in it. Anatomy, he said. Anna looked and then quickly closed the book, her face all red.

Over lunch we told stories and laughed about some colorful characters in Vineland. Religious Anna had secretly packed a Bible in the lunch basket and wanted to read from it. Ben suggested the Song of Songs but Anna flushed and said not in mixed company. So she read some psalms and proverbs and then for Ben's sake from Jeremiah about Jews in Babylon. "In the three and twentieth year of Nebuchadrezzar Nebuzaradan the captain of the guard carried away captive of the Jews seven hundred forty and five persons: all the persons were four thousand and six hundred." Clapping her hands, Anna happily exclaimed, "But Cyrus the Great restored worship in Jerusalem and saved them," and then with a big smile, she said, "That's part I like best. I just love stories about being saved, don't you?"

Olga jumped in and added, "I like it when evil are punished and good rewarded."

Ben looked strange so I told my sisters we weren't to talk about religion. They really annoyed me because I had warned them not to mention that kind of stuff what with Ben being Jewish. But no, Anna had to be sneaking her Bible into the basket and having her dumb say. And Olga too. At that moment, I wanted to kill them both.

For some reason Ben climbed up a tree and fastened the anatomy book with his belt to one of the branches. I guess for safekeeping while we all went swimming. Us girls went behind the bushes first to change into our bathing costumes and then Ben did.

"Last one in is prune," Olga yelled and belly flopped into the river, having forgotten her bathing cap. It served her right—her hair hanging in her face.

Anna sat at the edge and cupped water in one hand and let it slowly drip over her head and shoulders until she felt ready to hold her nose and take a quick dip. When she came up she said the water was "perfect" and wanted to know why I was such a "slowpoke."

My sisters stayed close to the bank because the current in the middle of the river could get hold of a person and carry them downstream. Then you would have to walk back through the woods, which could take a long time because of the underbrush and vines. But since I was the best swimmer of the Kasper girls I wanted to show off for Ben. He had teased me with a wolf whistle when I walked past him in my bathing costume. Well, now he would see how good I could swim. Diving into the water I quickly crossed the narrow part and stood on the far side waving to him. He swam to me and climbed the mossy bank. I pointed to a fallen tree about thirty yards downstream and dared him to race. "On your mark, set, go!"

At first we swam side by side but then I pulled ahead. Looking back to see where Ben was I missed the chance to stop at a tree and found myself caught in the current. As the river widened, the current made it almost impossible to get to shore. For a second, I thought I heard Ben's voice but decided I was wrong. Then I heard it again and again. I saw him stroking wildly, using the current to shoot him along. Trying to reach land slowed me down. A few minutes later he took my arm and the two of us made it to a sandy knoll at the river bend. We lay there several minutes gasping for breath. When we had rested, we started our walk back through the woods. He took my hand leading me through the brambles and over logs, while a million birds in the trees overhead were singing like a beautiful choir.

Suddenly we came to a small opening with a grassy patch, spongy underfoot. Ben stopped. Still holding my hand, he turned to me and said, "Shall we?" and from his needy look I knew exactly what he wanted and I said, "Yes." We hugged and kissed and fell to the ground. How long we were there, who knows? But I do remember the moment he slipped his fingers under my bathing costume and removed it. Never before had any man looked at me undressed, and never had I seen any man naked. But I felt no shame, no embarrassment. They say exercise heats up the passions. I think so because Ben and me were sweating in our love. Sometimes I would hear girls talk about doing IT. They said outdoors is worst because the ground is too hard. Not when it's mossy. I heard girls say it hurts the first time . . . it's no fun. Wrong. Mother swears that doing it before marriage puts a girl in hell. I say maybe that's the place I want to be, especially if there's the promise of more. Father says men want only one thing from a girl and once she's ruined they dump her. It all depends on which man. Our church talks about shame. I have none. I feel only glory.

Who would have ever believed that a man like Dr. Freedland would get involved with A. R.? A short, wiry fellow with curly black hair and a scaly eczematous face, he would constantly pull on his fingers, crack his knuckles, rub his palms, use a thumb to push back his cuticles, make a hand-washing motion. His frenetic paws seemed in search of a purpose.

As he rose to greet me, Mr. Boritski scowled and left the room. Dr. Freedland and Mr. Crenshaw had been playing chess or, to be exact, the former had been teaching the latter the game. I shook hands and exchanged names with Dr. Samuel Freedland and Mr. Allan Crenshaw.

Indicating the chess board, I said, "My father loves the game. Since coming to this country, he hasn't found anyone to play with."

"Bring him around," said the doctor and then, thinking better of that suggestion, added, "Maybe when things die down."

"If there's nothing you want," said Mr. Crenshaw, "I'll just go back to my own quarters."

With only the two of us in the room, the doctor suggested we sit and speak in Yiddish, "for ease of communication." He repaired to the couch and I to a badly stained parlor chair. Rubbing his palms, Dr. Freedland said, "I don't know how much A. R. told you."

"Nothing, other than you needed a courier."

"That's a discreet way of putting it."

Keen to learn about his current plight, I asked, "So what led you here? Did you rob a bank or take liberties with a patient?"

Dr. Freedland's expression suggested that I had exceeded the bounds of good taste.

"I was called to the bed of an Irish woman, Mrs. Mulhern, who was in the throes of a partial birth complication. The head of the fetus had emerged from the womb; it was alive but deformed. The only way I could save the woman would be to crush the skull and remove the fetus. So I asked how I should proceed. Mr. Mulhern insisted on making the decision. After agonizing about being a widower with a child, he finally told me he needed *her* to take care of the family. Saving the mother's life meant puncturing the head and pulling out the fully-formed fetus piece by piece."

"Let me guess. She turned you into the cops."

"Close. Grief-stricken, she felt impelled to seek absolution from her priest. A few days later, the police came to my office and took me away.

When I tried to explain that the family had requested the procedure I'd performed, the officer told me that the law was unequivocal about the matter. I was guilty of murder."

"Enter A. R. Right?"

"To defend myself I needed a great sum of money: for a bondsman, an attorney, expert witnesses, and a dozen other things. Although I had some savings, I didn't have nearly enough. In jail waiting for trial, one of the prisoners told me about a Jewish moneylender in New York who helped people like me."

"So A. R. bailed you out."

"*And* got me a lawyer."

I could figure out the rest for myself. Dr. Freedland had jumped bail and was in hiding until his lawyer could clear him, a tactic frequently used by guys on the run. Now I knew what Mr. Boritski did for a living. He hid lamsters. The house in the woods, the man of few words, the Negro who ran Boritski's errands, it all made sense. But having mapped the landscape, I realized that any favors I did for Dr. Freedland or Nathan Boritski would make me an accessory to murder.

"A. R. used the word courier. What does it mean . . . really?"

"I had no time to write up this case and fled without my files or notes. All the information my lawyer requires is in my head and has to be transferred to paper. I have just begun to put it all down, but frankly I'm not very well organized. Mr. Boritski can't do it, neither can Al. In addition, I need someone unknown to the law, which leaves out Nathan and Al, to carry the papers to Philadelphia and bring back a list of the questions my attorney thinks I'll be asked."

Longingly I gazed at the splintered light refracted through the pines. How I wished to be with Irina at the river.

"If I'm stopped, the papers won't get me in trouble, will they?"

He touched his cheek with a finger. "You see this awful skin condition? It started the day the police picked me up. Nerves. All I'm trying to do is clear my good name—and save my skin. Your part is merely to deliver some notes . . . on the Mulhern case. Let me repeat: I have to get them to my attorney, Mr. Stein. The police are watching him and my house, listening in on the phone, and have issued a warrant for my arrest. If I show my face, I'm sunk."

But what about me? I thought. Could I possibly plead that I had no idea what I was transporting from one place to another? If the police checked with the Vineland bank and learned that I had originally deposited $2,500, even though that sum had perilously shrunk owing to my wastrel ways, I could guess their conclusion.

"If you don't mind my asking, what's A. R. getting in return?"

"The rest of my life."

September 7, 1911

The last few days, from morning to night Ben is gone. He told Brotman he was running a fever and suffering from chills. Nonsense! I see him cut through the fields behind the house and disappear into the woods. Moonshiners live back in the pines. Surely he's not befriending those kind of people!

I followed Ben once before, in New York, and if I have to do it again, I will. He can have a grand future if he marries the April girl. I met Mrs. April in the post office and she said that her husband would be willing to help Ben get a start in his own business. She even hinted that if Ben married Erika, Ben could work for Mr. April, learning the trade. Such a chance! And yet I can feel in my bones he's going to *vecock* it. To listen to him you'd think everything was hunky-dory.

Last night I waited till Meyer went to bed and then cornered Ben.

We have to talk. About what? Is that any way to speak to your mother? About things. What things? Your future. Ben complained. There's that word again. My *future*. If you'd worry less—I interrupted. You'd worry more? Mom, what do you want of me? I want that you should be assuring the years ahead.

At that instant, I would say he wished his mother would just disappear. Ben has a way of looking. Such a look. I'm sure he learned it from his father.

Tomorrow I have to go to Philadelphia, he said, on business. For Brotman? No, someone else. Make your mother happy and tell her it's for Mr. April. All right, it's for Isaac April. I can tell you don't mean it. You wanted me to say it, so I said it. To your mother you can't tell the truth? Then who can you tell it to?

Suspecting that Meyer was at the root of the trip, I said, It's about your father's health, isn't it? Ben hemmed and hawed and then admitted he was going to see a chest doctor in Philadelphia. What's his name? Ben said, I have several names. Good idea. A second opinion is always a smart thing to do. He picked up his book. Can I get back to *Huckleberry Finn* now?

I had never read that novel, but a friend told me once it concerned a bootlegger father and a bad boy and his adventures. Maybe that's where Ben's ideas were coming from. Are you sure, I asked, you wouldn't prefer, perhaps, a different book? He peered at me again with that look, leading me to say, I was just joking. But I could see he knew that I had been serious. What are you trying to say, Mom?

When I see you go out the back door and across the fields, I wonder if you work now for a moonshiner. We had been speaking in Yiddish, but I used the English word to show him I knew it.

As a matter of fact, I came across one in the woods. His name is Barleycorn. He sells to the locals. I've been surveying some of the land next to ours. To make a farm work, you need more acres than we have. That's where I've been the last few days—surveying—looking out for our future.

I didn't know whether to believe him or not. Of late he'd been agreeing with his father that farming wasn't for Jews, but maybe he had in mind something else, something big, a cattle ranch or goat breeding. Then it occurred to me. What better way to impress Mr. April! So I said, It's a wonderful idea. The Aprils will be proud of you. The Aprils? You *are* hoping to marry Erika, some day? He closed his book and put it aside. Mom, he said, shaking his head, I'm bewildered. How did you connect our buying more land to the Aprils? Easy, it shows enterprise. Several seconds passed before he responded. I'm just trying to get my bearings in a new land. I agreed. No need to rush, but you do call on Erika. I know from Mrs. April. Yes, I go to her house, and we sit on the porch and schmooze.

Ever since Ben was a little boy, he had kept his habits to himself. Only to Fanny he would talk. Close is the way I would describe him, even secretive. So naturally I didn't expect him to tell me how he felt about Erika. They were seeing each other. That was good enough. Such a lovely girl, I prodded.

We plan to go swimming this Sunday at Parvin Lake. I originally suggested Saturday, but Mr. April nearly had a heart attack. On the Sabbath? he asked. Only kidding, I said.

My blood pressure, already too high, nearly went through the roof. You and your father, those socialist ideas of yours, don't you realize how radical they sound to believers, even to me who knows why you say them? And in this country, church people feel strongly about religion. They're like the Russians.

From the first time I met Dr. Samuel Freedland, I felt drawn to him, as if he had some arcane knowledge I needed. But I still don't know why I volunteered my services to do what I most dislike: paperwork. It happened almost accidentally when he said that he hadn't yet finished his notes and asked me to return.

"I can come back tomorrow."

"But I may not be done."

He had papers strewn everywhere: desk, tables, chairs, floor.

"From what I can see, you may never finish."

He scanned the farrago and admitted, "I've never had a talent for organization. In medical school, my class notes were always a mess. A friend used to lend me his."

"As much as I dislike clerical work, I do have a sense of order and how things ought to fit."

"Would you be willing to act as my amanuensis?"

"Sounds important. What is it?"

For almost a week, as Dr. Freedland paced the length of the living room, dictating, I took notes. At the end of each day, I organized them into a coherent chronology of Mrs. Mulhern's abortion. Although he could write English far better than I, my ability to categorize and sort eclipsed his. The story of an illiterate woman ordered by her husband to undergo a procedure that she regarded as sinful and then regretting her consent held less interest for me than the doctor's opinion of my father's condition, which I described in detail. He hazarded that my father had lung cancer and urged me to take him to see a specialist he knew in Philadelphia, a Dr. William Baker. A letter of introduction would be too dangerous. I would just have to make the approach myself.

Dr. Freedland's concern for his safety led me to ask him about the laws governing his alleged crime. From Cherry, I had learned that the girls at the brothel often had abortions, and that the doctors who performed them were known to everyone in the community. Abortion, as far as I could tell, was widely practiced, freely discussed, and accepted by many people. So what made Philadelphia different?

"Good question. Although abortion is officially illegal in America, the authorities turn a blind eye unless a woman dies—then there's a coroner's inquest—or the Church gets involved. In either case, the police have no choice but to act. The fact is that most Americans tolerate abortion, even Catholics. How else can one explain the estimated two million abortions in this country each year?

"But as I just said, once a girl dies or a priest or a rabbi gets involved, then suddenly what everyone knows becomes a crime. If I were to lose my medical license, I would have no choice but to move to a new city and set up business as an abortionist."

During the period I worked for Dr. Freedland, Al Crenshaw, who had once been a linotyper for a New York newspaper, converted the handwritten notes into print, thanks to a Remington that belonged to Mr. Boritski. The doctor took the fifty-two sheets of paper and put them in a manila envelope, which he placed in a briefcase that he locked, entrusting me with the key. He also gave me twenty bucks for expenses to and from Philadelphia, including, he said, "the cost of a consultation with my old friend Dr. William Baker."

Before I parted from Dr. Freedland, he told me the code words to use with the lawyer. My next task lay ahead of me—persuading Pop.

Adamant at first, he agreed to accompany me to Philadelphia when I promised him we'd visit the Yiddish vaudeville. Keeping my visit to the attorney's office secret, I detrained in the north end and took a cab to Mr. Stein's unprepossessing brick building, which stood in a neighborhood of middle-class houses. Except for a small sign in the corner of a front window announcing Andrew Stein, Attorney at Law, you would have had no way of knowing that this was a law office, let alone one whose clientele included some of Philadelphia's most notorious hoodlums. I was greeted by a well-manicured matron of forty or fifty running her hands over a typewriter with the speed and skill of Al Crenshaw. When the woman said, "Yes?" I whispered that I had a special packet for Mr. Stein. Unlocking the briefcase, I slid the unmarked manila envelope across her desk.

"And from whom shall I say I received this?"

I leaned toward her and mumbled, "Tell Mr. Stein that the contract has arrived from Cumberland County."

She immediately sprang into action, putting my envelope in a small wall safe and removing another that she tucked under her arm as she closed the safe and spun the dial. "I'll be back in a minute," she muttered and disappeared behind an oak door.

My father asked me in Yiddish what was going on. When I told him that Mr. April had requested I convey some important papers to his lawyer, Pop said, "So, you work for him already?"

"He knew I was coming to the city and asked me to drop off an envelope. There's nothing more to it than that."

The secretary reappeared in the presence of a dark-haired, round-faced swarthy fellow with lively eyes and a warm smile that made you feel at once that he was well disposed to like you. He invited me into his office, but not Pop, who understood the situation at once. As the door closed behind me, Mr. Stein said:

"How is our friend? No names, please."

"Our friend is looking well, but is anxious to get back to work, if not in Philadelphia then in New York."

"I quite understand."

Without another word, he took my briefcase and slipped in the envelope I had seen the secretary take from the safe. Raising a finger to his lips, he smiled and shook my hand. As I exited with Pop, I figured that silence never betrays, a necessary precaution when you legally represent gangsters like John "Duffy" Dougherty.

From the north end, we took a trolley to an area near Fairmont Park and the home of Dr. Baker, a tall, lean, taciturn fellow dressed in a tweed suit. His good looks must have appealed to the women patients because his waiting room, on the first floor of his house, overflowed with pretty ladies. Surely, I thought, they can't all be suffering from chest ailments. But after further scrutiny, I noticed that most of the women had a sickly pallor and retching coughs, probably from the factory worker's disease, tuberculosis.

Although I had made an appointment in advance, calling from the public telephone in the Carmel post office, we still had an hour's wait. Finally, a nurse called Pop's name. In the examining room, the doc, after a few introductory words, set right to work. Pop cooperated brilliantly, coughing with his usual basso resonance and bringing up a sputum sample that the doc bottled for a laboratory analysis. Hoping he would tell my father to quit smoking, I prompted him by asking whether my father could do anything to help himself, like giving up cigarettes. Of course Pop, had he understood, would have scowled at the suggestion.

"At his age it doesn't matter," the doctor said.

On the way out, I told Dr. Baker, "A friend sends his regards."

"And who would that be?"

"Dr. Freedland."

A rather pale fellow to begin with, he turned the color of bone. "How do you . . ." he began, but thought better of finishing.

"He recommended you."

"Please thank him for me and . . ." But again he couldn't find words safe enough to continue.

On the way back to Bridgeton on the train, I apologized to Pop for our not having enough time to attend the vaudeville. Pop seemed particularly contemplative. So I asked him what he had on his mind, a question that led to the most revealing conversation we ever had.

"I'm thinking of Jacob—and my last visit. It was my impression he wanted to unburden himself, but couldn't quite come out with it."

"What do you suppose he wanted to say?"

"Judge for yourself. He said that when he found his first job, at the sawmill in Kobyhcha, he liked nothing better than when Rissa would bring him a hearty lunch. One day, he said, she arrived early and took a turn through the town; passing the schoolhouse, she caught sight of a child, a little girl, whose smile reminded her of a dead cousin. She stopped and talked to the child, giving her a coin and stroking her cheek. 'Who are you?' the child asked. 'Your aunt.' 'Why do you give me money? I've been warned not to accept money from a stranger.' 'Yes, that's quite right, but as I said, I'm your aunt.' 'If you are my aunt, why don't you come to see my parents? I will run home to tell Mamma that my aunt has come to see me.'"

Pop gathered that Jacob was clearly fascinated but also pained by the story. He continued.

"He said that Rissa tried to persuade the child to stay, explaining that she had no time now to visit the family, but promised to return another day. Then she left. For weeks after, instead of bringing Jacob his lunch, she timed her arrival for the end of the school day. When the little girl appeared, she would accompany her a few blocks and then leave. She kept asking why Rissa did not come to see her family. Always Rissa gave her excuses.

"One day, while Rissa waited at the school, the girl's mother suddenly appeared and begged Rissa not to speak to the child, who was finding her visits unsettling. She agreed not to return, but asked Jacob to learn what he could about the family and made him promise that if anything should ever happen to the parents, they would adopt the girl.

"Jacob then abruptly stopped the story—and launched into a tirade about children and mothers and stupid social conventions. Obviously he was thinking of Rissa and Esther; but when I probed, he became evasive, apologizing for his outburst."

I took Pop's confessional story as his way of acknowledging that in all likelihood he would not live long. Why else would he make me privy to his innermost thoughts?

The train clacked on through the countryside, and we said little until the conductor announced our next stop, Bridgeton.

"Your mother will want a religious service," he said apropos of nothing. "Don't permit it. A cantor, maybe, but not a rabbi."

"Pop, you'll outlive us all."

"That's the great paradox, Ben, that we die of life."

September 20, 1911

Olga says that Ben, like the iceman, comes regularly to the April house, and last Sunday went with the family to Parvin Lake. They took my sister along to set up the beach umbrellas and serve picnic food from wicker baskets—chicken and potato salad and tomatoes and bread they call hollow. She also helped clean up. Olga told me all of it, like which kind of plates they ate off of, plain ceramic, not china. Mr. April hired a large hay wagon, and on the way to the lake they sang popular songs, "Bill Bailey, Won't You Please Come Home?," "Give My Regards to Broadway," and "In the Shade of the Old Apple Tree." She said they also sang in Hebrew but she couldn't tell whether they were songs or hymns or prayers or something else. At the lake they spread several blankets next to the water and cleared a spot for badminton. I smiled when I heard that Erika played the game like an oaf, not as good as her brother and sister. She also whines. Ben won't like that! He often makes faces at what he calls kvetchers. He said a kvetcher is like a child who makes "squeezing" noises for attention. When I sigh, he says tell me the matter, don't gasp. I think his mother must be a kvetcher, otherwise why be so touchy? Or maybe it's his father. Anyway, I know he doesn't like it.

Everyone went into the water except Erika. She said it would ruin her makeup. Olga says the "princess" took along a vanity case with a scent bottle and a powder box and still kvetched about the sun hurting her skin. So after playing badminton for only a short time, she quit and sat under one of the umbrellas. Ben asked Olga to fill in and Erika didn't like that one bit. Ben and Olga played Erika's brother and sister AND WON! Mr. and Mrs. April were trying to get Erika to play again but she refused. I wish she wasn't always looking so perfect. Olga says she does her nails every night and changes her clothes three times each day.

After lunch Ben rented a canoe and wanted Erika to ride with him across the lake. She said she would go if her brother and sister came also. So they paddled to the far side and were gone for an hour. When they returned, Mrs. April asked them what they did and Erika said they looked for arrowheads. I knew whose idea that was since Ben loves finding things left over from Indians. He reads whatever he can about tribes that were living in this part of New Jersey. Erika probably thinks he's peculiar. I hope so because Ben and me have become, well, how else can I say it? Special. Now that he's back working at Brotman's we are seeing each other every day. Whenever we can, which is often, we meet at Halbert's Grain and Storage after closing. In the back are several haystacks. We hide among them and play. One Sunday after church my family went to Bridgeton. Ben and I hitched a ride to Parvin Lake and in the cabin across the lake in the woods, we played for two hours on a blanket I brought. Then we swam in the Maurice River, but the Carmel company that makes nurses' uniforms had dumped blue dye into the water again and we came out looking like Indians, blue all over. When I got home I snuck into the bathroom and sat in the tub until Anna started banging on the door. When I finally came out I smelled of bleach but no one asked why.

I can guess what SHE would say if Ben took her swimming and they came out covered in dye. You'd probably hear her complain for six months. Ben can't really want someone like her. When we are alone he's so natural. Even though he's much smarter than me I can tell my being ordinary pleases him. She's so snooty.

I told Ben how I feel. No more playing if he likes her. He says her father can set him up in a good job but I keep telling him he's getting in deeper and deeper. If he works for her papa he can't not be nice to her. And if her papa helps him buy his own business he'll expect Ben to court his daughter. I know how these things work.

In bed at night I wonder what he would do if I got in trouble. Would he marry me or leave me? Except for the first time he's been careful, but accidents happen. He says he has a doctor friend who would help us. What does that mean? Mama asks if I've been a good girl. I get angry and tell her of course but she stares at me like she knows. Some girls say you can look in the eyes of another girl and be able to tell. If that's right then Mama knows. She would never say anything because Papa would kill me. I don't want Ben to be forced to marry me and then live the rest of our lives with him hating me.

September 22, 1911

Dearest Diary, Ben and Papa arranged a picnic at Parvin Lake—actually Father did most of the planning. He insisted. But that's the way he is, always at the head of the band. A hay wagon took us there, driven by an old man who makes liquor in the woods. He sang a song about whiskey, and then the rest of us sang tunes from New York shows. I was the only person who knew all the words.

At the lake, which is a pretty spot surrounded by cedars and pines and home to beavers and deer, Ben rented a canoe and asked me to join him—alone! But I said I wouldn't go unless my brother and sister came along. Did I tell him that because of Mama's fears, or because I actually did not want to be alone with him? I wonder.

We paddled to the far side of the lake, and Ben suggested we look for arrowheads. Pretty soon Ruth and Morris lost interest, and I found myself alone with Ben after all. Of course he didn't do anything improper. But he did lecture me, the way Papa sometimes does. Miss Pritchard used to tell us that well-bred people are never didactic, especially on social occasions. He told me I should learn more about southern New Jersey. Americans, he said, know little of their own history. They often don't even know about the places where they live. What's so bad about that, I asked, annoyed at his always bringing up unfamiliar subjects.

(We then had the following discussion.)

—How can you fully appreciate your town or village or city without some idea of who founded it and why, what happened there and which events formed its character?

—Knowing the history of a place doesn't mean I'll like it any better.

—True, but you'll understand why the streets are laid out and named the way they are, what brought settlers to your town, who lived in your house—all ingredients that make for a richer stew.

—Knowing what went into a dish doesn't improve its taste.

(He grew silent when I used his own example and stumped him. His next comment felt like a slap in the face.)

—Do you always kvetch when you're annoyed?

(I hadn't noticed, but my voice had become whiny—to show him how I felt. Not knowing what to say, I pleaded manners.)

—A gentleman should not be accusing a lady of "squeezing."

(Actually, I liked him for saying what he did. When Papa reproves me, he always assumes I'm a child. But Ben didn't. So I bent, saying,)

—Agreed: no kvetching.

(He continued to look for arrowheads and said nothing for what seemed the longest time. When he finally found one, he held it up for me.)

—The stone in this arrowhead does not come from around here. That means the Indians who left it originated from somewhere else. My guess is Delaware, the Lenni-Lenape tribe.

—Really, from that far away?

—I thought these things didn't interest you. I'm impressed.

(We both laughed. Taking my hand, he led me through the woods. But at no time was I frightened. In the trees I could see a ratty cabin with a storage shed. An adjacent swampy field had rows of trenches. Ben was reluctant to approach, until I told him I'd go by myself.)

—Buildings like this one were used to control the flooding of the cranberry bogs, also to store equipment and provide a resting place for the workers, maybe even to lodge some of the boggers.

(I pushed open the door and entered. In one corner, on a bed of hay, was a blanket in surprisingly good condition.)

—Someone must have been here recently . . . or plans to return. This blanket seems kind of new.

—I think we'd better get out of here.

(We left the cabin and stood looking at the ditches and the irregular furrows behind it.)

—They ran water through those ditches. The sandy marshes in this part of the country are fed by a huge underground aquifer that keeps the soil wet. Ideal conditions for cranberries.

(In the mud, I found a bent crucifix, which I brushed off and showed to Ben.)

—I'm not surprised. Many of the field hands were Italian immigrants.

—Should we just leave that blanket in the cabin?

—Whoever left it there will probably return. I'm sure some poor laborer comes here to sleep.

—But it has no running water, no plumbing . . .

—How many houses in Vineland and Carmel do? We still have a pump and an outhouse. Yours is one of the few houses with indoor plumbing.

—Papa paid dearly for the convenience.

—It's the same in Russia. Unless you pay, you get nothing.

—Well, then, why complain about America?

—Because this is the richer country, with a government that prides itself on being democratic and caring for the welfare of the people.

—Conditions will improve. Daddy says when the workers learn what's good for the factory owners is good for them, everyone will grow rich.

September 29, 1911

At the Bridgeton train station, Mama, Papa, and Ben greet me and Dr. Peter Alston. He insisted on making the journey. To guarantee my safety, he said, and to meet my parents. My family looks at Peter and me strangely. Because we converse in sign language. Mama asks, "What is she saying?" Within minutes, Peter through Ben is talking for both of us, and it feels completely natural. To them, as well as to me. He says he must return to Philadelphia on the evening train, and he will wait at the station. But Papa says, "You must have a meal with us." I hope Peter is thinking of courting me. Surely he knows how I feel. Mama will want to know whether Peter's Jewish. I must remember to call him Dr. Alston.

On the road to Carmel, Vasily and Alexandra are walking toward us. She throws stones at the crows in the trees. He walks with his usual slouch. When she sees who it is, Alexandra runs to the wagon and puts her arms around me. I am touched. Peter also. She has not improved. Making her usual gurgling sounds. I have told Peter about the child. He signs to me that I could do her a great deal of good. That Peter thinks I can help Alexandra pleases me immensely.

Ben introduces the men. Vasily smells of liquor and scowls. Surely he doesn't think I could ever have any interest in *him*! He jerks Alexandra from my lap where she has perched. He is claiming his property and wants me to know it. I can see from Alexandra's expression that she hopes I will care for her as before. Peter reads my fingers and whispers to Ben. Ben nods and says to Vasily, "When you are at work, Fanny would like you to leave Alexandra at our house. She would like to school her."

"Why can't she come to my place? She used to. I like that arrangement better."

I shrug as if to say, "We'll see."

They leave. Peter signals to me that Vasily is not to be trusted. Is he jealous? To think that I, speechless, might have two men caring for me . . . who would have ever thought it? But neither is Jewish. One Greek-Orthodox, the other a Methodist. As Peter and I continue to talk with our hands, my family, as if by magic, begins to follow suit, making gestures and pointing and manipulating their fingers. Peter tells them I have brought along a book. One that will enable them to learn rudimentary sign language. Ben says he will study it immediately. Papa grumbles. Mama's silent.

At the Carmel house, I revert to the slate and chalk. Mother invites everyone to the table for a first dish of borscht. Quickly taking Ben aside in the pantry, I write, "Do you have a favorite girl?" He says, "It seems so strange that you can hear but can't talk. The answer is no." He repeats his promise to learn signing. Ben and I sit at the table. Mama inches toward the subject of religion, no doubt puzzling about Peter and me. As she circles the question, I recall how I used to dreamily wonder if I would ever let myself be courted by a gentile. What I didn't realize was that when you care for someone, the question doesn't arise. You are just suddenly there. Like falling asleep on a train and awaking at a station that you never intended to visit. Mama always used to warn me about getting serious. As if one had a say in the matter. I didn't. It happened. One day my feelings arrested my reason.

"Alston," mother says, at last enunciating her concern. "May I ask, what kind of name is Alston? Was it Alstein? I knew a Pauline Alstein in Russia. She came from a fine Jewish family."

As always, Peter is unruffled. The room silent. His well manicured nails and long fingers are spread on the table. His hair, parted down the middle, vaselined. I can smell his cologne.

"Mrs. Cohen, my family is English. They settled in Boston, where my great-grandfather started a small press. He was a printer. As you probably know, Boston is a center of publishing."

Bravo! He will win over Papa, who immediately offers to pour him a glass of wine. Which is exactly the wrong thing to do.

"Thank you, Mr. Cohen, but frankly I am a member of the Anti-Saloon League. I think alcohol has ruined more lives than any other single American habit."

Papa is taken aback. But not for long. "Even worse," he counters, "than child labor and sweatshops?"

I drop my head on my chest. If Peter has any interest in me at all, he now has to overcome two obstacles. Religion and politics.

"I couldn't agree with you more, Mr. Cohen." Peter has rallied! "The group I belong to—the Evanston Methodists—deplore equally drink and the dehumanization of the working man."

Silence. Mama sucks in her lips. Breathes deeply. Papa strokes his chin. Ben, where are you? Come to my aid! I kick him under the table. Instead of praising Peter for his humanitarianism, Ben changes the subject, fleeing the field.

"Are you familiar with my sister's infatuation with Sarah Bernhardt?"

"I share it."

"Really?"

"The first time we left the school grounds together—in the company of others, of course—we went to see a Bernhardt film. I adore Sarah!" Peter smiles impishly and says, "I trust, Mrs. Cohen, you won't mind my making a confession in front of the family."

"What kind of confession?" asks Mama guardedly.

"I learned from one of Fanny's roommates that she was an admirer of Sarah Bernhardt's. That's why I suggested the nickelodeon."

October 12, 1911

At the kind invitation of the Aprils, the two families had a wonderful dinner to celebrate Yom Kippur. First, we all went to shul, except Meyer, who is at odds with the rabbi about whether it is permissible to smoke on the Shabbos. After the service, we gathered at the Aprils' house for matzo ball soup and boiled chicken with potatoes, carrots, and peas. Meyer, sitting next to me, nearly ruined the whole evening by asking for butter to put on his challah. I kicked him under the table and tried to pretend he was only teasing. The Aprils take kosher seriously. Ben had warned Meyer, but he's hopeless. After each dish, he would whisper a complaint. Though he grumbled that the matzo balls could be lethal, I noticed he finished every one. When Mrs. April looked our way, I smiled and told her they were light as air, the best I had ever tasted.

The boiled chicken, which was falling from the bone, led Meyer to mumble that it could pass for soup. Again I grinned, telling Mrs. April how wonderful the chicken tasted. She said she made it herself because she had given Olga time off for the Jewish holidays. But isn't Olga Catholic? I asked. Mrs. April said she was, but had rewarded her for being so respectful of Rosh Hashanah and Yom Kippur. Smart girl, that Olga.

When the dessert came, a bowl of fresh fruit, I warned Meyer not to ask for cheese. He said nothing, but did peel the orange by removing the rind in one piece, like a long wood shaving. The Aprils quartered their fruit, and ate it delicately.

Ben, seated next to Erika, occasionally leaned over and spoke in her ear—and she would smile. Good signs. Everyone noticed. The Aprils' son talked about wanting a pony to ride, and his father told him maybe for his bar mitzvah. Mr. April asked Meyer what he intended to plant in the spring. Unless, maybe, said Mr. April, you're putting in fruit trees and bulbs now. Meyer said he had other plans, a reply that made Mr. April prick up his ears. What plans? he asked. Meyer explained Ben might buy our farm and the adjoining land from the Baron de Hirsch Fund. The money, Mr. April asked, where will you get the money? Ben, who seemed annoyed by Meyer's introducing the subject, said he had stocks. This was the first time I had ever heard Ben mention the subject. Mr. April inquired kindly if Ben had given up the idea of cosmetics. Ben said no, he had a couple of irons in the fire, and Mr. April said, only half-kiddingly, A *gonser knocker*! A big shot. Ben observed that to get ahead one had to be enterprising.

Mr. April seemed to like that reply because he went on to talk about his brother in Atlanta who ran the factory there. It was my first factory, he said, and did well enough to let me start another here. The starting is the hard part, the running the easy part. But my brother Howard is rotten at both. Mrs. April nudged him with her elbow, and he abruptly stopped talking. For a moment the silence was embarrassing, but Ben came to Mr. April's rescue by talking about the first factory ever built in Carmel.

Fanny, of course said nothing, even though she had brought along her slate and chalk. I guess she was lost in thought about that . . . that doctor friend of hers. Heaven forbid!

I helped Mrs. April with the dishes so the two of us could be in the kitchen alone. She must have felt like me because she told her younger daughter to play checkers with her brother and stay out of the way of the adults. When the door closed behind Ruth, we quickly got to the subject of Erika and Ben. She asked me what I knew of Ben's personal plans for the future, but I just repeated that Ben planned to double the size of our farm. To what purpose I couldn't say, but knowing my son, I told her, whatever he turns his mind to will be a success.

And Erika? I prompted. My Erika, she said, is not some coarse peasant girl. She has had all the advantages. A finishing school in Atlanta she went to, where they taught her how to dance and play the piano, also how to set a table, cook, sew, crochet, keep a house, and talk like a lady. No expenses were spared. Only the best for our own. Carmel is just temporary. My Isaac will build up this factory and then move to Newark. He already has his eye on a building. If Ben and Erika really care for one another, and only they can say, Isaac will offer the Carmel factory to Ben. But you didn't hear me say it. To be official it will have to come from Isaac.

I was thinking any young man would pray for a father-in-law ready to train him and give him a business. It was like a miracle. But God is full of goodness. Mrs. April interrupted my wonderful thoughts, saying, My Erika will want to keep kosher. And Ben? I nearly blurted out that Meyer had filled his son's head with a lot of meshugas, but thank God, I spoke cautiously, remarking, So who would talk against kosher? If a family can afford two sets of dishes and kosher meat, I say nothing could be better. Ben is easy to please. A wife who can do all the things your Erika can will be like a priceless ruby. Mrs. April beamed and said maybe we should talk more about *particulars*.

Like for example? I asked. She replied she came from a good family and knew a lot about music and wanted me to tell her about the Cohens. So I told her about Meyer's parents and the distillery, but about my own, I said very little. After all, what's there to say about an itinerant family of needleworkers? To give things a little better sound, I told her my parents were masters of their craft, and people from all over sought them out, especially to make bar mitzvah suits and wedding dresses. And you, she asked, you can sew too? Not as good as my blessed daughter used to once, before the fire. But I too can sew. She clapped her hands and said, What a blessing! Then you can measure and cut Erika's wedding dress. I took her hands in mine and said, Aren't we putting the cart before the horse? She looked puzzled and said, How so?

How so? I repeated. We don't even know they love one another. She shook her head as if I were a ninny. Believe me, I know. Didn't you see at dinner the whispering and holding hands under the table? Really? I said and confessed that though I saw them speaking softly, I did not see them hand-holding. Well, I saw it! she said triumphantly, as if joining fingers meant a wedding. Still, I said, they're both young and need time to understand one another. She arched her eyebrows and said coldly, Understand!

My marriage was arranged, she added, as if it was the most natural thing in the world. Well, I replied, mine wasn't. Better, I think, in America young people should get to . . . understand one another before they take such an important step as marriage. Pretty soon, she said, my Erika will be in her twenties. She'll be an old woman. I believe girls should wed in their teens. Boys can wait till they're older. Exactly! I replied. A moment later, Mrs. April realized what she'd said and tried to take it back, but it was too late. Ben, she stuttered, why he seems, if I may say so, older, more like a man in his twenties, don't you agree? No, I said, which she didn't expect, and you could see the wind come right out of her sails. Of course, I wanted Ben to marry her daughter and inherit a factory and be rich, but not for a while. So I said, What's wrong with a two-year engagement? In that time they will become very close and see each other's warts and be ready for the chupah. Two years, she repeated, sounding defeated. I'm not sure Erika would be willing to wait that long. Erika will be only nineteen, I said. Mrs. April frowned. I didn't want to ruin a good thing by insisting the couple wait, but on the other hand I felt Ben was too young. Besides, I needed him around the farm. Once he started to manage a factory, he wouldn't be showing up much to help his father and me. Was I being selfish? With Meyer coughing more than ever and the doctors thinking he had cancer, I would be in a terrible spot if he died and Ben wasn't around to lend a hand. Two years would be enough time to put the farm in order and maybe hire an overseer. Also, my own health was scaring me. Lately, I'd been having heart shakings or whatever they call it when the heart misses a beat. No, two years would be perfect.

October 15, 1911

The display board in front of the shul had advertised a special event for today's service: a hazan, a cantor, from Philadelphia. As I approached the temple, Rabbi Kolodny made a face. When I reached him, he shook a finger reproachfully and resumed the old argument, asking how I could possibly smoke on the Sabbath. Well aware of his lack of humor, I said joshingly, "I just strike a match and inhale."

He told me that I should be ashamed of myself and that I brought disapprobation on the Jewish community for not observing the Shabbos laws. I could not help but inquire:

"Where in the Bible does it say that smoking's forbidden?"

"The Rabbinate—"

I interrupted. "Not Maimonides, not Rabbi Loew, not Hillel."

Other men gathered around us, all of them drawn to the dispute. I deliberately turned and asked them the same question: where was the biblical authority for this ukase? In less than a minute, an argument broke out among the men and had it not been for the arrival of the hazan, I think that the Saturday service would have been cancelled so the disagreement could continue, because there is nothing the people of the book like better than a good debate about the law. I must admit, though, that I had deliberately provoked the argument, knowing that neither the rabbi nor the congregation was well enough schooled to be persuasive.

The splendid cantorial music put me in a meditative mood, so when it ended I chose not to stay for the rabbi's harangue, but stood on the back porch smoking and thinking about the day I took Jacob to see my Aunt Rachel in Kishinev. We heard shouting and, looking out the window, saw what no human should have to witness. Kishinev, 1905, the time of the great pogrom. The fire. The ash.

They always pick a Saturday, because they know that most of the Jews will be in shul. In the house of prayer they were surrounded and their heads battered with hammers, nails driven into their ears, their eyes gouged out. The rioters burned homes, pouring petroleum over the sick and elderly. Women and children had their brains dashed out as the so-called righteous threw them out of windows. Had it not been for my Aunt Rachel, Jacob and I would never have lived. She had feared that one day a pogrom would come to Kishinev and had prepared a crawl space in the attic behind the chimney. We could hear the killers looting the house. One even complained that it was empty, leaving no Jews to slaughter.

The Kishinev massacre turned Jacob into a radical socialist and a despiser of injustice. In fact, the last time I saw Jacob we talked about that infernal day—and the revolution we both hoped to join. But when? Jacob was sanguine, but I told him that revolution would come to Russia only when the czar's insatiable greed had exhausted the granaries, and the poor were left to feed on air.

I tell myself I'll see him again, but I know that such faith is irrational, based on nothing more substantial than a hope. I'm like those who want to enter heaven and therefore believe in one, even though all our senses and science say the opposite. The truth is that if the found existed, there would not be this eternal seeking.

Behind me the door of the shul opened and the hazan appeared. We greeted each other in Yiddish and, in deference to him, I extinguished my cigarette. We spoke briefly about music and the lack of resources in the small towns to support a chorus, *meshorerim* singers, especially on festival days.

"You are not like the others," he said. "Your education sets you apart."

"So does yours."

He sighed and regretted the decline in importance over the years of hazans. "In the big cities, they still appreciate a knowledge of biblical and liturgical literature. But in places like this . . ."

His elision needed no explaining. "At least, you had the privilege of bringing out the rolls of the Torah."

Ironically, he added, "But where were the trumpet blasts from the roof of the synagogue, the lighting of lamps, my invitation to stand on the bimah and read aloud from the Pentateuch?"

"I think you know the answer," I said.

"A man like you, how do you stand it here?"

October 27, 1911

Taking off from Brotman's early, I returned to Carmel to meet Mr. April, who wanted to show me his factory. Having used on occasion two of his men, sewing machine operators, to help me seed our land, I had some idea of the working conditions. The factory, covered outside with decaying ivy, had small windows that admitted just a whisper of light. Dusty and dank, the building lacked heat, forcing the operators to bundle up in sweaters to ward off the chill.

Fifty-two people comprised the work force: six rows of sewing machines, eight people to a row, two cloth cutters, a floor manager, responsible for the behavior of the operators and the quality of the work, and a part-time janitor. Upstairs, Mr. April had his office, employing one secretary, who sat in front of a small desk with a kerosene floor heater.

The factory made dresses for the immigrant trade, so the profit margin was slim. I gathered that Mr. April wanted to migrate north to Newark to produce petticoats and slips because in that line you could earn a lot more. It didn't take a genius to see that if you wanted to compete with other dress factories selling to the poor, you had to cut your expenses. How? Reduce wages. Without a minimum-wage law, and with the surplus of workers in Carmel, Mr. April had the upper hand.

After a quick look around the main floor, we ascended to his office. The secretary gave us lukewarm coffee from a thermos bottle, and Mr. April had thoughtfully brought in some fresh bagels and cream cheese. He asked me what I thought, and I chose to avoid any hard feelings by saying that I really hadn't seen enough to judge.

"What more would you like to see?"

"I'd just like to poke around."

"Go right ahead."

When we'd finished our nosh, we returned to the main floor, and I walked among the dimly lit rows of machines, observing the operators, with flying hands and squinting eyes, each stitching a particular part of a dress and then tossing it into a bin in front of his workstation. The floor manager would collect the pieces and move them along to the next station, so that an orderly and cumulative process took place. But what would happen, I asked, if someone along the line had to relieve himself? Did the whole line stop and have to wait on the absent person? With apparent obliviousness, Mr. April replied, "Every hand is allowed two toilet breaks a day, three minutes each."

Since I did not wish to embarrass him in front of his workers, I saved my objections for later.

The workers spoke mostly Yiddish and Italian. Mr. April explained that the floor manager, Mr. Sapperstein, knew a number of languages, an invaluable asset if the system was to work smoothly. I marveled at the ease with which he moved from one to another, and figured he was probably the best paid of all.

I excused myself to inspect the bathrooms. The men's room had no running water, but rather a cistern suspended over a sink, and the toilets, two wooden seats side by side, functioned exactly as an outhouse: the filth fell into a hole. Toilet paper consisted of newspapers cut into squares and hung on a nail. On the floor, in a corner, stood a box of camphor balls to neutralize the smells. I saw no towels, not even a rack, and concluded that the people dried their hands on their clothes. On one wall someone had scratched the Russian word for shit, *govnaw*. I thought the sentiment well taken.

In the factory, I fingered the piece work dropped into bins for distribution to the next person down the line. The materials, all of them, were flammable, but nowhere did I see any extinguishers except for two pails of sand with hand shovels in a corner. To be fair, I must say that on every wall hung a large NO SMOKING sign. But I knew that smokers would undoubtedly sneak a puff in the bathroom. If they tossed the match into the trash, the room would immediately explode into flames. Fanny must have worked under conditions like these, except that most of the Triangle exit doors had been barred and in Mr. April's factory they remained open.

"Let's step outside," Mr. April said expansively, "where we can share a good cigar."

The clean October air felt good after the cold stuffiness of the factory. Mr. April removed a silver case and cigar cutter, but before he could offer me one, I reminded him that I never smoke.

"Pity," he said, "they're pure Habanas." He lit up, inhaled, savored the smoke, and slowly exhaled, obviously contented with not only his tobacco, but also the tour. "So, tell me, what do you think? Is it your kind of work?"

"In all honesty, Mr. April, I don't know."

"What's there not to know about?"

I truly wished to stay clear of politics and the subjects of wages and labor conditions. "Surely there's more to the job than what I saw. What about the buying and shipping of the raw goods? The delivery of the finished dresses? Then there's the patterns . . . which designs will be in fashion and which won't? I saw you have cutters. Someone has to buy the patterns and tell them which cloth to use. In addition, I know nothing about the financial end of the business . . . the keeping of books."

"By the time Erika finishes tutoring you, you'll know all about debits and credits. As for the rest of it, in one week I can teach you the ins and outs of how to run a factory."

Seeking safe ground, I praised the linguistic talents of his floor manager and remarked that he was probably handsomely paid for his efforts. That innocent comment invited Mr. April's anger, which I had never seen before and which frankly scared me.

"Sapperstein!" he roared, "he's nothing but a dried-up teacher who couldn't get a job in a schoolhouse. I took him on as a favor and then he has the gall, after one month, to ask for a raise. He's damn lucky just to have job. That's the trouble with too much education—it makes a person unfit for ten hours a day of labor. Real work gives a man calluses."

I nearly choked on a rush of bile and, unable to contain my resentment, said sarcastically, "Sitting in front of a sewing machine ten hours a day gives you piles, not calluses. It ruins your urinary system, breaks your back, and gives you respiratory problems."

Mr. April, who had taken a long drag on his cigar after his outburst, nearly choked. He started coughing and spitting. "What in hell . . . ! Have you lost your wits, Sonny? In case you hadn't noticed, there's thousands looking for work. I can hire anyone I want with the snap of my fingers."

"That explains the conditions in your factory."

"Meaning?"

"No real toilets, no fire protection, no proper lighting, no heating. And you probably pay as little as you can."

My putative father-in-law stared at me realizing he had just seen the true Ben Cohen—and didn't like the portrait. "You, boy, had better come to your senses. Otherwise . . . otherwise you can just forget about Erika. I won't have her marrying an anarchist—or worse. The way you're talking, you sound like a socialist, one of those types who prattle on about pay for injuries and benefits and insurance. The next thing you know, the workers will want to run the factories. Communism, that's what it is."

I had to smile at the transit from anarchist to communist.

October 27, 1911

Dearest Diary, How quickly events can go from sweet to bitter. Tonight, over dinner, Papa told us about the fracas at the factory. No one dared speak, not even Mama. When Papa blows up, there's no reasoning with him. Mama stared at her plate, Ruth and Morris stole glances at one another, and I just waited for the storm to pass. Even though I have my concerns about Ben, who seems so "European" and has radical political opinions, I think Papa is overreacting. If he would do less shouting and more explaining, he might be able to convince Ben. But then again, Ben, like Papa, is set in his ways. At Parvin Lake he said the measure of a great country is how well it treats the poor. I'm just glad Papa wasn't present. I know what he would have said: that attitude is just a prescription for free lunches. Because of their opposite views, I think it would be a mistake for Ben to work in one of Papa's factories. It would make much more sense for Ben to start his own business, without Papa's help if possible. When relatives become business partners, it hardly ever works out. Just look at Papa's brother. Uncle Howard insists he's barely breaking even, and Father says that he's stealing. The two men can't be in the same room together. Mama was right! Papa should have just sold his factory to Uncle Howard. But Papa insisted the factory was worth a lot more than my uncle was willing or able to pay. So Papa stews about his brother cheating him and plots ways to get even.

I'm the only one who will speak up to him, probably because I'm the oldest child. Of course it's unladylike to contradict, but his criticizing his brother is one thing, attacking Ben quite another—which led to the following exchange.

—Papa, I know how you feel, but would you rather have a man working for you who cares about himself or his workers? At least Ben was not trying to line his own pockets.

(Papa nearly strangled on the potato in his borscht. Pieces of it exploded from his mouth as he turned his anger on me.)

—I would have had more respect for the man if he tried to improve his own condition than worrying about the factory hands. In the long run, it would cost a lot less money paying Ben twice or three times as much than having to raise the pay of all the factory hands.

—Papa, you're a religious man. Generosity is the mark of piety. Isn't that what the Talmud says?

—Since when has the Talmud become a business textbook? Religion and commerce don't mix. I've said it before, and I'll gladly repeat it again: religion depends on faith, business on facts.

(Mother was signaling me to be still. Morris, who had taken a liking to Ben, tried to speak, but Papa told him to "stay out of it.")

—Papa, let me ask you this question: if religion and commerce don't mix, then how can the goodness of Judaism affect how we treat others in the marketplace?

—The ethics of one are not the same as the other.

—Oh, what then are the ethics of business?

—In one word, profit!

—And nothing else matters?

—Not really.

(I decided to be bolder than I ever had ever been in my life, though admittedly I put my statement in Ben's mouth rather than my own.)

—No wonder Ben says the workers will revolt.

(Papa sputtered and gesticulated like a madman.)

—He . . . that boy . . . Ben Cohen's going to land himself in jail one of these days. But maybe I shouldn't blame him entirely. That father of his is a dyed-in-the-wool communist. He fights with the rabbi and is known about town for his heretical opinions. Besides, he's a ne'er-do-well. I just hope his son hasn't inherited his father's work ethic, which is to do as little as possible.

—The man reads a great deal.

—A lot of good that does to support a family.

—It makes for interesting talk.

—Exactly! Talk, not work. If talk could put food on the table, we'd all be philosophers.

(Mother, obviously unhappy with the current of the conversation, tried to redirect it.)

—Isaac, did you know that Ben has a brother? Mrs. Cohen told me.

—Really? Where is he?

—Still in Russia.

(Papa, for all his anti-labor speeches, has a generous heart when it comes to family. So I was not surprised by what he said next.)

—Maybe the Cohens can't afford to bring him over. If they can't pay his passage, I will.

—Mrs. Cohen says he has a wife.

(Papa mulled over that fact and still came to the same conclusion.)

—They can give back the money later, if times are good.

(Papa asked me if I knew much about the brother, but I had to admit that Ben never told me. Then Mama added:)

—Let's not forget Fanny and what the Triangle Shirtwaist Factory fire did to her.

—That damned day! It gave business a bad name.

(The table fell silent for several seconds. I could see from Papa's face his emotional struggle. But was it for the loss of business or the loss of life?)

—You have to admit, Papa, it explains a lot of things: like Mr. Cohen's political opinions and Ben's attitude toward the workers.

—We will dedicate a stained-glass window to the victims. Then everyone will know where Isaac April stands. I'll tell the rabbi first thing tomorrow.

(In the doorway to the kitchen, Olga was staring.)

November 5, 1911

Although Peter and I correspond regularly, I haven't seen him since he ate at our table. The single teachers and nurses at the school used to talk about him. Eligible. Unmarried. A good catch. Those were the kinds of words that passed among them. I have no doubt that those same women are running after him now. His letters to me are sweet but restrained. I tell myself if he didn't care, he wouldn't write.

He's so handsome. Gentile, yes, but also a doctor! He says he has to be in Bridgeton in a "fortnight." On business. He invites me to spend the day. Saturday, November 18. Surely his intentions are honorable. Otherwise he would not have recommended our meeting in a public place, the train station. In novels, lovers take their mistresses to a hotel room. Of course, I have no way of knowing whether he has booked one at the Cohansey Hotel. If he did, what would I do or say? Is doing the prelude to saying, or is saying the prelude to doing?

To get to Bridgeton will take some planning. From Monday to Friday I am with Alexandra. Each morning, I come to the Zeffin farm, where Vasily lives in a bunkhouse. Three rooms: a kitchen, parlor, and bedroom. Alexandra sleeps on a cot in the parlor. No bathroom or running water. An outhouse and pump. Since Peter wants to meet on a Saturday, I will have to beg off from attending shul with Mama. One good thing: with all the Jews at prayer, there will be less chance of running into neighbors.

My tutoring of Alexandra has progressed of late. Her initial recalcitrance has given way to a readiness to learn sign language. I convinced her it was fun—a game—making figures with one's hands. Though she is still learning, we communicate fairly well, except for yesterday. She seemed to be trying to tell me something, I think, about Ben. And Irina. Concerning a haystack. At night. I'm sure she's confused. I smiled and told her we'd return to that subject another time. She did make it clear that her father stopped at the tavern, and she was told to wait. Outside, in the November weather. She wandered about to keep warm. She seems to think that she saw something important. But at that point her story becomes fuzzy.

Vasily pays me a pittance. Understandably. His own pay is paltry. I write on my slate that I am being paid in a different currency. The pleasure of teaching his daughter. He is ambivalent about her. One minute he hugs her, the next he strikes her for not obeying him. He brings me small gifts, like a chocolate chew. It's clear that he wishes me to join his household. I feel sorry for Vasily. And especially for Alexandra. But not enough to marry him.

Each morning Alexandra and I sit on the floor and play at some game or other while I teach her sign language. Her capacity to learn amazes me, and her laughing smile is a constant pleasure. When she makes a mistake or misses a move, she slaps her forehead as if to say, "How foolish." I often use jingles to make learning more fun. She wants me to hear one she's composed. "Fat and skinny had a race. Fat fell down and broke his face. Skinny went on to win the race." I laugh gleefully. "You rascal, I taught you that one." She answers thievishly, "I was hoping you forgot."

I am becoming her mother. And liking it. She takes my hand. Sits on my lap. We go for walks. I explain the natural world to her. She is really quite a beauty with long heavy yellow hair. I put it in a single braid, which nearly reaches her waist. Like many Ukrainians she has high cheekbones and limpid blue eyes, thin lips, and Nordic coloring. Skinny as a blade of grass, she jumps around like a rabbit. Except when Vasily is in one of his dark moods. Then she sits in a corner eyeing him carefully. Trying to read his thoughts. Often, when he's been drinking, she'll steal out of the house and stay with the Zeffins. But Vasily beats her for "running off."

She frequently asks if she can come live with me. "Father, won't mind," she says. I tell her how much I would like to have her. To have a child. Alexandra my own. But Mother would object.

"My mother is old. Has little patience. Complains. Some day, perhaps, but not immediately."

Alexandra studies my face and says, "Not too long, I hope."

"No, not too long."

On weekends, when we are apart, I feel incomplete. I cannot explain the feeling to Mother. She would be insulted. Father understands. I write the words on my slate. He nods his head sagely and says the same thing each time, "She's a mitzvah."

Poor Vasily, he asks me to teach his daughter the credo of his church. But his religious beliefs are so mixed up that what he says is always a muddle. A confusion between faith and fact.

I associate the start of the whirlwind with Al Crenshaw's walking into Brotman's on the first day of the month, a Wednesday. He took me aside to whisper A. R. had been in touch and I should accompany Dr. Freedland to Mr. Stein's office. The lawyer would then turn him over to the authorities and proceed directly to trial, a deal entered into between Mr. Stein and the prosecutor.

Having kept this matter from my family, I had some difficulty explaining why I had to depart for Philadelphia and might be gone for a few days. My reason was not entirely untrue: that I wanted to look at factories for rent that might lend themselves to the manufacturing of cosmetics. I had definitely decided Mr. April's shmattahs were not for me, and I now had to select either New York or Philadelphia to start my own business. Pop seemed satisfied with my explanation, but Mom looked as if she doubted my word. Eventually she tipped her hand.

"It has nothing to do with your father, does it?"

"What do you mean?"

"His condition . . . his coughing. I thought maybe you wanted a second opinion."

I assured her that I would be looking at factory lofts. Where would I stay? At the Franklin Hotel, where Mr. Stein had reserved a room, though that part of the story I omitted. When would I be leaving for Philadelphia? The next day.

Al Crenshaw drove Dr. Freedland and me to the station. The doctor bought two tickets, and we boarded a train for Philadelphia.

Met on the platform by Mr. Stein, we parted company at the central police station. I went to my hotel, and the other two, after shaking my hand and thanking me, pushed through the large oaken doors. Fortunately I had brought an umbrella, because a few minutes later a cloudburst drenched the City of Freedom.

The young clerk at the front desk had me sign the register and I walked up two flights of stairs to my room. On the bed lay a gift-wrapped box, which contained an expensive new camel's hair overcoat and a card that read: "A benny for a Benny. Thanks for your help. Call me at Marty's, after ten, *without fail!* A. R." That evening, after eating at a diner, I found a telephone exchange and rang Marty's. It took a few minutes before A. R. growled:

"Yeah, who is it?"

"Me, Ben."

"By seven o'clock tomorrow morning a fellow will come to your hotel room with an envelope. I want you personally to hand it to Mr. Mulhern before he goes inside the building. But for Christ's sake, don't let anyone see you pass it to him—and then skedaddle."

I started to protest, but he cut me off. "It's the last favor I'll ask in return for what you owe me, which isn't peanuts."

What could I say? I had been regularly borrowing more and more money. "Do I dare ask what's in the envelope?"

"Don't act like you got a *goyisha kup*."

"Just as I thought."

"Gotta run, kid. Call me the next time you're in New York. We'll go to a ball game together."

Sure enough, shortly before seven, I heard someone lightly knocking on my door. The kid who handed me the envelope looked like an Irish street waif hoping to pass for a gangster, with a fedora pulled down over his forehead and a cigarette dangling from the corner of his mug. As I reached for my wallet to tip him, he waved me off.

"It's all taken care of," he said and disappeared down the hall.

In a misting rain, I stood outside the courthouse and waited. Just moments before the trial was to begin, Mr. Patrick Mulhern turned a corner—alone, thank God. I figured his wife's absence boded well; if she wanted to see Dr. Freedland prosecuted, she would probably have made it a point to attend. Wearing a battered derby and a ratty raincoat with a turned-up collar, Mr. Mulhern shuffled toward me. The rain had driven most of the people indoors, but three men stood at the foot of the courthouse steps. To put some distance between them and me, I advanced toward Mr. Mulhern and, pulling my hat down to suggest that I was blinded by the rain, collided with him. He muttered, "Hey, look where you're goin'," but before he could pass, I shoved the envelope into his hand and hissed, "Pocket it! Don't ask," and darted across the street. Standing in the rain, I stared at the glowing courthouse windows and thought of Dr. Freedland, weighing my affection for him against A. R.'s admonition to leave the scene.

On my way to the hotel, I detoured through a park where a crowd had gathered. Families with children stood listening to a frumpily dressed, but peculiarly attractive, round-faced woman with curly hair, deeply set dark eyes, and a bulbous nose. Her message made her look beautiful: the necessity for anarchism in America so that doctors would not be prosecuted for performing abortions. Mesmerized, I listened under the protection of the trees as she spoke passionately atop a milk crate, while two women held umbrellas over her head.

"As Thomas Paine said, 'government at best is a necessary evil, at worst an intolerable one.' Sadly, the Revolution did not go far enough. If it had, women would now have the right to govern their own bodies and control the size of their families. Instead of children being treated as a commodity, as mere hands, they would be treated as individual minds and souls."

The crowd encouraged her with shouts of, "You tell 'em, Voltairine," "An end to government," "Women must be free," "Democracy or dynamite," and the like.

She argued that child bearing had reduced a woman's life to sheer drudgery, and that the domination of men had a corrosive effect on the female spirit. "The trial of abortionists is just another example," she said, "of procreation having become an arithmetic of industry."

She concluded with a plea that the faithful not let the state convict Dr. Freedland and limit the freedom of women.

Early the next morning, I bought a paper and read about the "shocking" speech given by the anarchist, Voltairine de Cleyre, and the "audacious" move that Mr. Stein had effected in court.

"Sensational Court Case"

—*Philadelphia Inquirer*, November 10, 1911

The case of Pennsylvania versus Dr. Samuel Freedland took a bizarre turn as the defense called to the stand in support of its "accident theory" the prosecution's key witness, Mrs. Patrick Mulhern. The mother of the child who Dr. Freedland was alleged to have aborted testified that the doctor had tried to save her life and in the process accidentally punctured the skull of the fetus.

Mr. Billings, the prosecutor, beside himself with anger, questioned the woman with no little acerbity.

"Did you or did you not tell Father Joyce, *and* swear, that Dr. Freedland aborted your child?"

"I used the word to mean removed, not like you're sayin' . . . somethin' unlawful."

"Are you now contending that you misapprehended the definition of the word 'abort?'" Mr. Billings then waved a dictionary and read. "Its verbal form means 'to end a pregnancy prematurely, to cut short, to terminate.' Is that what you're now saying, you failed to understand the word in question?"

Mrs. Mulhern remained steadfast, saying that the baby was not taken from her prematurely, it was "dislodged" when it stuck fast in the birth canal. "That's what I meant by the word 'abort.'"

The prosecutor warned her that lying could damn her eternal soul, a comment to which the defense objected, and the judge sustained.

Mrs. Mulhern, dabbing her eyes, asked, "Are you tryin' to weary me even more than I am?"

Mr. Billings now found himself in the disturbing position of having to rebut the one witness he had counted on, Mrs. Mulhern. Some in the court wondered why he didn't just withdraw the charges against Dr. Freedland and abandon the trial. But he persisted, calling to the stand Father Seamus Joyce, from the north vicariate.

Mr. Billings asked him to recount Mrs. Mulhern's statement, "the one that led you to the police."

"I couldn't do that now, could I, when it took place in the confines of the confessional."

Mr. Billings, looking beset by demons, hopped around the room and said in a raised voice, "Surely you're not telling me that the crime you asked the police to investigate is confidential information?"

"Not the crime, just the confession. All priests are sworn to protect the inviolate sanctity of the confessional booth."

Looking utterly bewildered, Mr. Billings asked, "What made you go to the police?"

"A fear that a grievous crime had been committed."

"Based on what Mrs. Mulhern had told you."

"Yes."

"But you can't say what she said."

"Correct."

"In that case, wasn't your even going to the police a violation of confidentiality?"

"You might say I skirted the edges."

Unable to persuade Father Joyce to disclose what Mrs. Mulhern had told him, Mr. Billings excused the priest and in short order began his summation, followed by Mr. Stein's closing comments to the jury.

Two hours later, the jury brought in a verdict of not guilty.

November 18, 1911

With Mama at shul and Papa and Ben walking in the woods, I go to the cemetery to meet Mr. Wolfe, who has promised to take me in his wagon to Bridgeton. For which I pay him fifty cents, even though he is going anyway. I arrive an hour early and wait at the station, burying myself in a newspaper so as not to be seen. In the Professionals Wanted section, I read that Gallaudet College in Washington, D.C. is hiring specialists in sign language. What if Peter and I could be together there? In the nation's capital!

When he enters the station, he smiles warmly but does not, as I hope, embrace me. Instead, he shakes my hand. His attitude is proper. Formal. Thanking me for meeting him. I was hoping he'd bring me a gift, but he carries only an umbrella. The day is sharply cold. We walk into town, and he suggests we stop at a bakery with tables to have hot chocolate and a nosh.

Of the four tables, three are occupied. The ones closest to the kerosene heater. We wear our overcoats and order hot chocolate and sponge cake. Peter asks me about Alexandra. Conversing in sign language, we attract the attention of the customers, one of whom is heard to say, "Who are those loons?" I tell Peter about Gallaudet College and study him for any clues to his feelings. A barely perceptible smile crosses his face. He studies his hands and breathes deeply, as if priming himself for a revelation. In *Tosca*, Sarah Bernhardt behaves in a similar fashion before she leaps to her death.

"My mother—" he says and breaks off.

I tell him that I know all about mothers.

"She lives in Boston. Father died several years ago."

I balance my chin on my hands and listen attentively.

"Her health is precarious."

His expressions tell me as much as his language. He is uncomfortable. Torn. But between what and what?

"I should be with her."

He plans to leave Philadelphia for Boston.

"Gallaudet College, in fact, contacted me. But I had to say no."

His face indicates the pain of that "no" and suggests the hope that it's not permanent. Or am I reading more into his gestures than are actually there? I am in no position to ask, What about us? Apparently, there is no "us."

He pays the bill and we walk silently down the boardwalks until we come to a millinery shop. "Let's see what we can find in here," he says playfully. The window dressing is quite extensive. In the shop he feigns interest in numerous items, but all the while keeps darting his eyes to the hats. Glances that give him away. I now see what he intends. After further attempts to act as if nothing in particular has arrested his attention, he stands in front of the hat display. They are stacked on short wooden poles. He points at one and then another: "That one," and the salesgirl removes it from the third row.

"Would the madam like to try it on?" she asks.

Having no way to indicate that I am unmarried other than to remove my hands from my gloves, which I refuse to do, I let the mistake stand. And try on the hat.

"It's perfect," Peter enthuses, as I admire myself in the mirror.

The hat, "Alice blue," is quite stylish. But what would I tell my family if I arrived wearing such a headdress? Mama would at once be suspicious. Thinking me a kept woman. And when would I ever have an occasion to wear it? I couldn't even hide it. Where? Not in the house. Reluctantly I tell Peter that his generous gift would invite my family's disapproval. His face exudes disappointment even though his words say otherwise.

We leave the millinery store and enter a leather shop. Among the belts and purses are racks of gloves, mostly for work. But some for fashion. Peter has undoubtedly noticed that mine are inelegant and frayed. He insists I pick out a pair of kid gloves. Is this to be his parting gift? His going-away present? His way of saying our flirtation has been pleasant but now it's over? If so, then I will accept the gloves as a reminder of someone I once cared for. The gloves are black with many tiny buttons. I can tell Mama that Ben bought them. He'll back me up.

Peter treats me to lunch and continues to apologize about his mother. "The doctors say she has a few months at most. I am taking a leave from the institution." He reaches across the table and touches my hand. The gesture profoundly moves me. It is the first sign on his part that I am more than a dalliance. More than a temporary companion of a bachelor who wishes to dispel his loneliness.

A gesture of love.

After my father and the rabbi had quarreled, instead of attending Shabbos services, Pop spent his Saturdays, weather permitting, at the school grounds about a mile away, watching the Negro farmhands play horseshoes. On this particular Saturday, as Dad prepared to leave the house, I offered to accompany him since he had become so frail.

He walked with difficulty, complaining about the lack of circulation in his legs, which accounted for his leaving our place almost an hour before the matches normally began. His wheezing had become decidedly worse and his parchment-colored skin seemed to fade more with each passing day. He leaned on a cane with a hand grip in the form of a silver horse head. I had bought it in Philadelphia. The moment I presented it to him, he had tossed away the several sticks he kept in a corner. Often, he would polish the grip.

As we passed the cemetery, Pop asked me what I intended to do with my life. "I spoke to the Baron de Hirsch people. They know nothing of your acquiring additional land. That was just an excuse you gave to your mother."

"Yes."

Although I rarely confided in my father, I knew that whatever I did tell him would remain just between us.

"Those morning detours of yours through the woods . . . I'm guessing they had to do with that lawyer we saw in Philadelphia."

I told him the whole story about Dr. Freedland, eliciting only one comment, "So why didn't you invite me to play chess with him?"

"Because I was afraid Mom would learn of his presence and cause problems. And that's the truth."

"She's unpredictable. Some things she would die before telling and others would take no prompting at all."

Leaning on the cemetery railing, Pop directed my attention to all the small headstones. "Children. Who knows what marvelous contributions they might have made to society." He paused. "You've bought two plots, one for me and one for your mother."

"Yes. I didn't want to say anything for fear of upsetting you."

"The mortician sent us a letter of confirmation."

"I specifically asked him to address it to me."

"No matter. You did the right thing. In your place, I would have done the same." He rubbed his eyes with his sleeve. "You know what troubles me most? Not dying, but being buried apart from Jacob and his family. It would be impossibly expensive to have my remains shipped to Bobrovitz, but I am saddened by the dispersal of our family and their resting places." Then he stood, head bowed, leaning on his cane, unabashedly crying.

I tried to embrace him, but he shrugged me away and continued silently down the road. Several minutes later, he asked me if I intended to resume painting miniatures.

"There's nothing I'd rather do, but how am I to support myself?"

"Perhaps if you spent more time at it . . ."

Pop was right, and I had no real excuses. Pleading work or women would merely have invited his censure. So I uttered a half truth. "No one can make a living from art."

"A great many painters did."

"Yes, but not in America. Besides, it takes real inspiration."

The spot where he stopped in the road will remain forever fixed in my mind. Oblivious to the horse carts, he turned and said, "There is no such thing as inspiration. I have read enough in my life about poets and artists to know there is only hard work. As Tolstoy and Zola said, you get up in the morning, you go to your desk, and you wrestle with words. If you feel you have nothing to express that day, then you sit and think or make notes, but you don't leave your desk to do something else. Art is a craft, a lapidary one. You must practice and polish all the time. Of late, you have become . . . like me . . . aimless. Nothing is accomplished without discipline. Yes, I know, who am I to talk, the perfect idler. It is because my life has been a disappointment that I know the ingredients of failure. Don't follow in my footsteps."

As we passed the synagogue, Rabbi Kolodny gestured, summoning us. Pop murmured that he was probably going to revile us for not attending Sabbath services. The morning prayers had already ended and a number of men drifted out of shul, appearing to make a point of ignoring me and Pop. But the rabbi greeted us warmly and asked us to step inside the sanctuary. Pointing to a plain window in the south wall, he told us that Mr. April had commissioned a stained-glass window, a representation of Ruth, in remembrance of the Triangle Shirtwaist Factory victims, and that soon a brass plaque would be mounted on the wall indicating the number of dead and injured in the great fire. Pop was visibly moved, and I must admit that my opinion of Mr. April changed radically.

November 27, 1911

I am heart sick. Olga says Ben and Erika drove off at noon and spent the whole afternoon ALONE. While I was in church praying for us he was . . . where? I must find out what he's really thinking. But how? Lately when we're together he's so quiet. Maybe it's because of my bad English. If we could talk in Polish, I think he would see me differently. But many people talk best when they're silent. Their feelings speak for them. Just holding Ben's hand is like speech. It means fondness. And when we love, no words can describe how we feel. Still I worry. He talks to her and not me. Olga says they talk about trifles. Worse—small things are life's glue.

He knows I worry about him and Erika, because last time we met he tried to make me feel good by mentioning her childlike habits. She collects postcards and has bookcases full of dolls, even one dollhouse real in every way. He swears he's never even kissed her though Olga has seen them holding hands. Moving to Carmel took him from me and put him near her. I worry most that Erika's father will offer Ben a job with lots of money. How can he refuse this pretty girl and her rich family, which will support him?

Some men have mistresses. Is that what Ben thinks I am? If so, I will NOT be his mistress. Irina, what are you saying? You are his mistress already. He gives up nothing to have you. And you give your most precious jewel. Think clearly! Your jealousy is confusing you. Maybe Ben is telling the truth when he says he calls on Erika to keep his mother from nagging. But I can hear the street tattle. Mr. April is an important man. People know him. They say he has set his eye on Ben for a son-in-law and what he wants he buys. Olga thinks Ben is just trying get a start in business and once he's his own boss he will forget Erika. Whether Olga is right or not it's bad. Do I want some man who uses a woman to get ahead and then turns his back on her? No! But Ben could never behave in this way.

Last time we played it was growing late. My family was in bed. Ben borrowed a Buick car and we rode to Parvin Lake and took a rowboat to the other side. We stayed in the cabin a long time because we heard bootleggers outside storing stuff in the storage shed. Wrapping ourselves tightly in the blanket, we listened and hardly breathed.

"I heerd the 'nooers picked up Ray's brother. And Ray spilled the beans."

"Guys who squawk oughter be shot."

"Yeah, like a rat."

"Chrissake, it's his brother."

"Loyalty don't count for nothin' these days."

When at last they left, I was shaking. In my left hand I felt something sharp, my silver crucifix. I had grabbed it at the first sound of the men and had pulled it free from my neck. My grip must have been tight or the silver old because it bent. I was afraid to twist it back and maybe break the cross. So I asked Ben to fix the chain but I guess a link broke because when I got home it was gone.

My grandmother gave me that crucifix for my confirmation. At Czestochowa she had it blessed. I remember I wore a white dress and polished white shoes. Mama put up my hair with combs instead of a bow to make me look older. I was filling out and she said the service was to confirm me in the church as a WOMAN. She used that word and not girl. I was very proud.

The next morning I went into Brotman's to tell Ben about the missing cross. He said he would check with the man who loaned him the car. But nothing. The last time I saw Ben I asked him again about it. He looked odd and said he didn't think it would be found.

"Why?"

"It's probably lost in the woods forever."

"Maybe someone will be finding it."

"And if they do, how will they know whose it is?"

"On back of cross are being my initials, IMN, but to see you must real hard look. I've sucked on cross for so many years, they've much disappeared."

Ben promised he'd continue to search.

Since that night I've thought about what those men said. One brother or lover turning in another seems to me sinful. How could a person tell on a loved one? I would never say a word about me and Ben and our playing. Even if my parents threatened to kill me I would rather die than betray Ben. I know if I were to become pregnant, Ben would admit it's his child. But if he can't I still won't. Just last month in Vineland some father shot his daughter, who refused to name the fellow who got her in trouble, and hundreds came to her funeral. I wonder what her lover feels now, with his girlfriend dead and her father in prison?

December 5, 1911

How should a Jewish mother respond when a Catholic woman stops her on the street and says, I would like to talk to you about marriage between your Ben and my Irina? Mrs. Kasper is a nice lady. I have nothing but nice to say about her. She has good manners. Her husband, that drunk, is another matter. But what should we talk about? That her church accuses Jews of being Christ killers, that the worst murderers of Jews are the Poles? We have nothing in common. The very idea of her Irina and my Ben took my breath away. But worse was to come. Like the serpent in the garden, she tried to tempt me. My Irina, she said, will convert. Then there will be no problem.

No problem! We will have Catholics for relatives? No problem! Irina can convert till the cows come home, but the first time a baby appears, she and her family will want to have the child baptized. I would eat dung first. How can you wash away years of being brought up as a Catholic? The die is cast, as they say, during the first few years of a child's life. Were not the Jews secretly practicing their faith in the cellars of Spain while professing to be Catholics? She'll be like them: a secret believer.

In all fairness to Irina, Mrs. Kasper shouldn't ask such a thing of her daughter. I believe in letting people be what they are. Irina may say she'll convert, but in her heart, I'm sure, she'd always be a Catholic, and who knows what secrets she'll whisper into her child's ear. Mixed marriages are like lobsters, they're neither fish nor fowl. The children of such marriages never know whether to kneel or to stand, to sit upstairs or downstairs, to cross themselves or to daven. This is a life?

A minute after she walked away, it hit me. For Mrs. Kasper to say what she did, Ben would have to be seeing her daughter. Maybe those jaunts through the woods were to rendezvous with Irina. Since he no longer goes that way, he must be meeting her elsewhere. Every time I ask, he says there's nothing between them. Nothing but *that*! If he puts Irina in a family way, he'll have no future. A wife and baby at his age . . . nothing could be worse. I was so upset by what Mrs. Kasper said to me, I didn't even hear Mrs. April.

Yoo, hoo, she called. Have you got a moment?

She took my arm and led me into the general store to escape the rawness outside. Mr. Fleischer, busy with a customer, didn't mind that we stood in a corner and talked. Mrs. April had her back to the display case, but I was looking right into it. An omen, I thought, and tucked my thumb into my palm. Staring at me from the display case was a bridal outfit and a man's wedding suit.

We need to talk, she said. So who's stopping you, I wanted to say, but instead whispered, I hope it's about our children. She whispered back, Isaac and I have been talking. I answered, Talk is good. It keeps sorrow away. She looked at me strangely, as if she had never heard the adage. I told Isaac what you said in the kitchen . . . about Ben being too young and waiting till he's twenty. Isaac agrees. She smiled as if there was nothing further to the matter. But I immediately began to wonder why Isaac April would be glad to see the couple wait for two years. Did he think my Ben wasn't good enough for his daughter and wanted to keep an eye on him? Or maybe it had to do with that disagreement Ben mentioned, between him and Mr. April.

When Ben told me that he and Mr. April had words, I nearly died. Here's a man who's willing to give Ben a business and teach him the ropes, and my son has to be Mr. Defender of the Downtrodden. It's all Meyer's fault. He filled the children with his rubbish, which one day, I'm sure, will land Jacob in Siberia or worse. Offending Mr. April is as good as being sent to Siberia. But the good news is Mr. April has a big heart. Didn't he pay for a colored window to be installed in the sanctuary in honor of the Triangle dead and injured? The day the rabbi told me, I cried. Meyer, who reads books by the yard, knows all about symbolism and that kind of mumbo-jumbo. But it wasn't lost on me that the window depicts Ruth. I knew what Mr. April intended. It was his way of saying his daughter would be faithful to Ben. Whither thou goest, I will go. Aren't those the great words of the Book of Ruth? I was deeply touched.

Of course Meyer scoffed at my interpretation. Although he's often full of theories and literature talk, the window to him is just a humane gesture, meaning no more than a local glassblower made a few dollars on the commission. He's really impossible. What he sees, I don't. What I know, he disputes. Only to God would I say it, but I married too young. At least Ben and Erika will wait. And Fanny will stay single (enough with shadchans) and look after me.

Taking Mrs. April's arm, I said, So nu, while our children wait for the chupah, does Mr. April have any plans? She shook her head yes and added, I'm glad you asked. As you know, he is wanting to open a factory in Newark, and will be spending a lot of time getting it started. The Carmel factory will need a manager. It didn't take a Talmudic scholar to see what she was saying. You mean Ben, I said, hardly able to contain my joy.

Of course, Isaac will want certain things done. I nodded in agreement. Don't you worry, I will see to it.

※

The Lord be praised! Yesterday, Ben started work with Mr. April. But instead of sitting down with the account ledgers, Ben insisted on learning the job from the bottom up. He began by asking one of the operators to teach him how to take apart and put back together a sewing machine. Then if one breaks, he can fix it himself. You're not a mechanic, I complained. Leave the fixing to others. Learn about debits and credits. He said Erika had already taught him as much bookkeeping as he needed to know, and his place was in the shop, not in the office. I wanted to scream because I could taste again Meyer's influence. If Ben would only see that his father is full of advice he never applies to himself. To have given me such a husband and son, God must be testing me. Neither one has a cupful of sense.

Over dinner, I asked Ben what his plans were once Mr. April left for Newark. Though his answer was no surprise, it did alarm me. He said, I will review all the salaries, look at the profits, and see if I can't raise everyone's pay. I put down my fork and stared him in the eye. Didn't Mr. April warn you not to meddle with salaries? Ben returned my look. How do you know that? For once I had the upper hand. I know it because Mrs. April told me. We were standing in Fleischer's store, and she related what her Isaac expected.

I wouldn't give raises immediately, he said. I just want to be prepared. Slapping my forehead for emphasis, I replied, you're some manager. The first time the boss leaves, you'll throw a wrench in the works. You're like his brother Howard in Atlanta. Ben leaned across the table as if he had a great secret to convey. I've spoken to him, and his side of the story is very different. My heart began to flutter like it does of late, causing me to start panting. The next thing you know, I said, you'll be making a revolution with this Howard fellow and driving Mr. April out of his own business. Is that what you're aiming for? But before he could answer, I asked, How did you come to speak to him?

Even Meyer looked interested, leaving his second lamb chop uneaten and putting down his knife. The secretary called to me and said

Mr. Howard April was on the phone. Isaac had left the premises so I took the call. Ben paused as if collecting his thoughts. Impatient as a groom on his wedding night, I said, So, so, I'm waiting!

All right, but what passes at this table, he warned, must not go any further. Are we agreed? I knew Meyer could never summon enough energy to repeat a good story, but for me it was different. Promising to keep a confidence was hard, especially when it came to the welfare of my children. Nevertheless, I agreed. Howard, said Ben, talked about business for a few minutes—he's having trouble getting certain patterns—and then asked me was I new in the office. I told him I was going to manage the factory while Mr. April worked in Newark. He warned me that his brother was a slave driver, explaining that when his wife had influenza and he took off a week to be with her in the hospital, Isaac April begrudged him the time off. That was the start of the split between them. And your wife, I asked. She died.

December 8, 1911

Dearest Diary, Papa took the train to Newark and plans to stay several months. But the good news is he found a house across the street from a park, Weequahic, an Indian name, and he wants us to visit every weekend. I told Mama that would be impossible because I had to make time for Ben. She said she couldn't leave me and the other kids unchaperoned, so we would have to go with her on her trips. I grumbled, but Mother said she saw no rush since Ben and I hadn't even become engaged yet, and a marriage was still a ways off. Our conversation was not very satisfactory.

—My friends in Atlanta are already getting married. Why must I wait?

—It's been decided. Mrs. Cohen and I talked.

—Does Ben know these plans?

—Erika, I beg you to leave these matters to me and your father.

—My life?

—Your marriage.

—They're the same thing.

(During dinner, I excused myself from the table and went to my room. I wanted Mama to see Charlotte's wedding invitation, which I had left among my jewelry. On entering the room, I found Olga holding a piece of my Sienese lace that held the bent silver crucifix I had found near the cabin.)

—Where are you getting this?

(The cheek of the young woman. Caught red-handed, she was asking *me* where my things came from, as if I had stolen them. My first reaction was to fly into a rage, but I remembered what I had learned at school: hysterics are for fishwives, self-control for ladies.)

—I found it in a muddy field.

—I am not believing you.

—What nerve! I catch you stealing, and you accuse me of taking something that's yours.

—Maybe you've forgotten, you are asking me to dust room and polish hairdressing set.

—Yes, not take my jewelry.

—Drawer was open, and I saw bent crucifix laying on a piece of lace.

—Lying, you mean.

—I'm not lying.

—Never mind.

—It couldn't be yours, it is belonging to Irina.

—Your sister?

—Yes. The cross is special, being given to her by my grandmother, who had it blessed at Czestochowa. That's where Black Madonna comes from, a holy shrine to Polish people.

—How could your sister have lost it in a cranberry bog?

—I don't know, but if you are looking hard at back, you'll see her initials, IMN.

(Turning the cross over, I could just make out some scratches at the bottom. I took my magnifying glass, which I used to pluck my eyebrows and to admire the small print on my postcards, and peered through it. Olga was right about the initials. At that moment, my mind was a storm of riotous thoughts.)

—Do you know, Olga, how it got where it did?

—No idea, ma'am.

(I could feel the blood pulsing in my temples and felt unfit to continue the conversation, so I dismissed her, telling her in the future to resist the temptation to look at people's possessions. After she left, I sat on my bed in a state of utter confusion. Eventually Mother came into my room to ask why I had disappeared.)

—Mother, sit down next to me. I want to ask you a question.

(For the first time, I showed her the crucifix, which nearly caused her to jump off the bed.)

—Where did you get *that*?

—I found it the day we went to Parvin Lake with Ben.

—So?

—Would you believe it belongs to Irina Kasper?

(I then told her the story of the cabin.)

—Child, you have the most active imagination I've ever seen. What is your fear?

—Inside the cabin was a blanket on a bed of straw.

—Maybe a tramp lives there.

—A tramp, indeed!

(Mama finally caught on.)

—Irina's parents are strict Catholics. They keep a tight rein on those girls.

—What if Irina and—

—Ben? Never in a million years. I'll cut off my right hand if I'm wrong.

—If you are, I'd prefer you cut something else off.

—Erika April!

"Dr. Tried on Abortion Charge Reinstated"

—*Philadelphia Inquirer*, December 11, 1911

The Pennsylvania State Board of Medicine on Friday morning reversed its initial decision to strip Dr. Samuel Freedland of his medical license for fleeing to avoid prosecution. In light of the jury finding of not guilty to the charge of performing an illegal abortion, the Board felt it had no other alternative but to reinstate Dr. Freedland. The Board, however, did take the unusual step of chastening Dr. Freedland for running away.

Given all the public interest in the case, the chairman of the Board, Dr. Harrison Harlingford, called a press conference to make the announcement. Dr. Harlingford explained that when birth complications arise, the line between delivery and abortion is "a very fine one indeed." He regretted Dr. Freedland's hiding to escape the law, but said "some of our laws are outmoded and need to be reexamined if doctors are to render the best possible care to their patients."

Freedland, in the presence of family members, told reporters he was relieved to have his license restored. But he said that adverse publicity had cost him so many patients, he planned to resettle in New York City and start anew. He pointed to the front of his house, where some agitator had painted the word "Murderer."

The Chief of Police, Capt. Randall Fillmore, said that as long as the laws on the books remained as they are, he would be obliged to arrest physicians, like Dr. Freedland, who perform partial birth abortions. "The law is clear," he said, "and I will enforce it."

December 12, 1911

While a customer was talking to me about pillowcases, Erika April walked in. I knew from my Saints' Days calendar this day would be special. She looked at sheets, not really intending to buy. Thank God, Mama had gone home for lunch. After the last customer had left, I asked Miss April if I could help her. She opened her purse and took out a piece of lace holding a silver crucifix. If she expected me to be surprised, I wasn't. When Olga told me Erika had found it, my heart went thump but I didn't show how I was feeling or what I was thinking. Why had Ben taken Erika to OUR place? She wasn't, I had told myself, that kind of girl, and then got mad at myself because it meant I was. Then I refused to think about it. Like Mama says, things don't very much bear looking into.

She handed me the crucifix and I thanked her.

"Do you know where I found it?" she said.

"No."

"Outside a cabin near Parvin Lake . . . in a cranberry bog."

I pretended amazement. "Really?"

"Although I have no right to ask, I was wondering how it got there. Do you have any idea?"

"No."

"I thought perhaps you might have been hiking in the area or swimming nearby in the lake."

"No."

I could see she was annoyed.

"Well, when did you lose it?"

"Months ago."

"And yet it's not rusty."

I shrugged. If she thought she'd make me talk so she could smile at my bad English I just wouldn't say more than a few words.

"A miracle maybe."

"You know Ben Cohen, don't you? Of course you do. He used to work next door at Brotman's until my father hired him."

"How nice."

"He made him the manager of the Carmel factory," she said proudly, lifting her nose in the air. "He was with me when I found the . . . your jewelry."

"You must being friends."

Erika, very huffy, said, "Ben and I are more than acquainted."

MORE THAN ACQUAINTED! Is that what they taught her in school—to talk like a stuffed turkey? She would faint if she knew how ACQUAINTED we were.

"I gather you like him."

She must have thought I was an idiot. I saw through her like a window.

"Neighbors, that's all."

"Olga told me he used to call on you."

What a big lie! Olga would never say such a thing. From Erika's questions I saw she was jealous. Good, maybe she'd fight with Ben and he'd never want to see her again and maybe even lose his job as manager. If that's what it takes to pry him away from her I would gladly work twice as hard to make up for the money he'd lose.

"In his store sometimes I see him."

"If you're wondering why I have taken the liberty to ask you these questions, it is because Ben and I will shortly be engaged."

Liar! I forced a smile and said, "Congratulations."

"I am not a possessive person, but I will insist that he discontinue having women friends. Even though I know such friendships are harmless, one can never be too careful. I do hope you'll understand and still value our trade, because of course we'll soon be shopping for linens and blankets."

She then walked over to the blanket shelf and pulled one from the pile. It was the same as the blanket I had left in the cabin.

"Curious," she said, "I believe I've seen this design before."

I took a big chance and made up some story. "If you promise no one to tell . . ."

She touched her hand to heart. "Me? Never." Her eyes were as big as soup bowls.

"A boy from Norma, we, well, you know."

Her whole body seemed to relax. Then she hugged me and said, "I promise. Not a word, ever."

She was so glad to hear it wasn't Ben, she thanked me and bought several towels.

"If you marry your Norma boyfriend, be sure to let me know. I'd love to give you a wedding gift."

December 13, 1911

Dearest Diary, I decided to take the bull by the horns and went to Vineland to see Irina. She's a pretty woman with beautiful skin, but utterly uneducated. She could hardly speak more than a syllable or two. I gave her the crucifix and tried to learn whether she and Ben had been to the cabin, but I couldn't get anything out of that girl. She's as thick as an ox. She did finally confess that she had a beau in Norma, probably someone equally stupid. I wormed this information out of her because I found a blanket on her store shelf that was the same as the one I had seen in the cabin. She all but told me she used that place for her trysts with the fellow. I wouldn't be the least bit surprised to learn she's expecting. She looked a little plump and large in the bosom. Although I'd never be caught dead at a shotgun wedding, I will send her a gift.

In case Ben has any ideas about Irina, I'll just let him know she has a boyfriend, and I might even hint that she looks, as they say in the south, like she has a watermelon on the vine. It's not that I've ever seen Ben and Irina together, because I haven't, but gossip is a pipe played on by many mouths. And I've heard the tune once or twice before. That's why I asked Ben to drop by after dinner. He explained he had a lot of work at the factory, but I said I wanted to show him a pendant with the face of a girl in miniature. I reminded myself to encourage his painting. He always likes it when I do.

I thought he'd never arrive, but at eight-thirty he knocked on the door, looking weary. At first we talked about the factory, and then he told me his father wasn't well, in fact quite ill. Before coming to our house, he had returned home to see about his dad.

—I think he's dying.

—Did you call a doctor?

—The one in Bridgeton's a drunk. I made a call to Rosenhayn, to Dr. Feldman. He's on his way. That's what kept me. I went back to the factory to use the phone.

(I was annoyed that Ben would use the business phone for personal matters. Lucky for him, Papa wasn't around.)

—I guess that means you can't stay long.

—What's this about a pendant with a miniature portrait?

(I took it from my pocket, and he examined at it from several angles.)

—I wish I had a magnifying glass . . .

—Wait here.

(I brought the one from my dresser. After studying the miniature, he said it was a "first-rate imitation.")

—Of what?

—An English one by Richard Cosway. The woman, whose name is lost to history, was a famous courtesan.

—That's rich! I don't suppose Mama would be too happy if I told her whose portrait was hanging around her neck.

—Then don't tell her.

—You'll never guess the owner of the silver crucifix I found. Do you want to guess?

—No idea.

—Irina.

(I scrutinized his face for any revealing signs, but could see only bewilderment.)

—Who told you that?

—Olga.

—That's hard to believe.

—I don't like being bullied!

(My complaint stopped him in his tracks. I learned that trick from Mama. When Papa gets too overbearing, she complains about his bullying, and sometimes even cries for effect.)

—My father . . . I have to go.

(He put the pendant on the table and left without a further word or gesture, not so much as a peck on the cheek.)

The sound of the door shutting behind Ben resounded in my head for hours. I decided the only way to work things out was to sit with you, My Dearest Diary, and tell you exactly what I fear. As much as I'd like to get married and start my own home, I don't want to select the wrong man. Although my preference is for someone who knows his own mind and will make a good living, I will not be gainsaid. For all my admiration of Papa, I don't wish to marry a man like him. I prefer a softer nature. Ben is kind, but he doesn't defer to me the way I would like. At Miss Pritchard's, a number of boys would come to the school to court me, but none of them Jewish, so I knew I couldn't take them too seriously. But if Ben had their manners, how much more I would like him.

Were I to list debits and credits, they might look like this:

Debits	Credits
Too European	Jewish
Too political (radical)	Tall
Prefers low company	Thin
Lacking in formal manners	Handsome
Doesn't care what other people say	Blue eyes (pale)
Better read than I	Loves his family
Dresses poorly	Speaks well
Smarter	Supports women's rights
Speaks more languages	Likes music and art
Close, almost secretive	Discreet
Not romantic!!!	Realistic

When I look at my list I ask myself: if you had to pick one aspect that matters more than all the others, which would it be? I'd select "Too European," which is related to "Not romantic." Papa says I shouldn't worry about romance and passion. Time will pass, he says, and you and Ben will find that you are very much suited for each other. Most people aren't what you'd call well-matched, he insists, but when two people live together, affection does develop, and somehow they get by while they're waiting.

One evening in the garden, when the moon was down, Ben made a suggestion that was anything but romantic. I chided him, saying, "If that is all I mean to you, then I am sad. Because I am more than just a pretty girl to satisfy your appetites." He looked hurt, and replied, "How different the things you need, the things I need."

After I'm married I don't want to be tied to a farm or a factory, not even a family, at least not for several years. When I picture myself, I am in a white summer dress, standing on the porch of a great house. My husband, formally attired for dinner, pushes me on the swing. My hair blows in the wind. Or in February, in a steam-heated carpeted living room with a silver tea set, the heavy rain is beating against the steamy windowpanes, and my husband and I are planning our next summer abroad, in Paris and London.

December 21, 1911

With Erika making demands and Pop lying ill—Dr. Feldman said nothing more can be done for him—I had neglected Irina. So last night I hitched a ride to Vineland with one of the local farmers in his ramshackle Model A, and threw pebbles at her bedroom window until she saw me. Opening the front door a crack, she agreed to meet me at Halbert's Grain and Storage after the family had gone to bed. I hung around town playing pinochle at the Peterson house, where I used to gather with some of the boys. My luck seemed particularly bad, as I lost every hand. Excusing myself about ten, I rendezvoused with Irina. Wrapped in my overcoat, we embraced and made passionate love in the hay, feeling no cold.

As we picked the stalks from our hair, she said she heard someone stirring. I wanted to make love again, but she insisted we leave. On the road, she took my arm and suddenly stopped.

"That man in woods," she said, "on day you took us all to Maurice River. In the newspaper, I read him. It mention Vineland."

I knew the article she referred to and could guess her thoughts. "Yes, it was the same person," I said, "and you are wondering how I could have been mixed up in that business."

"Yes."

Seeing no good reason to lie, I related the story.

"You in trouble?"

"No."

The rest of the way home she said nothing, looking perplexed. I told her I would wait outside her window until she pulled the shade up and down to indicate she was safe. A minute later, she gave me the signal and a quick wave. I then started out on foot to Carmel. During the more than two-hour walk, I had plenty of time to think, especially about Erika. Deeply troubled by our last meeting, I tried to make sense of our courting.

A pretty woman with penetrating eyes and thick curly hair and a fetching slim figure, she would be a good catch for any man. Throw in the fact that her father had gelt coming out of his ears, and she became a whale of a catch. But I felt no special bond between us. At times, she seemed attuned to the injustices of the world, and other times, indifferent. She praised the arts and learning, but preferred comfort more. Her feelings switched on and off like an electric light, available when the cause at hand demanded no more than money or lip service, but never really committed. She reminded me of those upper-crust suffragettes, the ones willing to walk decorously in parades, but unwilling to go to jail. I often had the impression that she would not dirty her hands for anything short of a disaster. We were like water and oil. She seemed better suited to be my daughter than my wife. She was a domesticated animal and I a feral one. Whatever the comparison—and I've never had a gift for metaphor—I didn't think we could make a success of marriage. But I did worry that if Pop's illness proved costly, and if Mom's heart flutterings worsened, I would need to continue as manager at Mr. April's factory. And the factory workers, who feared for their wages, also depended on me.

With all the money I'd make, I could spend the rest of my life painting miniatures in an airy New York studio, and whether they sold or not would make absolutely no difference. Now there's a thought: working at what one loves without regard to its commercial value. Such thinking could transform America. Why doesn't such a rich land bestow its bounty on the opera and ballet, actors and artists, musicians and singers? We already have a surfeit of sporting events. Vaudeville is a stale palette. The music hall panders to the lowest tastes. What is it that makes this country so afraid of arts imbued with thought?

Here I am bouncing from one idea to the next just so I won't hear the sound of my own footsteps on the road to Carmel—and just so I won't consider my own failures. Pop, for all his fecklessness, is right. Art is nothing more than a craft that one has to practice and polish. Polish the silverware. Polish is a nationality. In English, pronunciation, not grammar, is the difficult part. While I have been "polishing" my Polish Irina, as well as my managerial skills, I have completely neglected painting. Although I keep telling myself that I will pick up the brushes again, I worry I won't. The world is rife with people like Pop and me, idealists who dream of becoming artisans, but who won't put in the time to master our craft. Where, at what moment, did I quit? I would like to retrace my steps and take a different direction.

Tomorrow, tomorrow I will take up my brushes, expend more time, try harder, and one day instead of my having to justify my laziness, my work will justify itself in every brush stroke. Yes, I'm resolved!

And so on the longest night of the year, I kept walking into the darkness.

December 25, 1911

Only a short time after morning Mass, Ben drove up in a big car! He called it a Buick and said he got a good deal on it used. My sisters ran outside to see. He was carrying a bag full of presents, one for every person in the family, even Daddy. It's not my place to say, but lately he seems to be spending lots of money. I just hope he's not borrowing from Mr. April. When he handed me a small box in Christmas wrappings I guessed right it would be jewelry. How I wished for a ring. Inside the box I found a silver chain strung with a crucifix and a Star of David. I nearly cried. On seeing it Mother smiled, my sisters giggled, and Father snorted.

I showed him our Christmas tree which he called a Hanukkah bush. My sisters and I had trimmed it with decorations we made at the kitchen table using paper and glue and scissors. Our presents under the tree looked sad, a pair of socks, a scarf, woolen mittens, a box of candy, and a tin of pipe tobacco. Ben's presents were nicer than all ours. Even Papa smiled on seeing the new pipe Ben gave him.

Mama insisted that Ben stay for lunch. It was only the first time he ate at our house so I worried about Papa saying grace. He sometimes talked about Roman and Jewish crucifiers. But I hoped with his new pipe he would behave. Which he did, giving thanks for the food, and then we all waited for Daddy to slice the ham. Ham! My God, I thought, Ben is Jewish. I quickly whispered to him, "If you want something else, I'll see what's in the icebox." But he insisted on eating the ham. After the meal, he whispered, "Don't ever mention this to my mother. She'd have a heart attack."

We all ate so much that we had to stand in line for the outhouse.

December 25, 1911

Vasily, a Greek Orthodox, doesn't celebrate Christmas until January 7. But I feel sorry for Alexandra, who will see all the other children showing off presents. So I buy her a woolen hat to go with the mittens I knitted. For Vasily I have food. A salami and sausages and other meats that he likes. It is late afternoon. Lowering clouds obscure the little light left. I ask Ben to drive me to the Zeffin farm and to wait for just a few minutes. Only fifty yards away, I can barely see the bunkhouse candles. Before I cover half the distance, I can hear Alexandra's muffled moans. And a thwacking noise. Without knocking I enter. Vasily, a bottle of vodka in one hand and a belt in the other, is whipping his daughter, who is kneeling on the floor. Her hands over her head. Her back, exposed to the lash. I can see bloody stripes. Vasily looks at me with bleary red eyes, too drunk to say more than, "Brat won't behave."

He strikes her again. My presence doesn't matter. Alexandra reaches a hand out to me. Then I remember. Cherry's razor, still hidden in the large handbag—unused for months—that I took from the closet to stuff with presents. Reaching behind the lining, I remove the blade. Vasily stares. I open it and hold it over my head and glare at him. He seems stupefied. I move two steps toward him. He retreats. Dropping his arm. The one with the belt. Alexandra runs to me. At that instant, I make a decision. In sign language, I tell her to pack whatever clothes she needs for a trip. As she scoops up her belongings, Vasily slumps on the couch, drops the belt on the floor, and guzzles from the bottle. Is he stoking his feverish engine to confront me? I decide not to wait. Grabbing Alexandra by the arm, I lead her coatless from the bunkhouse to the car. Ben sees her bloody back and drives off immediately for our house. But mother asks how is she to cope with a child. Meaning she can't.

So we drive to Vineland, parking in front of the Kaspers' house. The family, I feel certain, will gladly house Alexandra. If they can. I signal to Ben, who has learned much of my sign language, to offer the Kaspers money. He removes a ten dollar bill. A lot of money. Mama has said many times she thinks he has a cache. The entire Kasper family can probably live on that amount for two or three weeks.

Mrs. Kasper opens the door. Seeing Ben, she calls "Eee-ree—" and stops when she notices me and Alexandra. The child stands pressing her back against my stomach. Ben quickly explains. Without mentioning

Alexandra's injuries. Before Mrs. Kasper can answer, he hands her the money. Mr. Kasper appears. She speaks to him in Polish. He eyes us suspiciously, looks at the bill, rubs the back of his hand across his mouth. He speaks to his wife in Polish. Ben and I know just enough to understand. He has asked, "For how long?" By now the four girls have materialized. Irina's face glows. Ben tells the girls what he has just told their mother. Anna volunteers to care for Alexandra herself. They can sleep together. She will be like a little sister. To Ben's question, Anna replies, "If he is asking, I'll just tell Vasily she's for now staying with us." Ben asks, "And what if he doesn't come?" Anna looks baffled. She speaks Polish to her father. His reply needs no translating. It is abrupt. Angry.

I communicate to Ben I will be responsible for Alexandra. But I need two weeks to make the arrangements. He looks puzzled. I tell him I'll explain later. Alexandra seems pleased with her new family. Mrs. Kasper gasps. She has just noticed Alexandra's back. She rushes her off to the kitchen to wash the wounds and apply iodine and gauze bandages. Mr. Kasper, who has taken the money from his wife, disappears. Olga and I join her mother in the kitchen to help with the nursing. Ben and Irina fade into another room.

Plans for Alexandra and me are quickly taking shape in my mind. Would I be breaking the law? Probably. But such things happen every day. One problem. I have no money. So, I will have to share my idea with Ben. He, as Mama says, knows the rhythm of rubles. But what if he objects? Not to the money but to my plan? Surely he won't. In the meantime, I need to pacify Vasily. If money won't work, I'm sure religion will. For Alexandra's future, I must make what I am doing look like part of God's plan. Perhaps several bottles of vodka, *as well as cash*, will do the job. Imported vodka. Not the clear. The brownish kind he likes best. Rubles and religion. The man is the perfect czarist Russian.

But for all my planning, I wonder: would Peter make a home for me *and* Alexandra? The last time I mentioned her, he said, "Poor child, she's probably destined for an orphanage."

Christmas Night, 1911

After Ben and his sister left, we Kasper girls took Alexandra downtown to see the carolers (she can't hear them) and the decorations. We wanted to make her feel better. She walked between us. We put our arms around her. One of the singers looked familiar. When he turned his head I saw Philip Gura, who I hadn't seen for a year. He had a beard and let his hair grow. He looked like a Bohemian. He used to live in Vineland before moving to Bridgeton. I liked him but not THAT much. He played the guitar and banjo and we would sometimes sit on the front porch and sing songs. Those days now seemed very innocent—and long past. A few times he'd tried to kiss me and I pushed him away. If he only knew. Why is it that to one man you say no and another yes? I went from being a nice girl to a bad one all because of Ben. But my changing, is it really his fault? How I wish we had a priest I could talk to. The one we have now is rigid like a rod. He fills me with guilt just for my confessing petty sins.

Anna never notices other people. She's too busy trying to be a saint. Mother thinks she ought to become a nun but I would bet that underneath all the Bible stuff she really likes boys. Olga is much different. She loves laughing with the lads and teasing them and having them rib her. If anyone knows about me it's Olga. She hears things from all sides: Mama and Papa, me, the Aprils, and even the people who come to the April house. We often tell each other secrets. Just a few days ago she told me that a boy she likes tried to put his hand on her breast and she slapped his face. When I asked her if she was finished with him she said, "Just for being fresh? Of course not."

December 27, 1911

Dearest Diary, Ben has requested that we spend New Year's Eve together. Will he ask me to marry him then? I certainly hope so. With Charlotte getting married and Dolores engaged, I feel matronly. From the old friends, Alice and I are the only ones still not spoken for. Once I'm married I can stop taking piano lessons and pretending to care about all that long-haired music Mama so loves. She thinks a "lady" has to be accomplished on the piano and play Beethoven for her suitors. I'd rather listen to popular songs on the gramophone—and dance all the new steps.

How much fun I'll have being engaged. Charlotte and Dolores have told me about the kitchen appliances they've bought and their matching bedroom sets. I can't wait to visit department stores and start furnishing my own house. Of course, we won't stay in Carmel very long, just until Ben can learn the business; then he'll work in Newark or New York, so we can be near the family. I'd never spend my life in a town like this one. Daddy agrees. Hasn't he gone to Newark to look for a building? We could sell the Carmel factory and use the money to start a cosmetics business, which is really the kind of manufacturing Ben wants to do. It sounds better anyway. The shmattah trades, even the upscale ones, are for immigrants. I'd rather tell friends that my husband sells mascara than housedresses or petticoats. Ben gave me one of the compacts he used to make. It's rather pretty with a lid of inlaid tortoise shell. I don't think Papa would object, just so long as Ben could make a good living. Papa says that a husband's first task is to support his wife and family so they never have to accept a handout. I would die of shame if I had to ask for charity.

Were I to share these thoughts with Ben, I know what he'd say—I'm already living off charity, my family's—but that's because *he* feels guilty that Papa is setting him up in business. We don't pick the family we're born into. Some of us are just luckier than others. But I do believe that those who have had good fortune should help the less fortunate. When it comes time to buy linens for my new house, I will patronize the Kaspers' store for some of those goods, though of course I will have to find the finer fabrics in Philadelphia and New York. But sheets and pillowcases are the least of my worries. Now that Papa has found a house in Newark, I assume he'll soon be bringing us north. But how can I be engaged and live there while Ben is living here? The best thing would be for Ben and me to get married as soon as possible. Then we could stay in this house until we moved to the city. Although Mama is adamantly opposed, I would change the decor and maybe hire an interior decorator from Philadelphia. As long as we have to live in Carmel, I see no reason why we can't live comfortably, surrounded by handsome things. When I mentioned my plans, Mama furiously accused me of ingratitude. She's mad because I don't share her tastes. But I can't wait to say good riddance to the stove and the icebox, as well as the furniture and the fixtures.

Mama and Papa sleep in separate bedrooms because Papa snores. I think in general it would be a good idea to have our own rooms, just for the privacy. Perhaps Ben would like to read late, and I would want to turn off the light. Or maybe I'll want to spend time at my dressing table when he wants to turn in. Yes, I think it best to keep the bedrooms just as they are, apart.

January 4, 1912

I am almost seven weeks late! My time of the month always comes every twenty-nine days. For two weeks I have felt nauseous so I sent for Ben to come RIGHT AWAY. In the meantime I thump my stomach and jump up and down. I am even drinking extra doses of castor oil. One of the married girls told me that if you leave something inside, like a piece of cloth, it will bring on your monthly. But I'm afraid of an infection or worse. I wish I knew more about my body.

Ben was at the door around dinnertime. Mama asked if he wanted to eat cabbage stew but he said he'd walk on Delsea Drive and be back later. I could hardly eat. After we cleared the dishes I asked Olga to wash them for me since it was my night to clean up. Mama said Anna should go with me. So the two of us walked down Delsea and spoke in Polish. Anna chattered away about some miracle reported in the church newsletter. Finally I saw Ben in the distance. He greeted us with hugs. After I gave Anna a mean look she said she wanted to window-shop and Ben led me by the arm to the corner. A cold wind was coming down the street so we huddled in the doorway of Biaggio's drugstore, where Anna couldn't see us.

"You now can kiss me," I said.

He bussed my cheek and I wondered why not on the lips?

"Your note said, 'Right away come! It's very, very important!'"

My heart was beating like a drum. "I think I'm having baby."

"How do you know?"

Then I told him about my missed time and my nausea, which girls always mention. I also said I was trying to shake it loose.

"Let's wait one more week and see what happens," he said.

"And if nothing, what?"

He put his arm around my waist and comforted me walking home, knowing I was so scared of everything, my family, his family, him staying with me, the baby, bills, everything. Anna walked ahead of us alone, which was how I felt.

❧

Święta Mario, Matko Boża, byłam złą katoliczką, ale nie straciłam przecież wiary. Wierzę w Ciebie, naprawdę wierzę. Błagam Cię, pomóż mi. Spraw, by Ben się ze mną ożenił, a za to ja będę się do Ciebie modlić trzy razy dziennie, nawet jeśli zostanę Żydówką. A przed śmiercią wybiorę się z pielgrzymką do Częstochowy, żeby się pomodlić przed Twoim obrazem. Przysięgam Ci na wszystko co najświętsze, przysięgam. Zdrowaś Mario, łaskiś pełna, Pan z Tobą błogosławionaś Ty między niewiastami i błogosławion owoc żywota Twego, Jezus. Amen.

Dear Mary, Mother of God, although I've been a bad Catholic I have not lost my faith. I believe, truly I do. Help me and I will make you a promise. If you convince Ben to marry me, I will pray to you three times each day even if I become a Jewess. And before I die I will make a pilgrimage to Czestochowa to pray at the feet of the Black Madonna. I swear it. By my heart's blood I swear to you. Hail, Mary, full of grace, Lord is with thee; blessed art thou among women and blessed is fruit of thy womb, Jesus. Amen.

January 6, 1912

When the divine Sarah walks out on her lover in *Camille*, she doesn't have to worry about a child. But I know that if they'd had one, she would have taken it with her. When I hand Vasily a bundle of dollar bills and a basket with six bottles of his favorite imported brown vodka, he cries. From joy, I'm sure. He has known since the day after Christmas where Alexandra is living. Ben told him that if he objected, he would tell the sheriff about Vasily beating his daughter. Having no choice, he accepted her absence. As if he cared. Beating her the way he did.

Although Ben knows the truth, I tell Mama and Papa that I am seeing a throat specialist in New York. Ben pays for the trip. As in the past, I don't ask where the money comes from. I will stop in the city to see Cherry. To tell her how thankful I was for her razor. I have even packed my slate and chalk, so we can communicate. Ben and I drive in his Buick to Bridgeton. We wait together on the platform for the train. I give him Peter's telephone number. He warns me not to get my hopes up. I say I won't but I have. In Peter's last letter, he says how much he would like to see me. Since he can't leave his mother, I have shamelessly offered to come to him. Purely as a guest. For four days. I am not blind to the many letters in the newspapers from women led astray. Promised marriage. Seduced. Abandoned. But Peter would not do that. And surely not under his mother's roof.

I hope I am not misreading the signs and being driven by self-deception. A whole week away from Alexandra. What will Peter think when I tell him about my taking the child away? Perhaps I ought to wait. First, see how our visit goes, then decide. Don't prejudice matters beforehand. A gift, I must remember to bring her one. As well as the Kaspers. Maybe something for the house. Ben bids me good-bye with hugs and kisses. Lost in my imaginings, I have no sense of time. The train trundles forward while I retreat into remembrance. I am back at the institute. Dr. Alston is not in his office, which I often pass, in hopes of catching his eye. The door is open. I enter. On his desk is a pipe. The fine-grained one he rubs along the side of his nose. I sniff the bowl and enjoy the familiar tobacco scent. On a windowsill rests a tin of Prince Albert. He owns several paperweights. All of them scenes encased in glass. Some you shake and it snows. The one I remove from his desk and take to my room is a miniature bouquet of flowers with dew drops on the petals. I have it with me in my valise, intending to give it back to Peter if our reunion goes as I hope.

When he asks how it came to be in my possession, I already know what I'll say. So many times I've rehearsed it. I'll begin by teasing him. Saying that language may provide truth but is by no means obliged to. He will give me his wry Harvard smile and tell me I am "begging the question." After we joust for a minute or two, I will bite my lip, look at the floor, and confess. I wanted something of you I could hold. To remind me of you in your absence. It is too easy to misremember. To forget. To reconceive. A large glob of glass is stable. Unchanging. Although it can bring to mind innumerable fantasies, it is what it is. Peter will accuse me of being too abstract. Of finding meanings in objects that will not bear the weight of my reading. Then I will say, I return it to you freighted with all my imaginings. And so more valuable than before.

Cherry is waiting for me at Mrs. Shirley's new "house." She has put on weight and lavishly uses mascara. As well as layers of rouge. After I greet Mrs. Shirley and some of the girls from the old days, we go to a tea room. At first we say silly girlish things. Comparing notes about cosmetics and fashions. Then I ask, "Do you miss Ben?"

She bravely responds, "Men! Here today, gone tomorrow."

I pray she is wrong. She rambles on about the "house" and a man named A. R., Mrs. Shirley's boss. The name sounds familiar. Then I remember. The horseshoe roses. "He's a slick operator. Before Mrs. Shirley could say boo, he had her in his books. Ben knows him. You can tell your brother his old friend is a crook."

She says "crook" with such bitterness I can feel the hurt that Ben's absence has caused her.

"I don't suppose he remembers me," she says, obviously wanting me to contradict her. Which I do.

"But he never writes. Or comes to the city."

What can I say to her in a phrase, chalked on a slate? In Russia, Ben and I exchanged confidences. Shared our deepest secrets. Only once since our arrival in Carmel has Ben spoken of himself. Actually his predicament. Two women seeking his attentions. We were painting my bedroom:

"I sometimes feel like Joseph with his coat of many colors."
Shrugging, I hold up my palms.

"Why? I will tell you why," he says. "One minute loved, the other envied, depending on the mood and the person."

I write on the wall, "You are speaking in riddles."

He paints over my words and replies biblically, "And she caught him by his garment, saying, Lie with me: and he left his garment in her hand, and fled, and got him out."

"Who is she?"

"If I could answer that question, I'd know the way to Xanadu."

Cherry asks, "Do you think I'll ever see him again?"

I shake my head yes. But I am lying.

Her eyes tear.

Then I leave for the 180th Street station and board a coach of the New York, Westchester, and Boston Railway. I will have to make numerous changes. No one line runs directly to Boston. A system of interurban railways connects the two cities. The train passes through Mount Vernon and into Connecticut. In Hartford, I spend the night in a small hotel run by a Greek woman. For a dollar extra, she serves me dinner. Moussaka and a sweet wine.

In the morning, I board the train north for Springfield and Worcester. The last stretch to Boston. A cab drives me to Beacon Hill. Peter's house, a three-story red-brick Victorian, canopied by sycamores and oaks, looks stiff and imposing. An omen?

A man in livery admits me to a dark drawing room with floor to ceiling windows and damasked linen wallpaper. Although the drapes are drawn, the scant winter light barely breaches the room. I see only dried rain streaks on the windows. A bell. Peter appears. He holds out a hand.

The man in livery asks, "Tea or coffee?"

I request tea. So does Peter.

"Shall we sit?"

We each fall into overstuffed chairs and virtually disappear·in the upholstery.

"Let me tell you what I have arranged. Cook will bring you breakfast. Afternoons I will show you historical Boston, and in the evenings we can attend the theatre and return here to dine. How does that sound?"

"Delicious," I answer. And ask about his mother.

"She has a nurse and looks forward to meeting you."

Until now, I had no idea of Peter's wealth. At least his mother's. A servant, a cook, a nurse . . . what else?

After tea, he shows me to my room.

To my surprise, the house is equipped with an elevator. For his mother. Who comes to dinner in a wheelchair pushed by the nurse. Her name is Martha, and her skin looks like spotted parchment. The varicose veins in her hands resemble long blue worms. Shrunken and frail, with a hunched back, she is mentally agile. And sharp tongued. She sits imperiously at the head of the table. At the other end, Peter. Mrs. Alston talks about ancestry. Peter and I communicate in sign language, which his mother does not understand. He says his mother has blood clots. She could go any moment. Or hold on indefinitely. She seems strong to me. Before the sorbet dessert comes, Martha says sweetly:

"So many immigrants change their names. Did your family, Miss Cohen? And if they did, what was it in Russia?"

I answer through Peter, who replies, "Fanny says that in Kiev, the family name was spelled Kohen. They simply changed the first letter, so as not to be thought German."

"German," repeats Mrs. Alston. "They are an industrious people. Just look at their composers. Why, may I ask, would one not wish to be German?"

My reply: "Because we are Ukrainian."

"I should think . . ." she starts to say. But breaks off.

Peter changes the subject, mentioning the opera we are to see the next night, *La Traviata*. Mrs. Alston observes, "For the life of me, I have never been able to understand why anyone would want to celebrate a courtesan."

What would she say if she knew of my friendship with Cherry?

❧

The first three days fly by. Museums. Shops. (With Ben's money, I buy presents for everyone on my list.) The Boston Commons. Harvard Square. Faneuil Hall Marketplace. The opera. How Cherry would have cried over the death of Violetta Valery. But would the opera have convinced her to value herself? On the third evening, Peter comes to my room. Sits on the bed. Talks. It is the first time we have been truly alone. He touches my curls. Kisses my forehead.

"Let me tell you about Alexandra."

"Please do."

"Her sign language improves from day to day."

"She sounds like quite a gifted child."

"You'd love her."

He smiles but doesn't reply. I remove from my bag the paperweight. He immediately understands, making my rehearsed speech unnecessary. "I am touched," he says. "Such gestures speak volumes." He pauses. "Mother, would like to have a word with you, if you don't mind." I ask what about. "No idea."

I dress and pad down the long carpet to Martha's room. She is propped up in bed with several pillows. She points to a chair and asks me to sit. "I will come right to the point. You are a dear girl, Fanny, a sweet child, but not right for Peter. I have long planned for him to marry Muriel Kurtz, whose father is a prominent merchant in this city. Peter and Muriel have known each other since childhood. They both attended splendid colleges. If you truly care for Peter's future, you will discourage his attentions. A marriage between Peter and Muriel is my fondest wish, the wish of a dying mother. I'm sure you can understand—and will respect—my feelings."

The whole night I am awake. Alternating between tears and anger. Why did Peter encourage my trip? He must have known all along that his mother opposed the union. Or did he? For him not to know would suggest that his mother makes all the vital decisions and tells him only later. In which case, he's weak. Terribly so. And yet I still love him. Fanny, what are you thinking? Look around! The very room you're sleeping in should tell you that never the twain shall meet. He's from wealth. You're not. It's a matter of social class. He and his mother, starchy. The both of them as formal as Boston society. You would never fit in. And Alexandra, the daughter of a defrocked priest, whose mother is anybody's guess? He would never accept her. What must I have been thinking? Years ago Ben was right when he said I let romance turn my head. Making one thing seem like something else. How else to explain my blindness? Romance and reality have little in common. Only now am I beginning to see.

Early the next morning, the man in livery knocks on my door. A phone call. It could come only from Ben. Is Papa ill? Or Mama? I come downstairs to the drawing room. The servant, knowing I have no means of speaking, says into the voice piece, "Here she is."

"Fanny! Ben. A terrible thing has happened. It's Vasily." Immediately I think of Alexandra. I gurgle my death rattle into the phone. "The Zeffins found him this morning. Carbolic acid. Alexandra doesn't know. I've brought her to our house. You need to be here when she's told."

I leave that day, though not until Peter and I retreat to his study to talk. At first we only stare. He then thanks me for making the tedious trip and hands me a check to pay for my travel. I refuse, telling him my brother has covered the cost. Are you sure? Yes. To avoid the real subject, he begins to talk about *La Traviata*. I interrupt.

"When you sat on my bed and said you had no idea why your mother wanted to speak to me, you knew."

"I couldn't be sure."

"Peter, don't equivocate."

"Yes."

"How long have you known?"

"Since I first told her you were coming."

"And you said nothing. No call to tell me of a change in plans." I feel a rush of resentment. "How could you?"

"I had hoped to persuade Mother."

Fury flushes my cheeks and with ill-concealed anger I sign, "Your behavior is contemptible. You belong in Dante's hell, in the circle reserved for cowards."

He feebly says, "I tried . . . but the opportunity never arose."

"Peter, I'm speechless, not blind. You would never oppose her."

"In her state, the truth might kill her."

"As well as you!"

Silence.

"I am sure everything will work out for the best."

He hands me the paperweight, which I let drop in the wastebasket.

January 11, 1912

For me and Ben to meet Dr. Feldman at night, I stayed late at the store. We drove to the law office of some friend of Ben's who was on vacation. The doctor was waiting for us. He had brought along two black cases of instruments. To examine me he used a table that felt like a slab. No doctor had ever looked at me THERE. Once when I had a bad sore throat the nurse took a stick and pushed down my tongue and checked inside. But this! I put my hands over my eyes from embarrassment. Even later I found it hard to face the doctor.

He took a long time and then while I got dressed, he went into the lawyer's waiting room to speak to Ben. A few minutes later both returned. Dr. Feldman said we should all sit and talk. Ben and I sat on the couch holding hands.

Dr. Feldman used a lot of medical words that I couldn't understand. So I asked him to explain things simply. For speaking up like Ben says I should, I was proud. With Papa I would never, but lately I have been telling Mama what I think. She just shakes her head and says if I don't learn my duty and place, no man will have me. Little does she know.

"I can't be absolutely certain," Dr. Feldman said, "but you show all the signs of being pregnant. You can go to Philadelphia for a blood test, but I believe it would be a waste of money."

The doctor gave me directions to make sure the baby would be born healthy and I would be okay. He said the nausea would pass and I would feel better in a month or two. Ben paid him and some extra for coming from Rosenhayn. When we left, the doctor wished me good luck. Ben suggested we take a car ride before going home.

"To shake loose baby?" I said kiddingly.

"To talk about what to do."

I noticed in the back of the car a tow rope, a lantern, and a box of stick matches. For emergencies, he said. We took the road to Norma. Pulling into a deserted track in the woods Ben turned off the motor. He looked kind of sick, so I touched his cheek.

"What are you meaning," I asked, "when you said 'what to do?'"

Staring out the window almost like he is talking to air, he said, "I'm in no position to get married."

"You're manager of factory now, aren't you?"

"I'll lose the job the moment Mr. April learns about us."

"Explain me."

"We can't have the baby."

At first I misunderstood. How could I NOT have the baby? You can't just make it go away. Then I remembered the doctor and the trial in Philadelphia. Suddenly, my mouth had a bad taste.

"Abortion?" I was hardly able to say such a word.

"We have no other choice. A baby now would ruin our lives."

"I think you are not wanting baby ever."

"In a few years, when I'm set up in a business of my own."

I knew, in some way, I had him caught. He couldn't marry Erika with me carrying his baby. But if I said nothing the child would be born really without a father. I did not want to raise a baby alone. My family would disown me and I'd have to move. How could I live? So I was caught too.

"Supposing I just had baby in another city. Girls are sometimes talking of special houses for laying in and adoption. But I am not knowing what to be telling my family."

At last Ben turned to look at me. "We have a great many wonderful years in front of us, Irina. An abortion would make you normal again."

A few married girls who came into the shop talked the same way. They said expecting made you abnormal so they wanted to put things right. Since I hated feeling sick every morning and throwing up, I wanted to be healthy again. The girls also talked about the dangers of childbirth. I think it was the danger part that made me say:

"Is abortion more safe than childbirth?"

"Dr. Feldman thinks so. That's what we were talking about in the waiting room."

"Being done where?"

"In New York."

"Your doctor friend who was hiding?"

"Yes."

Because I wanted the baby, I said, "Ben, I have idea. Rent house for me and Fanny. We can be living together with Alexandra and ours. You are saying, your mother has handful with Alexandra. Then she can be free. And you can be visiting any time."

Ben looked annoyed. "My mother may find the child a nuisance, but she loves having Fanny home. She would call our child a momzer, a bastard. Trust me, Irina, an abortion is the answer to our problem."

"Problem? I am having no problem."

January 13, 1912

The Lord, my grandmother used to say, is full of cruel jokes. Ben drove a stricken Meyer and me and Fanny to the hospital this morning, and as we passed the shul, all the Saturday morning *daveners*, lined up on the porch waiting to go in for the service, saw us driving on the Shabbos. Several of the men took off their black hats and waved them at us, disapprovingly. How fitting that Meyer should collapse on a Saturday and, as always, be breaking religious law. Of course, illness is always an exception. Meyer, lying on the back seat, could not see the annoyance of the faithful. If he had, he surely would have smiled.

He had taken ill in the early morning hours, his breathing labored, his body feverish. Toweling sweat from his face, Ben told him we would start out at once for the hospital. But Meyer insisted on first going through his thin leather briefcase with its precious papers: the original deed to the distillery, the Baron de Hirsch Fund correspondence, a letter from Nikolai Gogol, and a few other documents he held dear. Two hours passed by the time he had finished shuffling his papers and Ben and I dressed him, all but carrying him to the car. Though his eyes were closed and color ashen, he clutched the briefcase to his chest.

The very doctor Ben had wanted to avoid, the drunken one, was on call. Had there been enough time to get Meyer to Philadelphia, we would have driven through the rain and the night. Resting in a white metal bed with sheets stiff from starch, Meyer seemed hardly to care about his condition, just the briefcase. The ward had only two other patients, and thankfully, between Meyer and them stood several empty beds. By the time the doctor arrived, even I could see that Meyer wouldn't live long. When the doctor spoke, his breath smelled of liquor. Ben said furiously, If this man dies, it will be on your head. I swear I'll report you to the medical board for drunkenness.

To our surprise, the doctor acknowledged his condition and added, Even sober, I couldn't save this man, nor could any other doctor. So do what you will.

We stayed at Meyer's bedside all that day and night. Most of the medical words meant nothing to me, but I did understand pneumonia. His breathing difficulties increased and he fell in and out of sleep so that I could hardly tell if he could hear us.

As I fell from life, my sainted mother, who had died many years before, was sitting at my bedside, holding my hand, and repeating, "Meyer, my darling son." Drenched in sweat, my body feverish, I was yet again assailed by the dreadful dreams that illness brings.

In my phantasmagoric state, Mother told me that shortly after Vasily, the caretaker, came to work on our estate, he unearthed a locked box. She ordered it opened and discovered a jewel-encrusted book that bore the seal of Peter the Great.

Where is the book now? I asked. In the library of the Carmel shul, she replied, adding that the distillery could never be returned until the book had been brought back to Bobrovitz. Taking her hands in mine, I promised to recover it. Only then, she said, can we be rich again, and my spirit pacified. I'll be coming home, I answered, with the book. After all, what need of it does Rabbi Kolodny have?

Mother smiled and said, "At last, Meyer, we'll have restored to us the Holy Grail, our Bobrovitz distillery."

Shortly before he died, he asked Fanny to sit on the side of his bed. I took Ben's arm and we waited in the hall. After Fanny came out, crying, Ben and I entered the room. Put your head next to mine, he stammered to Ben and wrapped one arm around his son. After a few moments, he said, free of embarrassment, It's time to close the book. The story is over. I just wish it had ended in another country, in a better world. He then asked Ben to wait with Fanny because he wanted to say good-bye to me alone. Ben embraced his father and left.

Meyer held up a frail hand that I clasped in my own. Esther, we began a new life, and Ben will complete it. One day he will look back on our life in America to see if its completion marks for our family an end or a beginning. Only he will be able to say. Fanny . . . who knows? At least she has Alexandra. His eyes closed, and for a moment I thought he was gone. But his lids fluttered and opened, and he completed his thought. I will never see Jacob again, nor do I think you will either.

He groped for the briefcase, which Ben had put on the nightstand. Unable to reach it, he gave up, and his hand fell to the side of the bed. I put my ear to his chest. No longer able to hear Meyer's breathing, I knew.

I waited to call Fanny and Ben, and just sat on the bedside next to the man with whom I had spent most of my life. Eventually, my attention gravitated to the briefcase. What was it that he wanted to show me? Rustling through his private papers, which I had always treated as sacrosanct, I found an envelope with a letter from Jacob, as well as another letter.

Dear Father,
Your letters reach me regularly. News of your life is welcome, but I am pained by your frequent requests that I write in return. You must surely realize that I cannot write to you without writing also to your wife; and that I cannot bring myself to do. Call it spite, call it obduracy, but I am my mother's son. Once hurt, I never forget. To help you accept my longstanding silence, I have gone to the trouble of copying a letter Rissa sent me shortly after I asked her to marry me.

Dear Jacob,
I must tell you about a terrible thing that happened to me when I was sixteen years old. We lived close to an army camp. There was a large field between my parents' farm and the school. It was spring. The meadowlarks were sailing from fence to fence. School had let out. I was alone, crossing the field. An Army officer was lying in the grass, waiting. He offered to carry my books and escort me to my house. I tried to object. He said I shouldn't be afraid. When I explained that I was expected home, he gently touched my arm and insisted we become acquainted. Mayflies, like a black fog, descended on us. I told him I really had to get home. He removed his jacket and rolled up a sleeve. As the flies thickened on his bare arm, he said that soldiers were like mayflies, which live for years underwater. Then one day they surface, shed their skin, and take flight—for one day. But in that one day they make love, countless times, and then die. He removed his boots. I tried to leave. He put his arm around my shoulders and restrained me, snarling that a soldier must

take his love where he can find it—before he dies. I cried out, "No!"

For five years, the child lived with my parents as their own. When you asked me to marry you, I wanted to have the boy with us. So I asked your mother for advice. She told me the existence of the child had to remain a secret. I protested. Your mother said, "What can you expect? It's not his. Believe me, the presence of the child would be like a cancer in the family."

In the silence of death, I cried and then finished reading the letter.

I asked your mother if you shouldn't be the one to decide. But she said that you were unworldly about such matters and would fail to see the consequences of marrying a woman with a bastard.

January 14, 1912

A cantor sung and, as Pop had requested, we had no religious service. It all took place at the graveside, so that Rabbi Kolodny would not feel slighted that we had not asked him to perform the funeral ceremonies in shul. The large number of people who attended surprised me. Among them were the April family, several of the Kaspers, Mr. and Mrs. Brotman, the Negro horseshoe pitchers, many of the Carmel tradesmen, and, perhaps as a mark of respect, the sewing-machine operators who worked for me. I had bought two cemetery plots, side by side, at the foot of a great pine tree. For all the seasons of the year, Pop would have birds singing to him from the branches. I imagined he would be pleased. When the cantor concluded his canticles, the attendants lowered the plain wooden casket into the ground. Fanny and I threw a handful of dirt on the coffin, and Mother, to my surprise, invited the mourners to speak, perhaps because she found herself unprepared to eulogize her husband.

To my surprise, the first person to speak was Irina, who remembered Pop as a kind man who always smiled at her. I looked over at Erika and could see her chagrin. She never came forward, though her mother did, and spoke not about Pop, whom she really didn't know, but about the difficulties immigrants faced in their journey to America. Several tradespeople made perfunctory remarks and then all eyes turned to me. So I eulogized my father as best as I could.

"My family and I thank you for being here today. The fond habit we call life has come to an end for Meyer Cohen. It was a habit that he embraced through hikes in the woods and, especially, in books. To make sense of a life is difficult, with all its vicissitudes and variety. And yet running through my father's life was a single consistent thread, a dream that informed everything he did: his passion to live in a just world. That wish led him to remind me on endless occasions that people are different, in small ways and large, and that we must respect their different needs. If you would be a good man, he used to tell me, then you will treat equally the slow learner and the fast, the timid and the gregarious, the right-handed and the left-handed. He regularly voiced his approval of Emma Goldman and the suffragettes, saying that in his 'day,' as he called it, women did not enjoy the same opportunities as men. Fanny has asked me to say that our father tried in every way possible to provide for her. 'If I must,

I'll go without,' he would insist, 'but she will have every chance.' In his daughter, he saw the gentle feminine in himself and 'kvelled' at Fanny's every achievement.

"I would be delinquent if I did not admit that my wish for a world in which books and art matter more than riches comes from my dad's influence. Where will I ever find again a father such as this? Not only is the habit of his own life over, but also the habit that my mother and sister and I became so needful of: having him beside us. But now it's time for me, and all of us, to bid him farewell. And so I say to you kind people who have come today, be glad at least that his recent illness will no longer have dominion over him. He is with the earth. And to you, Pop, wherever you are, I say: Sweet passage, and may your socialist dream live until the end of time." Mr. April snorted.

Mother and Fanny and I stood at the cemetery gate and thanked the mourners for having attended. The winter day had favored us with sunshine, for me a reminder of those long ago times in the Russian woodlands when I heard foresters' songs and saw birds rise from the swamp. Irina pressed her cheek to mine, and Erika squeezed my hand, but I could see from her expression that she felt hurt. Ignoring Jewish tradition, we did not invite the mourners to our home for food and drink; instead the three of us walked arm in arm alone, back toward our house. At first, we said nothing. Then Mother sighed, always a forewarning of a complaint to come, and halted in the road.

"I saw."

"She was only paying her respects."

"To your father or to you?"

"Both."

"Ben, how many times have I told you? Marry your own kind."

"A gesture of condolence does not lead to the altar."

"Aha, you no longer even think in terms of the chupah, now it's altars, is it?"

"Mom, what do you want of me?"

"That you should stop seeing the Kasper girl and get engaged to Erika."

"I don't want to get married."

"Who said married? I said engaged. It was your father's dying wish. I swear."

"That Erika and I—"

"Yes!"

Fanny squeezed my arm, confirming I was right and Mother wrong.

"He said nothing to me."

"Of course not. He knows how stubborn you can be."

"She's still a child."

"That's why a long engagement is a good thing. It will give her time to grow up."

"Mr. April plans to move the family to Newark. If Erika is single, she'll have to go with them."

This disclosure slowed my mother's bandwagon. I could read in her brown study an idea taking shape: how to overcome the obstacle of a long-distance engagement. Planning was her forte. Once she made up her mind, she was indefatigable. And to think that she called me stubborn! The second she took my arm to continue our homeward walk, I knew she had concocted a scheme. Whether it suited me or Erika would be immaterial, so long as it pleased her.

"You can live at home with Fanny and me, but be a caretaker for the April house—and visit Newark on weekends. The factory doesn't need to be open six days a week. You always agreed with your father that five days were enough. Right?"

"Yes."

"Distance makes the heart grow fonder. Isn't that the adage?"

"How long do you think this weekend engagement can continue?"

"A year or two. By then she'll be ready for marriage. Didn't you just say she's still a child?"

"Some people remain frozen in time. Just read what the Viennese doctors say."

"Don't bring up those Austrian quacks with me. We know about them. When I think about it, two years would be perfect. Yes, two years."

January 21, 1912

Dearest Diary, For weeks Ben has been promising to take me for a train ride to Cape May. So when he pulled up this morning in that shabby Buick of his and said, "Hop in, we're going to Union Lake," I nearly refused. After all, the January weather was not what you would call conducive to a pleasant outing, though I do admit the day was unseasonably warm. It's just lucky that I overcame my annoyance and went. He had brought a basket with turkey sandwiches and a cucumber salad that looked like his mother's work. When I said good-bye to Mama, I could tell she wasn't too pleased at the idea of Ben and me motoring in his car alone, but since Ruth and Morris had left the house earlier, she would have to propose herself as a chaperone, and she knew what I would say to that!

Ben threw a carpet rug over my lap and legs, pulled on his goggles, beeped the horn, and put the car in drive. It lurched forward and bumped down the road. The springs in the seat felt as if they needed repairing. Trying to make a joke, I remarked that a person could be "impaled." He replied rather rudely, "They're good for a goose." Of course I didn't answer. We traveled several miles before reaching a sandy lane that led through the woods. Ben said it followed an old Indian path, which he observed was good for finding arrowheads. His preoccupation with historical artifacts does make me wonder. We stopped at the top of a hill, and Ben asked me whether I would prefer to walk down to the water's edge or picnic on the cliffs overlooking the lake. I said the latter sounded more picturesque. So we hiked up to a spot in the trees away from the breeze coming off the water and spread out a blanket, which he covered with an oilcloth. The cold of the ground seeped through both, so I pulled my coat around me and decided to make the best of a rough outing. It certainly was not how I wished to spend a Sunday with a suitor.

Off to our right stood the dam with the trolley periodically clanging as it came down the tracks. In the distance to the left, where Ben said the Maurice River ran into Union Lake, I could see a Negro fishing. Every time he cast his line, the canoe nearly tipped. As he drifted nearer, Ben said he knew him, "Al Crenshaw." On the opposite shore of Union Lake, a rowboat with three fishermen was just leaving the dock. We watched as the canoe inched toward the dam.

All of a sudden, Mr. Crenshaw got a bite and started twisting and turning as he tried to reel in the fish. The canoe kept tipping perilously.

Ben, worried, walked to the cliff edge to watch. The matter seemed settled when he had the fish dangling from the end of his line. But as he leaned over the side of the canoe to net the catch, the canoe flipped and pitched him into the lake. A moment later he came up for air, flailing an arm and shouting that he couldn't swim. He yelled to the rowboat, not more than twenty yards distant. The three fishermen waved, which led Ben and me, now standing side by side, to think that they would come to his aid; but they didn't.

We stood on the cliff riveted. Then Ben cried out to the rowboat to help, but they just laughed, as if it was all simply a joke. Before I could hold him back, Ben threw off his coat and slid down the sandy cliff. At the water's edge, he stripped to his underclothes and leaped into the water. Mr. Crenshaw was a good fifty yards distant. I watched as the colored man came up and went down. By the time Ben reached the canoe, Mr. Crenshaw had been out of sight for several minutes. Steadying himself by grabbing the overturned canoe, Ben seemed to catch his breath, and then dove repeatedly, disappearing from sight for more than a minute or two each time he went down. After about five minutes, Ben, who must have been paralyzed with cold, righted the canoe, retrieved the paddles floating nearby, and rowed to shore. I grabbed the blanket and oilcloth and, although afraid of heights, scrambled down the cliff to meet him.

Exiting the water blue in the face, his limbs rigid from the cold, he suggested I build a fire and told me he had a box of matches in the back of the car. But first I wrapped him in the blanket and oilcloth, rubbing his feet and hands to bring back the circulation. Then I ran to the Buick. Gathering up dry leaves and twigs and pinecones, I started a fire, which quickly came to a blaze. For someone unaccustomed to the outdoors, I was rather proud of how fast I had managed everything. It took Ben a while to warm up, and by the time he did, the rowboat with the three fishermen had slid into shore just a few yards away from the fire. They were chuckling as they approached. A gaunt fellow with a pockmarked face spoke first.

—Drowned, did he?

(Before Ben could answer, a second chimed in.)

—One less niggah.

(The third man, as wide as he was short, shook his head skeptically.)

—I don't know, mister, why ya bothered.

(Ben finally looked up from the fire.)

—Because he was a friend.

—Tom, Ray, hear that? The man's a nigger lover. That black man was his *friend*.

—Them kind is worse than the darkies.

—Right ya are, Ray.

(Tom then put his foot against Ben's back and shoved him toward the fire. Ben, falling forward, barely escaped the flames but could not avoid some hot ashes, which burned his left arm. As Ben writhed in pain, the men returned to their rowboat. I screamed that I would have the police arrest them, but they just laughed. The last thing I heard was the man called Ray saying:)

—You both oughter fry in hell with your niggah friends.

(Taking wet mud from the edge of the lake, I sat on the ground and gently applied it to Ben's arm, having read once that doctors often treat burns in this way. He said he appreciated my caring and my having threatened the men. Then I took my silk kerchief and bound his arm. He reached up and touched my face, saying:)

—We must contact the police.

—Should we be getting involved?

—We are already, in numerous ways.

"Tragic Drowning"

—*Vineland Independent*, January 23, 1912

Two days ago, a Negro, Allan Matthew Crenshaw, drowned while fishing in Union Lake. According to several eyewitnesses, his canoe capsized while he was trying to reel in a fish.

What happened next is unclear. Benjamin Cohen and Erika April of Carmel, in the area at the time, say that a nearby rowboat with three fishermen refused to aid the man.

The fishermen, identified as Millville residents Tom Biney, Ray Stecca, and Bobo Hodges, said they made every effort to reach the man, but by the time they pulled alongside the overturned canoe, Mr. Crenshaw had sunk from sight.

Mr. Cohen said that when the men made no effort to help, he swam out to the canoe, but owing to the great depth of Union Lake, an old quarry, he could not locate the man, whose body was recovered hours later at the site of the dam.

Miss April added that the fishermen assaulted Mr. Cohen for having tried to rescue the drowning man. Calling him a n____r lover, they shoved him into a fire Miss April had built to warm Mr. Cohen.

As evidence, Mr. Cohen displayed a nasty burn on his left arm that he said resulted from the incident.

The Vineland and Millville police are investigating.

A service for Mr. Crenshaw will be held at the African Methodist church in Vineland, Sunday, January 28, at 11:00 a.m.

January 29, 1912

At last an engagement! Ben has asked Erika to marry him. She said yes and her family approves. He will marry well, move into his father-in-law's business, make a comfortable living, raise a family. How proud Meyer would have been. I do have a worry, though. When I asked Ben if he'd told Irina yet, he said no. Does he think he can carry on like a king and have a wife and mistress too? If you don't tell her, I will, I told him. Mother, he said, you will cause more harm than good. I knew he was too polite to call me a "meddler," the word he used when I saved him from that Cherry tart in New York. But as I've said a million times, for the sake of my son, I would go through the fires of hell.

Tomorrow he plans to leave work early and drive to Vineland to buy a ring. Why Vineland? I asked, Bridgeton has more to offer. He said, I know the jeweler in Vineland. Humph! He met him once, maybe twice. He's going to Vineland to see Irina. I wouldn't mind if his intention was to tell her that he's engaged to marry Erika. But I'm sure he'll give the poor girl some cock-and-bull story about having to pretend to be engaged in order to keep his job.

I have little doubt Mr. April would fire Ben in a second if he knew he was shtooping some Polish-Catholic girl. That's why my son's little double game has got to end. He thinks I'm blind to his doings with Irina, but Mrs. Kasper's willingness to see her daughter convert let the cat out of the bag. He's doing more than holding Irina's hand. I was young once and know all about two people being in heat.

I've saved my children before. God expects it, blessed be the name of the Lord.

Clutching Mrs. Cohen's letter to my chest, I sobbed all through morning service. Mama asked me why I wouldn't kneel and take the wafer and wine. I knew I would choke from crying. After Mama confessed, she expected me to go next. I said no. She looked terribly cross and wanted to know why I was acting so strange lately. How could I possibly tell her?

Walking to our house after church I saw Ben huddled on the porch. I didn't know whether to run away or go home. My sisters waved so I had to talk to him. Mama offered him lunch. He thanked her but said he needed to get back to Carmel. We all sat in the living room, and I pretended to be happy. Mother, who could see that Ben was hoping to talk to me, sent my sisters upstairs. But I couldn't take the chance of Mama hearing us. So we went outside. Mama mumbled we were mad to stand in the cold, but I said Ben had something for me in his car.

I knew that even the porch wasn't safe because one of the upstairs windows opened above it.

"Not here," I said, and we walked to the road.

"My mother told me she wrote you."

"She said you engaged Erika April."

"It's only until I can get established."

"Then her too unfairly you're treating."

"I can't give you up, Irina."

"It's easy, marry me."

"Not until I have my own business."

Tears ran down my face so I turned my back to the house in case someone saw. Ben tried to hug me but I pushed him away.

"I am changing my mind," I said. "I won't do it."

Ben looked like he would puke. "We agreed!"

"That was before letter."

"I even bought two train tickets for New York city."

"Take your mother to theatre."

That was the cruelest thing I ever said to him but I couldn't help myself.

"You can't back out now. Dr. Freedland agreed to do it."

"Even after him being at trial and all?"

"As a favor to me, he said he would, but he wants a lot of money. It's almost everything I have left."

"I am saving you money if no abortion."

"A baby will cost a lot more. Why hobble both of us?"

"You are saying you can't give me up. Then don't. I'm willing to be working hard for our happiness."

"You don't understand, Irina, what I have now is a prize job."

"Well, I'm prize too."

February 9, 1912

If sleep would only come without its ghosts. I have the most terrible dreams, and they're always about someone drowning, often Irina. We are canoeing on Union Lake, heading for the Maurice River. She asks me where we are going, and I say upstream to see the beautiful stands of cedar and oak. Once out of sight of the lake, I tip over the canoe. She calls to me, pleading she can't swim. I slip under the canoe's air pocket and wait. After a few minutes, I come out, and she has disappeared. Then I wake up in a sweat. One night I even sat up in bed and cried out her name. This morning I decided that I would offer her what she and her family lack most: money. An hour later, I called A. R.—my stock in Liggett & Meyers and my bank savings were long gone—and asked him to wire me another thousand dollars. When he reminded me I owed him a bundle, I assured him I was good for it. I basely told myself that the sum was more than what the Kaspers earned in a year and would free them to leave Vineland to start somewhere else, where Mr. Kasper could find work. Without money, I rationalized, one cannot purchase favors or ward off the diseases that issue from want. What I could not rationalize was the shame I felt at my own corruption. Like Cain, I too was marked.

Given that most of the factory hands were Jewish, I let everyone go early for Shabbos, and I drove to Vineland to catch Irina in the store before closing. Her mother, as I guessed, had gone home to cook the evening meal, leaving Irina to lock up. A customer was haggling over the price of some linens. I thought he would never quit, but Irina proved even more tenacious. Finally, he shook his head no and marched out the door. Irina ignored me, folding the linens and putting them back on the shelf. At last she asked me what I wanted.

"I came to see you."

"Have you changed it, your mind?" A resignation in her voice indicated she didn't believe that I had.

"Irina, I have come with an offer. I still have the train tickets—they're for next week—and an appointment with Dr. Freedland. If you agree to go through with it, I will give you a thousand dollars. So much money will make a big difference in the future plans of the Kasper family. You'll see."

Her first response was to upbraid me for treating her like a harlot, "a paid thing." She cried that the baby belonged to us both, not just to her, and that I should assume responsibility for its life.

What could I say? Of course, she was right. But sometimes children come at the wrong time, when we're unprepared to support them. I had seen too many young boys and girls ruin their lives, in Russia and America, because they "had to" get married. A few of my factory men were in that very position, and I could tell how much they resented losing their youth to marriage and children, and all because they, like me, had been careless. I fervently hoped that the money would bring her around.

She sat at the table on which the store displayed its goods and scribbled some numbers on a piece of paper. Since I had no other choice, I patiently waited to see what would come of her jottings. At last she looked up and said with a coldness that I had never seen in her before, "Two thousand, I want. One thousand for family and one for me."

My indebtedness deepened as I realized that yet again I would have to turn to A. R. If I worked like a Trojan for years, maybe I could eventually pay him back. Just maybe.

"If you're willing to accept a thousand dollars now and another thousand in the next twelve months, we've got a deal."

"Yes, Americans so much love deal."

"Then we're agreed?"

She stared into my face with a contemptuous look that I remember to this day and slowly shook her head yes.

I offered to walk her back to her house, but she refused. She wanted to know whether she should bring any particular kind of clothes or eat a special diet for our trip to New York. Dr. Freedland had suggested loose-fitting garments, several changes of underwear, and a liquid diet twenty-four hours before the procedure. I remember clearly his calling it a "procedure" and not an operation, a distinction that gave me some comfort. One often read in the newspapers about people dying during operations, but rarely ever from a procedure. When I said this to Irina, in lieu of a reply she gave me an indifferent shrug and turned away.

As she locked the front door of the store, with her back turned to me, she asked in a flat voice, "When do I see money?"

"I can give you the first thousand in New York."

"Before," she said, "not after."

At first I misunderstood and complained that the person giving me the cash lived in Manhattan.

"I am meaning before the procedure, not later."

Although her insistence would necessitate my persuading A. R. to deliver the money to Dr. Freedland before our arrival in New York, I had no other choice.

"You can put it in your purse before the procedure."

February 13, 1912

Dearest Diary, Ben bought me an engagement ring, really just a band with small diamonds. Frankly, I had hoped for something grander. Seeing my expression, he stated sheepishly that he'd had expenses of late but that he'd soon buy me a diamond as big as the best. I think the next time, I'll accompany him and just point out what I want.

He leaves for New York tomorrow, but Papa, whom I telephoned, said that as far as he knew it was not for business. So I asked Ben. He seemed vague and, after I pressed him, divulged that it had to do with his health.

—Are you seeing a doctor?

—Yes.

—Which one?

—A doctor Rosenberg, a specialist.

—You didn't tell me you were ill.

—I don't know that I am.

—Now that we're engaged, you shouldn't be keeping secrets from me.

(He then went into a long-winded explanation about how his family had a history of breathing problems, chest disorders, weak lungs, or some such. I suddenly wondered if I wanted to attach myself to a man who came from a line of sick people. So I asked him what symptoms he had been experiencing of late.)

—None.

—Then why are you seeing a specialist?

—It's only fair to you. If I'm going to prove a burden, you should know now, and then you can decide whether or not I'm the right person.

—How considerate of you. You're terribly sweet.

During the train ride to New York, Irina and I spoke only in phrases, as if neither of us had the energy or interest to sustain a complete sentence. But she did tell me that with the money I gave her, she had arranged for the bank in Vineland to pay her family fifty dollars a month until the allowance ran out. In the city, we ran into rain. The rawness of the day made us feel all the gloomier. We took a horsecar to the west side, where Dr. Freedland had opened a basement office. I gathered from the letter boxes that he and his family lived upstairs. Dr. Freedland met us at the door, took Irina's valise, and handed me an envelope. A. R. was as good as his word. After counting the bills, I passed the envelope to Irina, who likewise counted the money. He then directed Irina to a dressing room and told her to get into the gown hanging behind the door. The moment she disappeared from sight, I asked Dr. Freedland if A. R. had sent him money, too.

"Suffering from the shorts, are you?" said Dr. Freedland. "That's what you get for fooling around."

"I've learned my lesson."

Dr. Freedland's Delphic reply, "Sex and beauty are inseparable," was certainly true in Irina's case.

Again I asked about A. R.

"Yes, he sent one of his boys to my office yesterday. You can sort out with him what you owe. I'm taken care of."

Dr. Freedland excused himself and retreated into his examining room. I sat down and started to read a book that I had brought with me, *The Red and the Black*. The doctor poked his head around the door and invited me to give Irina "a hug and a kiss" before he got started.

Irina was lying on a narrow padded table wearing a plain, square-cut nightgown that resembled a sailcloth. For the first time since I had offered her money to have an abortion, she smiled at me. I kissed her and told her she'd be all right. Taking my hand, she said:

"Ben, remember, Ben, blue dye? In Maurice River? Like Indians we are looking, blue all over. My family, they think maybe I am drowning in bathtub I take so long to scrub. And arrowheads . . . remember? I never forget."

Dr. Freedland suggested I grab some lunch. "Down the street, on the right, you'll see a small restaurant. A Mrs. Stresa runs it. Try the roast beef. By the time you get back, it'll be over."

The rain had not abated, nor had the cold. I pulled up my coat collar and turned down the brim of my hat. Along the street stood garbage cans waiting to be emptied. An army of cats had invaded the offal, dispersing the detritus of family meals across the sidewalk and road. At the eatery, which called itself the "Italia," I watched the customers at the other tables and wondered what their stories would be like. We all have one, I thought, and many are a lot worse than mine. Blind children, scrofulous fathers, malnourished mothers, the list could go on and on. One woman dandled a little girl in a pinafore. Would the baby have been a boy or a girl? The only thing that matters now, I told myself, is Irina's well-being. She was paying an awful price just for our having played. I consoled myself that Dr. Freedland had often said childbirth was far more dangerous than a procedure. But what if she died? She can't, not with someone as skillful as Dr. Freedland in charge. Yes, but what if she did? Impossible. And if she did? She won't, she won't, she won't! Suddenly, I hated more than anything else in the world . . . death.

My lunch wouldn't go down, so I paid the bill and walked back through the rain. The doctor unlocked the door in a panic.

"What's the matter?"

"She's hemorrhaging. A prolapsed uterus. I didn't know."

"Can't you get her to a hospital?"

"You can, I can't. They'd put me in jail."

"Which is the closest?"

"Presbyterian."

I ran into the street and hailed a cab, then dashed back into the house. Irina was lying on the table in a pool of blood, her face ashen and her lips blue. Wrapping her up in my coat, I carried her to the waiting cab. A newsboy was shouting that Arizona had just been admitted to the Union as the forty-eighth state. I told the cab driver our destination and tried to comfort Irina as we bounced down the uneven road.

"You'll be all right in a day or two," I said wishfully.

"Hail, Mary, full of grace," she mumbled, "Lord is . . ."

"I'll get you a priest," I whispered.

"You. Just you."

"Don't be afraid."

"I'm not. But I know I'm going to die, and I am hating it."

The hospital attendants put her on a trolley and wheeled her away. "Where are you taking her?" I shouted.

"To the emergency ward."

I paced the waiting area for over an hour before a doctor appeared. His glasses, perched on the end of his nose, gave him a censorious look.

"Are you married?" he asked. "She wouldn't say. My guess is you're not."

"Is she all right?"

"We did what we could. The next few hours will tell."

"Surely she'll live!"

"She's a pretty girl. Why didn't you marry her? Then this wouldn't have happened."

"I couldn't."

"If you couldn't, then why did you take your fun with her? You know it's the woman who pays. Men like you disgust me . . . your selfishness, your obtuseness about human biology. What's your name?"

A young man from the steamship came to mind. "Henryk Nawrocki."

"Which doctor performed the abortion?"

"She never saw one, I did it."

"With what?"

"A coat hanger."

"I don't believe you."

"Can I see her?"

"Not until you tell me the name of the doctor."

I came as close as I ever will to betraying a man. "Impossible."

"Perhaps the police will have better luck."

He briskly left. At least a dozen people were staring at me accusingly. I darted for the stairs to find a nurse's station, where I asked to be directed to the emergency ward. The nurse said "the first floor," the level I had just come from. "Is there another stairway?" She looked at me skeptically—until I explained that I didn't want to involve the girl's parents, waiting below. Only then did she point out the backstairs, which I took three steps at a time. After poking my head into several rooms and alarming one elderly woman who pulled her covering sheet up to her nose, I found the right place. A nurse was taking Irina's pulse. Irina's free hand clutched her silver cross. The other patients in the ward seemed oblivious. Identifying myself as the patient's fiancé, I asked if we could have a few minutes together. The nurse seemed unwilling to leave, but finally exited when Irina whispered, "Please."

"I am saying every prayer and every moment never letting loose of crucifix. Blessed Mary knows I am wanting to live so much. She'll forgive my sins, for sure. Don't you think?"

"I do, Irina. I do. I do."

"If death puts us with angels, why I am hating death? So much I want to believe. If Church is wrong, what is there else but death?"

Trying to make amends, I said, "Whatever you want, just ask," knowing the one thing that mattered to her most, I had denied her.

"Don't," she said and broke off.

"Don't what?"

She motioned for me to put my ear next to her mouth.

"Play with another girl . . . our kind of play."

"I swear it."

"Erika . . ."

"Yes?"

She said something in Polish that I asked her to repeat in English. With great difficulty she breathed, "After us, there will be no more us," which were the last words she ever spoke to me.

I subsequently read in the newspapers that she bled to death. But that information came several days after I had made my escape via the hospital's loading dock, from which I ran all the way to Marty's Pool Hall in the rain.

Obituaries

—*Vineland Independent*, February 19, 1912

Mr. Ernst Helmig, a longtime resident of Vineland and father of John Helmig, blacksmith, died of natural causes, age 89. An elder in the Lutheran church, he devoted himself to Christian charities and even spent a year among German communities in Canada spreading the Gospel. Services will be held at the Grace Lutheran Church on Thursday, February 22, with interment in the adjacent cemetery.

❧

Miss Irina Kasper died last Thursday in New York City's Presbyterian Hospital from multiple hemorrhages brought on by an undisclosed illness. Her family, shop owners in Vineland, were called to her bedside but arrived too late. The girl's body has been brought back to Vineland. Funeral arrangements are pending for a service and burial in the city cemetery.

3 Area Residents Die Violently"

—Vineland Independent, February 20, 1912

Tom Biney, Bobo Hodges, and Ray Stecca, the three men under investigation in the drowning of Allan Crenshaw and the assault on Benjamin Cohen, were found Friday shot to death in Mr. Biney's cabin east of town. No arrests have been made, but the police are looking to question Mr. Cohen.

The men had apparently been playing cards and drinking hard liquor. Capt. Stafford, of the Vineland Police Department, said that two of the men were found slumped over a table, each with a bullet in the back of his head. The third man, Bobo Hodges, was found lying on the floor shot in the right temple. A pistol was found on the floor.

Capt. Stafford has suggested two possible explanations for the crime. The first is that the men argued among themselves, and Bobo Hodges killed the other two and then took his own life. But Mr. Hodges's girlfriend, Selina Brown, pointed out that Mr. Hodges was left-handed and would therefore have been unlikely to shoot himself in the right temple.

The second explanation offered by Capt. Stafford is that some outsider killed the men and tried to make it look like a gambling dispute. The investigation continues.

"The Unremembered Dead"

—by Don Eron, the *New York Herald*, February 22, 1912

In a city like New York, teeming with people, the dead are often nothing more than statistics. But some have about them a great mystery. Such is the case with a young woman who passed away last week at the Presbyterian Hospital before her Vineland, New Jersey, family could reach her. As she lay dying, the attendants, looking through her purse for a name and address to summon her kin, discovered a thousand dollars.

This reporter has taken it upon himself to try to unravel the mystery. The girl, Irina Kasper, was brought to the hospital by a man who identified himself as Henryk Nawrocki. Dr. Ligner, the attending physician, said the man was about twenty, thin and tall with blue eyes and blonde hair. The man went to the girl's room and, when the duty nurse went to summon the doctor, bolted. The question is why? Was it out of fear or guilt or both? According to witnesses, he made his escape through the basement, leaving by way of the loading dock.

A quick check of the city register, woefully incomplete at best, shows dozens of families named Nawrocki, but no Henryks. Whether in fact the man gave his right name is impossible, at least at this juncture, to know. That he fled without removing Miss Kasper's money leads us to believe that theft was not the motive for his flight.

But what of the money? So great a sum is not easily come by. Mrs. Kasper tearfully insisted that her daughter was a good girl, and Mr. Kasper said the cash now belonged to the family. The police, having no reason to suspect the girl of felonious behavior, concurred.

Your reporter will update this story information permitting.

February 23, 1912

Dearest Diary, The last ten days have been horrible, but yesterday the very worst. An article in the *New York Herald* was reprinted this morning in the local newspaper. The man in the story resembled Ben to a T. Since then I have been frantic trying to decide what to do or say if he ever returns. To be continued after dinner.

Ben showed up late this afternoon, just in time to have Friday night supper with the whole family, including Papa, who came home for the weekend. Why in the world am I talking about food? I'm still so distraught I can't keep my thoughts straight. As if nothing unusual had happened in his absence, he waltzed in with a bouquet of flowers and a box of Barricini chocolates. Irina Kasper, dead! The three men who abused us, murdered! Ben, wanted for questioning! And he says not a word about any of it! Am I losing my mind—or is he?

He handed Mother the flowers and me the candy and stretched out on a parlor chair chattering about having gone to New York to have a medical examination and talk to the Baron de Hirsch Fund about deeds and land grants. But I wasn't buying any of it.

—For ten days?

—I also did a few other things.

(My family crowded around him to hear. But I knew better than to let them get involved, at least not at first. So I pulled him, trailing his coat and hat, onto the living-room couch next to me so that we could speak privately. Shooing the others away, I made it abundantly clear that I didn't want them listening in. "No keyholes, Morris," I said. If Ben hoped to avoid my questions, he was sadly mistaken.)

—You went to New York to see *her*, didn't you?

—Who?

—Ben, when you and Irina disappeared, your mother called your old employer.

—Mr. Cosin. And he told her he had agreed to hire Irina, but wanted me to bring her to the factory for an interview.

—So it's true. You and Irina were together in New York. In a hotel room, as Mr. and Mrs. Cohen!?

—That's not it at all. Irina went to New York to see a doctor.

—To have an abortion?

—No, to consult him about her tuberculosis.

—I don't believe you. What about Mr. Cosin and what your mother learned from him?

—It's all true. She sought a job in New York so she could be near a good hospital. I needn't tell you about the ones around here. Irina had T.B. and didn't want her family to know. She asked me if I could get her a job and locate a specialist, since I had once lived and worked in the city and had friends there.

—Which doctor did you send her to?

—I sent her to Presbyterian Hospital, where she died.

—According to some reporter for the *New York Herald*, a man brought her to the hospital and then vanished. Are you that man? You fit the description.

—No. I hate to admit it, but I went to speak to a gangster.

—This story becomes more incredible by the moment!

—When my family and I lived in the city, I borrowed money from a man whose name I would rather not mention. He has been hounding me for repayment. I went to see if I could work out some arrangement. Before I could meet with him, his father took sick—he lives in Syracuse—and the man was gone for over a week. I stayed at a fleabag hotel, the Chelsea Arms. I can even show you the hotel bill.

—Is it for two or for one?

—You have to believe me, Erika. When we arrived in New York, we took a cab to Cosin's factory and, after Cosin said he would hire her, she went to Presbyterian Hospital. Then I waited to see the money man.

(His story sounded so fantastic and yet plausible, I was virtually speechless. I knew that Mama was holding dinner until our talk was concluded, so I pushed harder for answers.)

—Was she hemorrhaging?

—Not that I know of.

—But they put her right into bed.

—The doctor must have seen something.

—Who was the man who accompanied her and came to her room?

—I have no idea.

(His replies were like quicksilver and made me want to scream.)

—Her funeral is in two days. Do you intend to go?

—I'll leave it to you. For several months we worked side by side. Our families lived one street away. I often spoke to her, and I even took Irina and her mother and sisters to Philadelphia for the day. Did I care for her? Yes. But did I want to marry her, no. Now tell me what I should do?

(He really had me over a barrel. I didn't like being put in the position of telling my fiancé that he couldn't attend the funeral of a woman he once had befriended. Like many girls my age, I can be silly and frivolous, but about matters of life and death I know how to act. So I told him that of course he should pay his respects, and that I would go with him.)

—I'm not the least surprised by your decision. That's why I want to marry you.

(I nearly threw my arms around his neck and kissed him. But I still had a number of questions that needed answers.)

—Have you heard about the three murdered men?

—Yes. I don't know who shot them, but I can't say I'm sorry.

—They were beasts, I agree, but murder . . . ?

—You say that as if *I'm* the one responsible.

—This gangster friend of yours . . . is he somehow involved?

—He hates guns. Money is his racket.

—I must tell you, Ben, I have this awful feeling you're behind it.

—Then I think it best that we part.

(At that moment, I didn't know whether or not he was bluffing, but I decided to call his hand, as they say.)

—All right, I'll tell the family we've agreed to end our engagement.

(I walked to the living-room door as slowly as I could without appearing obvious. My hand was on the doorknob and still he had said nothing. I turned it and looked over my shoulder. He had taken his coat and hat, and to my dismay was actually preparing to leave. Who knows what would have been the result had not Papa at that very instant burst into the room. Insisting that he had something important to say and couldn't wait any longer, he summoned the other members of the family into the living room.)

—I am selling the Carmel factory. The cheap shmattah business is now finished. Petticoats, as I told you, that's where the money is. Ben, I want you to come to Newark. I already found you an apartment near us. When the sale of the Carmel factory goes through, I intend to open another one in New York City, on the East Side. That place will be for you, Ben. I suggest you bring your mother and sister to Newark. They can decide later whether to follow you to New York, where I assume you and Erika will be moving once you're married.

(I knew that when Papa made up his mind, he was like a runaway train. Ben says his mother's the same.)

—That's very kind of you, sir, but I have my own plans.

—Cosmetics? Forget it. Petticoats! That's where the money is.

This morning, before the interment, a Mass for Irina took place in the Vineland Catholic church. Neither the Aprils nor my mother attended. Erika excused herself at the last moment. My presence seemed to hearten the Kasper family, who were already enjoying the fruits of their wealth, judging from their clothes. I couldn't help but think how they'd treat me if they knew the truth.

At the family's request, Irina lay in an open casket, but I lacked the courage to look at her, wishing to remember her alive and vital. Mrs. Kasper leaned over to whisper that immediately after the eulogy they would be sealing the casket and wouldn't I like to say a final good-bye. I pressed her hand and said I kept Irina's image dear in my heart and didn't want to see her any other way.

The eulogy left me bewildered. Instead of talking about Irina, the beautiful young woman with alabaster skin and blue eyes who had clerked in her family's little store and made them rich, the priest talked about Jesus, heaven, and the angelic hosts. Although those around me seemed to take comfort in the priest's assurance that Irina now reposed in the arms of the Lord, I resented him promoting the Church at the expense of a woman who, had the real story been told, had died for love of me. But as Chekhov says, the lie that elates is dearer than a thousand sober truths. The eulogy had one saving grace; it was so formal and lacking in feeling that, as much as I tried, I couldn't shed a tear.

After the burial, I drove back to Carmel to tell my mother and Fanny about Mr. April's "plans" and ask them to join me in Newark. The funeral had convinced me that I needed to leave this part of the country and start a new life somewhere else. To my surprise, they both refused.

"Since when does a son of Meyer Cohen's leave the workers to the greediness of the bosses?" Mother asked.

She was alluding to my having instituted several changes in the factory, among them shorter hours and higher pay, all of which the new owner would probably rescind. But I had to smile at the thought of my mother becoming a socialist for the purpose of convincing me to remain. When I tried to point out the advantages of New York, she said only that she "didn't wish to return." Her terse comment meant more than it said. New York was the site of Fanny's accident and my involvement with Cherry. And she didn't know the half of it.

Had she been present when I found A. R. at Marty's Pool Hall, after racing through the rain with my hat in my hand and the water dripping from my hair down my back, she would have been aghast. He was shooting pool against some teenage yegg, while Owney served as banker, handling all the side bets.

Hearing me panting from my run, he looked up from the table and said, "Get dried off, kid, and pull up a chair."

Marty asked me if I wanted anything to drink. "I usually never drink before six," I responded, "but today's different. Give me a slug of Scotch, straight. On second thought, make it a double."

A. R., abstemious as ever, leaned his pool cue against the table and, folding his arms across his chest, said, "Benny, I can see we need to talk. Asking Owney to "hold the game for five minutes," A. R. took me into a back room. "What's up, kid?"

I told him about the abortion and my taking Irina to the hospital. "But I never mentioned Dr. Freedland's name."

"You did the right thing keeping mum. The girl . . . you'll need an excuse for her coming to New York."

"I can call my old boss, Mr. Cosin, and ask him to cover for me."

"Get right to the phone."

When I returned, having secured Cosin's help, I related what had happened to Al Crenshaw, who had once done a job for A. R., and showed him the scar on my arm from the burn. He gingerly touched the discolored skin. I had never seen him so gentle.

"When I was a kid, a kerosene lantern fell on me. To this day I can feel the hurt of that burn."

"The doc said there's no pain like it."

"Give me the names of the three guys in the rowboat."

"How come?"

"That's my business. Stay out of it."

"But you're the guy who hates violence."

"I know some fellows in Philadelphia. They owe me a favor."

It seemed A. R. was always bailing guys out of jail, getting them lawyers, giving them seed money, helping their families. He had a legion of men in his debt, including me.

"About the money you lent me, A. R., it's going to take a while."

"Kid, I got the patience of Job. But a time'll come when I want a favor. Then I don't want to hear any ifs, ands, or buts."

June 21, 1912

The end of May, Peter informs me of his mother's death and his new position at Kurtz Manufacturing. He says he wants to try his hand at industrial hygiene, a new field. A more rewarding one. I can think of a number of rewards. Muriel. Money. And the Beacon Hill house. He says that the school I applied to in Washington, D.C. has asked him for a letter of recommendation. Which he has sent—"with the highest accolades."

I take Alexandra to the post office every weekday. A half-hour walk. But I have to wait three weeks to hear from him again. Mrs. Myshkin's face tells me that my prayers have been answered as she proudly hands me a letter. We both know the stationery. It's Peter's. Alexandra tugs at my sleeve. She wants me to read the letter and relate its contents. We walk outside and sit on the raised wooden boardwalk, with our legs dangling over the side.

Dear Fanny,

As you know, my mother's final wish was to see me pay court to Muriel Kurtz, who is a fine woman and comes from a good family. I can honestly say that I care for her. My feelings for you, I need not recount. Our hours together will always remain sacred.

Be assured that Muriel is not guilty of alienating my affections. She knew nothing of our friendship. My mother, who told me you would make an admirable companion, merely pointed out the cultural differences between us. Since mother's death, I have given her concerns a great deal of thought.

Had the fates been kinder to us, perhaps we might have had a future together. I apologize if I misled you. At all times, I tried to conduct myself as a gentleman. But I realize that emotions are often hard to disguise.

Last night I asked Muriel to marry me. We are now engaged. The ceremony will take place in a year. It is with fond remembrance and the greatest rue that I must ask you to discontinue our correspondence, as it would not be fair to Muriel—or to you.

Your devoted teacher,
Peter Alston

"Fates! What in the world does that mean?" I replace the letter in its envelope and, no longer able to restrain myself, cry. Alexandra puts her arm around me and in sign language asks, "What is it, Mother?"

Perhaps it is her gesture, or her word, or my having seen too many melodramas, but I sob all the more. Until I remember Papa's last words to me.

"Fanny, think of Alexandra and yourself as castaways on a deserted island, where you must create your own language, your own idiom. Bring forth, in accents pure, a new speech. So when others are swept ashore, you can teach them how to speak. Help the silent children of the world. It is you, and you alone of the Cohen family, who will make a revolution."

When I tell Mama about the letter—after all, she knows why I haunt the post office—she characteristically says, "Now, Fanny, you can invite that nice Jewish man. The furrier from Philadelphia. We can all sit down for tea like the quality."

She is thinking of Mr. Barisch, who does business in this part of New Jersey and tells Mama that her daughter is a *shana*, pretty, girl. I have made it crystal clear to Mama that I am not interested in this middle-aged man. Bald on top. With sidelocks that hang down his cheeks. She tries to tempt me by saying that few men are willing to marry a woman with a child. But I remain steadfast.

I know that Mama is desperate to keep me with her in Carmel. She repeats that Ben has agreed to support us, and that the Baron de Hirsch Fund will let us remain in the house. She even praises my decision to keep Alexandra with us, as my foster daughter. But Alexandra needs schooling. I can see she is lonely. And if she is to support herself someday, she must learn more than I can teach her. Now, though, it looks as if I may have a position at an Olmsted school in Washington, D.C., where she can use sign language and learn lipreading. Maybe even be taught to speak. What an opportunity! To be exposed to all the subjects that a regular school offers. Mama keeps repeating, like a religious incantation, families should never live apart. I think of how Peter stayed at his mother's side when she was ill. And what did it get him? Muriel Kurtz. And me? Nothing.

Suddenly I am angry and sign to Alexandra that we will be moving to the capital. She cartwheels around the house like a mad creature. When I call Ben with the news, he offers to send me money, saying jokingly,

"What's a little more against my account. The man won't mind. And besides, you'll need it, raising a kid and all."

Mama perseveres, saying, "The silver lining is that we will continue to live as a family."

I console myself by thinking that when I leave, Mama, as Papa used to say, will need as many grievances as possible to sustain her old age.

March 20, 1913

Dearest Diary, We moved north to Newark a year ago today. Fanny and Alexandra are now living in Washington. It seems like forever since I've written anything, but I've never in my life been so busy. At first I had to help Mother properly furnish our Newark house. That literally took months. Dealing with carpenters, drapers, and upholsterers nearly drove us both mad. Then I insisted that Ben let me furnish his apartment nearby, on Mapes Avenue. He wanted a place for his artwork and, had I not had my way, would have turned the living room into a studio. The apartment now has a fashionable charm with modern pieces. Then Papa opened a new factory on the Lower East Side in New York. Ben and Papa travel between Newark and New York every day, so I hardly get to see either one. For months my family kept asking me when I was going to set the date, but I couldn't pin Ben down and wasn't about to tell my family that.

The other day we finally agreed—to a June wedding. The moment I announced it, Papa ran off to buy us an apartment on the Upper East Side within walking distance to a trolley that runs three blocks from the new factory. So now I have to furnish that place as well!

Although I can hardly count all my blessings this past year, I mustn't forget to include how Ben settled the strike that took place at Papa's factory here in Newark. Lines of workers picketed from morning till night. I suppose it would have gone on for months and ruined the business if Ben hadn't arranged for some man in New York to put an end to it—with a minimum of violence, I'm told.

March 30, 1913

This past year with Ben and Fanny gone my only company has been Meyer. I talk to him every day, and though he never replies, I know exactly what he's thinking. That's what comes of our having been married for so long. My only other conversation is with shopkeepers. They ask me about the children, but what can I say? Fanny and the child, though they sometimes visit, are as good as dead to me, and Ben has abandoned his mother. A son who uses every excuse not to see his mother is like no son. His reasons would fill a book. He has to spend time with Erika and her family. His apartment has no furniture. Mr. April wants him to work in Newark and New York. The workers went on strike, and he had to settle it. The excuses are endless. But I know his real reason: that I wrote to Irina. He denies it, and says all that's behind us. Not for one moment do I believe him. He is trying to punish me—for doing the right thing! Irina would have found out soon enough about his engagement. And Erika? Didn't he owe her the honesty of being faithful? He was acting like a Mormon, having two women. Well, my letter fixed that and also, even if he won't admit it, secured for him a future in Mr. April's employ. The old man sold the factory here in Carmel and opened another in New York. Then he put Ben in charge of the operation—and made my son a rich man. He's so rich he bought me a telephone, which is the only way we speak. A few weeks ago, he called to say he would drive down to see me—at last!—and to exult that Mr. April had put him in charge of the Newark factory, and that he was already thinking of branching out.

I warned, Don't bite off more than you can chew. But he laughed and said, If a business doesn't grow, it dies. So, I answered, if you want to open another factory, what's to stop you from buying the one you used to manage in Carmel? Since you left, it's not doing well. The new owner wants already to sell it. He complains about the workers. He says you spoiled them. The sewing-machine operators pray you should return. Impossible, Ben said. Why? I asked. We'll talk when I see you.

Before I saw his car pull up, I heard it on the gravel drive. What met my eyes nearly bowled me over, a big machine—he called it a Franklin—with silver parts that reflected the light like dozens of mirrors. As he walked up to the house, I told myself to take a good look because maybe it would be the last time I saw him, what with my irregular heartbeats. If only he would move back to Carmel, I would know that God had heard my prayers. Oh, how I've prayed! Meyer would have called me selfish; well, with only one son left, what is the crime in wanting him near me?

He came through the door with gifts, everything from a fur coat to a gramophone. Erika and I, he announced, have decided to get married in June. I could feel my arrhythmia . . . that is what Dr. Feldman calls it . . . which takes my breath away. Ben, answer me your father's question. For what did we travel seven-hundred-thousand Persian miles? So you could work in a factory? We could have stayed in Russia for that. Democracy? The right of every man to be like every other man, dull, insipid, coarse. Sometimes I would ask myself—when your father was standing, late at night, smoking, looking out the window—I would ask myself if the golden world was only an idea leading us from one place to another, down unmarked trails in search of a southern passage to a new world that exists, if at all, only in dreams.

Now you sound like Pop.

I felt tears coming to my eyes. For all his failings, I said, I miss him. Loneliness can devour the world. Mom, he replied, you wanted Erika and me to marry. Yes, I said, but not right away. Well, he sighed, it's too late. I put my hand on my chest to stop the wild beating. Are you all right? he asked. I'm ill, Ben; as God is my witness, I'm really ill this time. He took my hand and said he would call Dr. Feldman right away. Don't waste my time. He'll just give me the same medicine I have on the shelf. Mom, what can I do? Tell me! To have you visit regularly would make me less afraid. When you are gone, I can't sleep at all . . . I'm so worried about what if I will maybe fall down and break a hip. It happens, you know. Worst of all, such terrible dreams I have. The people who come to mind. The reminders of youth, of pain. Please, Ben, if you can't come, call!

He kissed my hand and then my head. Embracing me, he whispered, I promise to telephone you every day. I said, Sometimes when I don't hear from you, I worry you've forgotten the number. He squeezed me all the tighter and said, Don't worry, I'll call.

Two days later he drove off. For breakfast I made him blintzes with honey, his favorite. Leaving the dirty dishes in the sink, I sat for hours staring at the empty gravel drive, arguing with myself about times past. Finally, I decided to tell Meyer the rest of the story, the part that Rissa's letter omitted.

After Rissa farmed out her son, she came back to me, Meyer, and said her pain was unceasing . . . she had to tell Jacob. And what will you tell him? I asked. I will tell him the truth. Her words still torment me.

I did what you wanted, she said. On November 5, 1907, I dressed Michael in the early morning light. There was snow on the ground. I put on his leggings and his winter coat, and tied his blue hat under his chin. He had the sniffles. I wiped his nose. Then we started down the road to the village station. He asked me where we were going. I said to visit a friend. He had just turned five the month before and had never been away from my parents' farm. We took the train to Kiev. The station was crowded. He clung to me. I assured him there was nothing to be afraid of. We stood together watching people vanish and reappear in the great steam clouds from the trains. I told Michael to wait under the great clock, and that I would return in a minute. He said he would wait. Then I walked out of Kiev station. I never heard of him again. I read the newspapers every day. But there was nothing. And now I must tell Jacob.

May 2, 1913

A month after I last saw her, she died. In the cemetery, Fanny and I stood under the great pine tree as they lowered her into the ground, next to my father. Dumb and dark, I heard nothing, except the grating of the shovel and the thud of the dirt hitting my mother's coffin.

When we left the cemetery, we sorted through her belongings, brother and sister, united again, briefly, before Fanny had to return to her teaching job at an Olmsted school in Washington for the deaf and dumb. In Mom's letters, I find one from Alexandra, in an uneven hand, telling her grandmother that she is learning to *talk*. My sister slips it into her purse. The various objects, including newspaper clippings, induce memory and desire: the morgue at Charities Pier; Pop, in the hospital, hugging me; Erika rebuffing my attempt to make love to her before marriage; my art supplies stored at the top of a closet; A. R. demanding partial repayment in the form of a contract to break up the strike at our Newark factory; Cherry, her lashes caked with blue mascara, seeing me on Broadway and complaining about A. R. exploiting the girls, but for "her dear Ben" it was free; Irina, whose ivory beauty now lay in a box, bleeding for love; sunlit fields and cool woods, Maurice River, and birdsong.

Do I remember these moments because of Mom's death, or because I am grieving for what I've become—a sweatshop boss—even going so far as to tell a reporter that strikers should be jailed for subverting the capitalist system? I have defiled Pop's dream and Jacob's hope. And now I shall live through a long chain of days and weary evenings pretending to listen to Erika's inanities, finding respite only in Fanny's letters and in trysts with Cherry.

Who will cry for me in this land of whorish opportunity and incessant loneliness?